From This
Wicked Patch
of Dust

Camino del Sol
A Latina and Latino Literary Series

From This Wicked Patch of Dust

Sergio Troncoso

THE UNIVERSITY OF ARIZONA PRESS

TUCSON

The University of Arizona Press
© 2011 Sergio Troncoso

www.uapress.arizona.edu

Library of Congress Cataloging-in-Publication Data

Troncoso, Sergio, 1961–
    From this wicked patch of dust / Sergio Troncoso.
        p. cm. — (Camino del sol: a Latina and Latino literary series)
    ISBN 978-0-8165-3004-5 (pbk. : alk. paper)
    1. Immigrant families—Fiction. 2. Mexican American families—Fiction.
3. Mexican Americans—Fiction. I. Title.
    PS3570.R5876F76 2011
    813'.54—dc22
                                2011014819

Publication of this book is made possible in part by the proceeds of a permanent endowment
created with the assistance of a Challenge Grant from the National Endowment for the
Humanities, a federal agency.

♻

16   15   14   13   12   11   6   5   4   3   2   1

For Rudy, Oscar, and Hajar

From This
Wicked Patch
of Dust

The Beatles in Ysleta
JULY 1966

Pilar Martínez stumbled into her mother's apartment, which had once been a church in El Segundo Barrio in downtown El Paso. Nineteen-month-old Ismael was limp in her arms. Her husband, Cuauhtémoc, had locked the pale green Chevy Impala in the darkness of San Antonio Avenue. She glimpsed her husband's grim face. His brown trousers were speckled with mud and ripped at one knee. Pilar's own face was streaked with an ashlike grime, and her jet-black hair seemed a ball of snakes twisting to escape their torture. Marching into the bedroom, she nestled Ismael into the rickety white crib and hurried to the living room. Cuauhtémoc unlaced his boots, and don Pedro and doña Josefina, her parents, waited in front of the rust-colored sofa. "Nos robaron el cobre. It's been stolen, Mamá," Pilar said, shaking the numbness from her arms.

"Cómo? Quién?"

"Probably marijuanos from the canal behind the lot. They stripped it," Cuauhtémoc said bitterly, his green eyes flashing. He imagined twisting a rebar with his hands around an anonymous neck.

"We talked to don Chencho already and he's coming back on Monday to redo the bathrooms, the kitchen. It'll only take a few weeks." Pilar slipped off her shoes, and fine grains of sand pattered on the floor. "Cuauhtémoc will do the plans for his new bathroom and living room to pay for don Chencho's work, as soon as he's able. It will be fine."

"But we'll have to move there."

"What? To Ysleta?"

"To Ysleta. Or the same thing will happen again. Another catastrophe."

"You don't even have running water! Or electricity! Y los niños?"

"Mamá, we don't have a choice." They had spent the day putting up a makeshift chain-link fence around the lot. "If we're not there, then our house will never be finished."

"Pilar, what you need is a good dog and a club," don Pedro said, hiking up his loose pants.

"What are you talking about?" Doña Josefina's eyes bore through don Pedro's shiny bald head.

Cuauhtémoc trudged to the kitchen and poured himself a cup of atole. Would anyone dare break into their house if they saw someone living there? He stirred the hot thick brown elixir with a spoon and lost himself for a moment in the clouds of steam. Pilar followed him, while doña Josefina and don Pedro shuffled behind.

"Pedro can bring milk every day, on his way to Socorro. Milk and eggs, and whatever else you need," doña Josefina said, wringing her hands as she sat at the kitchen table covered by a plastic tablecloth imprinted with yellow flowers and green stems.

"Seguro que sí. Whatever you need, you tell me. I can stop by every day after I'm done on the farm, too."

"We need to do this in a week, as soon as don Chencho starts installing the new pipes, or the same thing will happen again," Cuauhtémoc said.

"It'll be all right." In her head, Pilar was already making plans to register the children at the new school two blocks from their house. That had been the plan all along anyway; they just had to start earlier. She marched through another doorway in the kitchen to the darkened bedroom where the children were sleeping. The aqua-blue wall between the kitchen and the bedroom reached only two-thirds of the way to what once had been the church's ceiling, dividing the massive rectangular space like a gigantic I. Under the dome above the I, the pendulous air traversed every room in the house, vaguely connected its noises, and seemed to harbor a residue of bygone solemnity. Pilar returned and sat down. "Ay, que greñuda! I look like a witch with this hair!"

"Doña Pepita, I need to ask you for a favor," Cuauhtémoc said, staring at the cup in front of him. "We don't have the money for the new copper pipes . . ." His voice trailed off as he thought of what he had just paid for: the lot in Ysleta, the adobe for the unfinished rooms, more lumber, the chain-link fence.

"Por supuesto, Cuauhtémoc. Whatever you want, m'ijo."

"Seguro que sí."

"Not give. Lend. We'll pay you back in a few months, Mamá," Pilar said.

"If I find out who did this, if they come back again, I don't know what I'll do. Malditos. Maybe I should buy a rifle." A shiver raced up Cuauhtémoc's spine.

"We'll call the sheriff, that's what we'll do. No rifle."

"Call the sheriff? With what, Pilar?" There was still no phone service in Ysleta.

"Don't worry. There are plenty of gente decente in Ysleta. Don Chencho. Doña Lupe. Ramon. Pepe Chavez on Carranza, your sister Elvia. They will help us. Those potheads come out at night only when there's no one around. We'll be all right, you'll see." A siren echoed in the distance, on Paisano Drive. The canyon of red-brick tenements and old stone houses gave the street an ominous, permanent darkness that at night seemed to hide eyes behind every hedge and porch, even in the trees.

～

The Chevy Impala with fins rolled slowly east. It was followed by don Pedro's green and white Ford station wagon. Pilar inhaled the scent of wet dirt of the irrigated cotton fields on Alameda, which wasn't Alameda anymore but Route 80. The tangy smell reminded her of El Charco, the ranch in Chihuahua where she had lived as a child.

Pilar thought back to one day in 1944 when she had been nine years old. They were dirt poor, and her mother woke up every day before the sun rose to make tamales to sell on the street. Her older sister Estela and she cleaned and ground the corn meal before leaving for school, but doña Josefina also forced them to sell jamoncillo and piloncillo to the other children during recess and after school. One day Pilar decided to join a baseball game. When she returned to retrieve her homemade candy, the box was gone, stolen. Her mother slapped her across the face, smashed a broomstick across her back, and screamed, "You are a good-for-nothing! Why are you here? Why don't you just run away?" Pilar had never forgotten those words. For how long had she felt her existence had been a horrible mistake? What was it to believe you reminded your mother of her ill-fated decisions, her abandonment, the hardness of this earth? It had taken don Pedro to more or less heal this wound. This happy-go-lucky musician had intervened one year and fallen in love with doña Pepita. And she had not driven him away. Over the years, don Pedro had deflected her mother's bitterness and anger away from her children.

Don Pedro had worked as a bracero for an American copper company in Arizona, learned pidgin English, and moved to the border town of Juárez. He had first worked in Socorro for a commercial farmer. El señor Johnson grew to trust don Pedro and helped him apply for citizenship. Here was a man who worked the most difficult and dirtiest jobs, yet slapped the dust off his pants at the end of the day and genially waved to his boss, grateful for a glass of water. Without Papá, Pilar thought, they would never have left Juárez for El Paso, and Cuauhtémoc would never have followed her to America. Without Papá, where would they be now?

Through the rear windshield of Cuauhtémoc's Chevy Impala, Pilar glanced at her stepfather and mother. Don Pedro cautiously gripped the steering wheel, while doña Josefina stared fiercely ahead. She was always on a knife's edge, ready for a fight. Don Pedro was an angel in a plaid shirt whose greatest pleasures were a banana-peanut-butter sandwich, a can of beer before dinner, and a good joke.

Their cars ambled into the colonia of Ysleta, which was a misspelling of the Spanish *isleta*, meaning "little island." A misnamed, misplaced swath of earth in what had been a prehistoric sea. The gravel slipped under their tires. Elevated dirt mounds of irrigation ditches cut short the horizon. The most unusual and even gaudy structure was the Ysleta Mission, which had been founded one hundred years before the thirteen colonies of New England had declared themselves the United States of America. With its three-story cupola, crumbly white stucco walls, and rickety wooden fence, the mission had attracted a small settlement of adobe shacks. Mount Carmel was a warehouse-like new church with a gray asphalt roof and cinderblock walls, and lay to one side of the mission, anchoring a dusty little square against the grim and boundless desert.

Pilar pointed out the church to the children and explained its role in Christianizing the Tigua Indians, who still lived in Ysleta.

"Will they shoot us with arrows?"

"No, Panchito, these Indians don't do that anymore."

At the end of the road and dust, Cuauhtémoc finally found the old one-lane wooden bridge across an irrigation canal that joined Old Pueblo and Socorro roads. The Impala's white-walled wheels rattled each plank on the swaying bridge. Don Pedro waited till Cuauhtémoc's car was on Socorro Road before guiding his station wagon onto the bridge.

After a few minutes of bumps and near-stops, the cars turned onto a nameless street of hard-packed dirt. In the hazy morning daylight of the Lower Valley, Pilar could distinguish the few scattered shacks of their neighbors, as well as the wooden stakes and neon-pink plastic ribbons that marked the boundaries of purchased yet still empty lots. About halfway down the dirt street, the pale green Chevy Impala stopped in front of a chain-link fence and an unplastered adobe house with sheets of plywood for doors. One side of the front yard was a giant mound of gravel and sand for mixing cement; the other side was a gigantic four-foot cube of adobe, with stalks of thick yellow straw intermittently protruding from the rough brown bricklike crooked antennae. Behind the chain-link fence lay a small runoff canal cut into the sand and subsoil.

"This is our house, niños," Pilar announced before she pushed open the heavy car door.

"Here?"

"Yes, here."

"But, but, but there are no windows," eight-year-old Julia, the oldest, stammered.

"When we get more money, we'll get windows."

"What about the rain?"

"It doesn't rain in Ysleta."

"Never?"

"Almost never."

"What do you mean by 'almost'?"

"Rarely in the summer. Don't worry, Julia, we'll have windows in a few months. Before it gets cold in October. Now, take Panchito and Marcos and keep them busy outside. Don't go into the canal."

"What canal?"

"The one behind the house."

"Why can't we go there?"

"It's full of spiders and frogs and snakes and niños de la tierra. If one bites you, you will die."

"Will, will we really die?"

"Well, maybe you'll just get sick."

"Like throw up?"

"Yes, you'll throw up all day," Pilar said, searching for Cuauhtémoc, who had been unloading the Impala's trunk. "You cannot go into the canal. Is that understood, Julieta?"

"Sí, Mamá." Julia ran to the chain-link fence, waited for her father to open the gate's lock as he came back for another load from the car, and ran toward the mounds of sand and gravel. Francisco and Marcos chased her. Pilar lost sight of them as they hid behind the stacks of adobe. Only their giggles echoed in the deserted street.

"There are niños de la tierra in those adobe bricks too, and in the backyard. You didn't tell her that," Cuauhtémoc said, his head halfway inside the trunk of the Chevy Impala.

"I don't want them to get filthy in that canal. God only knows what's in there."

"You also didn't tell her about 'no Beatles.' Which reminds me, I need to buy several extra gallons of kerosene for the lamps and stove." There was still no electricity in Barraca. The electric company had promised Cuauhtémoc that by the end of the summer, maybe by early fall, they would put the posts and overhead wires in their neighborhood. Pilar had been outraged when he had reported the news to her. "You tell them we have children? Babies?" she had exclaimed. But other families with children had already been living in Barraca for years. They were only the latest arrival.

Pilar and Cuauhtémoc unloaded the final box of pots, pans, and canned food from don Pedro's station wagon. Doña Josefina hovered over the toddler Ismael, who walked cautiously to the fence, gripped the chain-link with his chubby hands, and gawked at the half-made adobe house. As soon as Mayello napped, Pilar thought, maybe her mother could help her ready the bedroom for the night, and cook lunch and dinner. Perhaps Papá could saw the plywood door for the outhouse so that Cuauhtémoc could fasten it to the frame before nighttime. For now, an old white sheet on nails would do. It was work, and more work, and in a few days progress, and in a few months . . .

"Mamá! Mamá!"

"What happened?" Pilar finished tugging the jug of kerosene into a corner, where the children would not knock it over.

"Marcos fell down, cut his leg. He's bleeding."

"Where is he?"

"In the back. We were playing hide-and-seek and I was about to count to twenty and Pancho and Marcos were running and Marcos fell down and Pancho stepped on his leg."

"My God. That's a deep cut, niño. Let's wash it with soap and put a bandage on it."

"Pancho pushed me! He did! He pushed me!" Marcos cried, his brown face streaked with dirt, tears leaving behind crooked white lines on his cheeks.

Pilar glanced at Pancho. The older boy was frightened. His white T-shirt was torn at the belly button, and his stomach bulged over his waistband.

"I don't think he meant to do that. Pancho, go fetch me a bandage from the bedroom, inside the black shoebox next to my shoes. Julieta, what is Mayello doing in that corner by himself?"

"He's playing with rocks."

"Go get him."

"Mamá! Está comiendo tierra!"

"Clean his hands. Bring him over to the faucet too. Now, Julieta!" Julia pushed Ismael to the faucet in the front yard, their only source of running water until their indoor plumbing was reinstalled and connected to the main water line by don Chencho. As Pilar kneeled to rinse Marcos's gash, she noticed Mayello was grinning. The baby's face was smeared with mud and grime. A muscle spasm rippled across Pilar's back like an electric shock. She closed her eyes and faced the ground on all fours, sweat suddenly dripping from her cold temples.

"You cannot eat dirt! You cannot push each other! You children need to help me! I can't do this by myself!" she yelled at the ground, her head half-dizzy. A migraine seemed to want to start and not start inside her head.

"We're sorry, Mamá. We promise to help you."

"I'm sorry too."

"Me too."

On her knees, Pilar blinked and inhaled. She whispered to no one in particular, "Why did we come to este maldito terregal? Why to this wicked patch of dust? What have I done?"

"We'll help you, Mamá."

"I know you will, sweetheart. You know I love all of you?"

"We love you too, Mamá."

"Yes we do!"

"Listen, tell me one thing and I'll let you go play again," Pilar said, as she struggled to her feet. "Say, 'I am not sorry for being a niño. I am proud to be a niño!'"

The children looked at each other quizzically. Pilar smiled to reassure them. "Just say, 'I am proud to be a niño.' Say it loudly, so even la viejita doña Hortencia can hear you. It'll make me feel better. Please, do this for your mamá."

"I'm a niño!"

"Niño!"

"I'm muy proud to be a niño!"

"Thank you. Now go play and be careful." Pilar watched them sprint to the other side of the house, beyond her view. Above, a biplane gently descended to the cotton fields on Avenue of the Americas. The biplane's buzz seemed to expand the reach of the blue sky. She walked to the outhouse, knocked perfunctorily, and pulled the sheet open. She stared beyond the chain-link fence to the desolate landscape. Suddenly the stench overpowered her, and she vomited into the rancid abyss.

The absolute silence and darkness unnerved everyone. They were used to El Paso's city buses rumbling up and down the cracked streets until midnight. Children ran, shrieked, and laughed on the sidewalks, in between parked cars, even in the alleys, until the streetlights flickered with a weak orange light. If the night air was warm and dry, the old men and women dragged out their lawn chairs or reclined against their stoops, and smoked and gossiped after dinner. But in Ysleta, beyond the city, the red sun sank behind the Franklin Mountains in the west, and darkness enveloped the earth.

When Pilar fetched a blanket in another room, the adobe walls and the unfinished doorframes were lost within a thick blackness. She felt as if she had plunged into the ocean's depths. The darkness quivered with her every step. Her hands touched the walls in front of her, the doors, the nothingness of space that wrapped itself around her like a black sheet. From one dark corner of the bedroom, Pilar overheard sobs.

"M'ija, it will be okay," Pilar said gently, crouching next to Julia.

"Why did you get me that record if we were coming here? Why?"

"It will take only a month before they put in electricity. Then you can have your Beatles."

"How much is a month?"

"Thirty days."

"That's still too long! I hate it here!"

"Julieta, things will get better, I promise you. This Saturday we can visit your abuelita and listen to your record some more. How's that?"

"Can I stay with Abuelita until we have electricity?"

"No, I need you here to help me with your brothers."

"I still hate Ysleta and I hate you for bringing me here."

"Julieta, I know you don't mean that."

"Yes I do."

"Well, I don't hate you. I love you. Let's go to sleep now and get up early. You say your prayers?"

"God, please take care of me, take care of all my family, and take care of me while I sleep."

"Good night, preciosa."

"Good night, Mamá. Mamá?"

"Yes?"

"Can I pray for one more thing?"

"What?"

"God, please let me hear the Beatles' *Second Album* in Ysleta as soon as you can."

"Good night, Julieta."

~

As she drove one Saturday morning to the Big 8 for groceries, Pilar saw a sign—"German Shepherd puppies $5." She stopped at the white brick house next to the farm, and the white-haired Anglo lady let her choose from the three puppies left. Pilar picked the strongest puppy, black and gray, the one that leaped at her knee as soon as she stepped into the backyard. His face and big ears were black. His eyes gleamed like black marbles. His chest, with a star-shaped patch of gray, seemed like a furry shield, his paws, also gray, like socks. Pilar brought him back in a cardboard box in the back seat of the Chevy Impala. She could not wait to see the children's faces. Carefully she set the box down in one of the unfinished rooms next to the kitchen, but when she stepped into the front yard, the children were nowhere in sight.

As she marched around the house, Pilar thought she heard Julieta behind the outhouse in the canal. She leaned over the chain-link fence and scanned the banks of the canal. She finally found them throwing rocks behind doña Hortencia's fence, partially hidden by the tumbleweeds and cattails scattered along the banks.

"Didn't I tell you not to come back here? Just look at you!" Francisco and Marcos sat halfway down the embankment, white with dust. Each boy clutched a rock in his hand. Julia was holding Mayello's hand at the top of the crumbly embankment. "Get out of there now!"

"I told them not to, Mamá. I told them, but they wouldn't listen to me," Julieta pleaded, guiding her youngest brother away from the canal's edge.

"You were throwing rocks too! Don't lie!" Marcos yelled as he scurried up the incline on all fours. The boys stumbled to the top of the embankment.

"Look at your pants and shirts! I just washed them yesterday."

Pancho seemed on the verge of tears. Marcos glared at Julia and kicked dirt onto her sneakers.

"She was showing Mayello how to hit the beer bottles at the bottom, wasn't she, Panchito?" Marcos said. Pancho said nothing.

"I was not!"

"Yes you were! But Pancho's the only one who broke a bottle! You weren't even any good!"

"Liar!"

"You're the liar!"

"You're just a tonto who doesn't know what he's talking about."

"You're just a girl!"

"Both of you stop it. I don't want you coming back here. What if one of you tumbles into that green water? What if Mayello follows you and cuts himself on the glass or rocks? Do you know there are scorpions and snakes in this canal?"

"I'm sorry, Mamá."

"Sorry."

"Go wash all your clothes in the washtub, then hang everything up in the backyard. I'm tired of cleaning up after all of you." Pilar returned to the house, all four prisoners following solemnly behind her. About halfway there, she suddenly turned around and said, "I have something to show you."

"What is it?"

"A surprise. All of you wait right here and I'll bring it out. Close the gate, Julieta." Pilar carried the cardboard box to the front yard and placed it on the hardscrabble grass. Immediately the puppy jumped out, wagging its black tail.

"Un perrito!"

"He's so fast!"

"Is he ours?"

"Yes, he belongs to all of you and it's up to you to take care of him. Mayello, he doesn't bite. Relax, niño. He's just excited to see you."

"He's beautiful. Look at his fur. He's so cute."

"Is he a boy dog or a girl dog?"

"He's a boy dog."

"Does he have a name? Look how he licks me! He loves me!"

"He's black like a wolf. Is he a wolf?"

"No, he just looks like one."

"Lobo. Let's call him Lobo!"

"Yes, Lobo! Here Lobo!"

"Mom, how big will Lobo get? Bigger than Papá? Mayello, he's not going to bite you!"

"Big. German shepherds usually get very big. Did you know German shepherds are very smart?"

"I'll bet he's smarter than Julia."

"Look, Mamá, Lobo's chasing a snake! Get it, Lobo! Get it! Atta boy! It went into the adobe!"

"Jesús, María, y José."

A Chance to Prove Himself

One year later, as Cuauhtémoc drove to work, he thought about where he could get the best prices for two-by-fours and plywood for a cuartito in the backyard. Pilar didn't want the handsaws, hammers, electric saw, paint buckets, or paintbrushes inside the house anymore. With a cuartito, he could also buy and store extra sacks of cement for the rock wall in the front, whenever prices were cheap, and yeso to finish the inside Sheetrock walls. Maybe in a few years, he could buy a used truck. The old railroad ties he and Pilar had hauled from Mendoza's Yonke had slightly bent the bottom half of the Impala's trunk. Now Cuauhtémoc needed a chain, discretely hidden, to keep the trunk from flapping open whenever he hit a bump in the asphalt. But those thick, oily, and unbelievably heavy ties had done the job: even after a few summer downpours, their cesspool had ceased collapsing into itself.

Even early in the morning, the air was thick and hot as he drove on Alameda. After Western Playland, empty lots and junkyards were supplanted by brick houses and convenience stores. The cool breezes of the Lower Valley yielded to the hot exhaust from eighteen-wheelers, construction dump trucks, jalopies, motorcycles, and city buses on their way toward downtown El Paso. The city had been inexorably expanding east toward Ysleta. New immigrants or retirees from LA or young married couples had nowhere else to go. To the west was the no-man's-land of New Mexico, to the south was Juárez, where many had escaped from, and to the north was Fort Bliss, bigger than the state of Rhode Island.

Cuauhtémoc turned onto Texas Avenue, the edge of doña Pepita's neighborhood of food warehouses, red-brick tenements, ornate yet nearly abandoned churches, auto shops, Mexican tile stores, and used-car lots. Today he would have lunch at his suegra's apartment, just as he had every day since he began working at Morgan Smith. His mother-in-law cooked the best frijoles he had ever tasted, better than Pilar's, with slices of Muenster cheese melted atop the mashed pinto beans. As he ate, she would entertain him with stories of how she survived the Mexican Revolution when Villa rode triumphantly into Chihuahua's El Charco and electrified the countryside with his spectacular victories and charisma. Cuauhtémoc believed his mother, had she lived, would have been much like doña Pepita: the pride of Mexico undiminished, the gumption and wit of the street personified, and la gente humilde embodied in one feisty, yet kindhearted señora.

Cuauhtémoc had never forgotten the last day he had seen his mother. In front of the kitchen sink, she had waved to him with her flowered yellow apron tight around her waist. But when he returned from school, his house was surrounded by neighbors. His sisters had stopped him from entering the house. Like a wild animal, he had screamed at them to release him and pounded them with his fists. His mother lay in the living room, bleeding from her brain.

Cuauhtémoc eased the Impala into the side lot of the Mills Building in front of the Plaza de los Lagartos, the heart of downtown El Paso, and found an empty spot in the back row. As he marched into the Mills Building, he said "Buenos dias" to Jeannie Apodaca, the receptionist, who didn't know much Spanish but always claimed to want to take a class to learn the language of her ancestors. Dylan Smith, Mr. Smith's youngest son, a construction manager who wasn't very reliable, lingered at Jeannie's desk, even though both were married.

Cuauhtémoc zigzagged through the labyrinth of front offices, cubicles for engineers, small offices for project managers, and toward the wide open space in the back. There the draftsmen worked at huge, elevated drafting tables, with long fluorescent lamps, on clamps, angled above the tables like impressionistic pterodactyls. Chuy Gomez sat at his table, somber as always. Rogelio Gandaria stirred his cup of coffee, waiting for their boss Manny Ramirez to walk in before he started to look busy. Most of the other draftsmen had not yet arrived. Nobody wore a tie or jacket in the drafting room, including Cuauhtémoc. That had been one of the practices that had pleased him most about Morgan Smith. Also, if you did your work, they left you alone. Manny handled the project managers and front office directly, absorbing the problems and criticisms, as well as the accolades, before they ever reached the draftsmen. He translated what was needed and what was unsaid into plain language, including Spanish.

Cuauhtémoc remembered the first day he had walked into Morgan Smith. It hadn't been Morgan Smith then, but Smith and Hunter, and their offices had been across the plaza in the Cortez Building. Cuauhtémoc was desperate for work. In 1958, he returned to Juárez from his year of mandatory service for the Mexican government in Apatzingan, Michoacán, as an agronomist. He hightailed it to the border, even though his bosses at the Department of Agriculture had offered him a job in Mexico City. He had heard rumors that his nóvia Pilar Del Rio had been spotted dancing at a club in Juárez. Cuauhtémoc had been sending Pilar money every month, to save for their betrothal. A gorgeous brunette who resembled Jane Russell, Pilar was also saving money. She worked at the department store as a saleswoman and occasionally modeled clothes at local fashion shows.

Twenty-two-year-old Cuauhtémoc stumbled into Juárez, after an all-night interstate bus ride, and barely muttered hello to his father and stepmother before boarding another bus to Pilar's new house in El Paso. Pilar had written to him about the generous offer of American citizenship to don Pedro from the owner of the poultry farm. That bit of news spooked Cuauhtémoc. Yes, El Paso was just across the bridge, a mere twenty minutes away if the traffic wasn't too heavy. But the love of his life might be slipping away while he had been busy creating and testing hybrid varieties of corn and rice in Michoacán.

Pilar told him he was crazy, that she had not been dancing with anybody at any club, that every day her feet throbbed with so much pain after she worked at the department store that she wanted to cut them off. From a closet, she retrieved a shoebox with a stack of money she had saved, much more than Cuauhtémoc had ever sent her. Cuauhtémoc felt like an idiot. For twenty-four hours from Michoacán to Chihuahua, he had endured an awful gut-wrenching fear: he might not be with Pilar the rest of his life. In one moment, this fear drained away from his face. He dropped to one knee, kissed her hand, and proposed to her. They giddily made plans to marry at the main cathedral in Juárez in a few months. He would not return to Apatzingan or Mexico City. He would find a job in El Paso and score a green card.

Every day, Cuauhtémoc and a friend, Hugo Jímenez, a classmate from La Agricultura, used day passes to walk across the Santa Fe International Bridge to look for work. They wore their best baggy, pleated khakis and short-sleeve white shirts, and shined their shoes meticulously. They gripped brown paper bag lunches with chicken or beef burritos and tortas, which later became misshapen and soggy. After two weeks, they sunburned to a dark, coppery hue under the merciless southwestern sun, wore out two pairs of leather shoes, and lost weight. The young men walked into random office buildings, chatted with whomever spoke Spanish, from genial janitors to stiff receptionists to well-dressed Mexicanos who might point them in the right direction. Most were at least polite and claimed they just didn't know of any jobs in El Paso. Some asked what they could do. A few even ushered them inside their offices and introduced them to their bosses, who usually had no idea what an agronomist was or how they could use one.

One day the two perfectly coiffed young men were eating their lunches on a wooden bench at the San Jacinto Plaza, arguing about why the alligators hadn't moved for ten minutes inside the enormous round fountain of blue and yellow Mexican tiles. In the palpitating heat, Cuauhtémoc declared he would try the Cortez Building, an imposing, ornate, stone-and-brick edifice across the plaza. He had seen a sign for a "compañía that designs buildings and roads." The receptionist (who was not Jeannie, but a Mexicana who knew Spanish very well) told them to wait in the lobby. As they waited quietly and gradually stopped perspiring from baking under the sun all day, Manuel Ramirez sauntered out and waved them inside. Manny was an older classmate from La Agricultura!

He told them Smith and Hunter was indeed looking for a draftsman who could do topographical elevations—but he needed only one of them.

Manuel Ramirez interviewed them one at a time, but almost without hesitation he chose Cuauhtémoc. He was younger and seemed eager—no, desperate—for a job, whereas Hugo waxed rhapsodic about his college days, more focused on the past than on the future. Hugo was surprisingly gracious about it, and even declared he looked forward to finally making the move to Mexico City, which he did a few weeks later. Cuauhtémoc was elated. He would start at $1.25 per hour.

From that day in 1958, Cuauhtémoc had worked for Smith and Hunter for six years, every year earning raises and, more importantly, respect. Two years ago, against the advice of many of his friends at work, he had loaded Pilar, the children, and their belongings in a U-Haul and moved to Santa Ana, California, for a new job with better pay. But Cuauhtémoc hated California, the high cost of living, the tense and interminable commute to work, and what he perceived as a harsher attitude against Mexicanos and Chicanos. Sure, El Paso wasn't sophisticated, or rich, but the power was inexorably shifting away from the clubby old guard of white businessmen and lawyers who had dominated city politics for decades. More common were people like Preston Smith, who rapidly adapted to the majority Mexican culture, married Mexicanas, and were creating a third culture, of Mexicanized Anglos and Americanized Mexicans. Last year, Cuauhtémoc had escaped from California, with Pilar and his four niños in tow, returned to doña Pepita's house without work, walked into the new offices of

Morgan Smith in the Mills Building, and gotten his old job back, with better pay and an abrazo from Manny Ramirez.

"Oye, Cuauhtémoc, I need to talk to you. You have a minute?" Manny asked. He wore a starched white shirt and tie, but had already loosened the tie knot and rolled up his sleeves twenty minutes into the workday. Slightly taller and more muscular than the compact Cuauhtémoc, Manny had black, slicked-back hair, revealing a streak of gray that gave him the air of a lothario.

"Que pasó? Are we okay with Santa Anita?"

"Of course. You caught all of Ganda's mistakes. Ese pendejo. I'm gonna fire him one of these days, as soon as his kids are out of college," Manny said. "But no, that's not it. We're going to bid for a new job, a huge, important job, and I want you to do the bid plans. Fort Bliss is contracting out for two thousand housing units for troops coming from Europe and other parts of the United States. The army hasn't created housing at Fort Bliss in decades. If we get this, híjola, it will be work for Morgan Smith for years. Como pegándole a la loteria mexicana. El viejo Smith himself wants to review the bid before we send it in, and we don't have much time."

"Seguro que sí," Cuauhtémoc said quietly, his round face betraying the slightest of smiles.

"Use that new method for elevations, for speed and accuracy. Forget about Ganda, but when you get a chance start teaching it to El Sério. A ver si le agarra la onda."

"Ándale pues." The "new method" was the one valuable skill Cuauhtémoc had salvaged from his brief foray into California: a way of calculating an average depth for any terrain, with dozens of reference points from the many hills and valleys within a particular plot of land. He used this average depth to determine where in the landscape to fill in, and where to cut in, so that the company achieved a relatively flat building site with the least movement of earth. When the quantities in question were tons of dirt over hundreds of acres, the right calculations could save the company significant money. Cuauhtémoc had learned this new method in California, but nobody in El Paso knew how to use it effectively yet. Even Manny Ramirez could only follow Cuauhtémoc's first few steps before losing himself in the dizzying array of plot points, united points, blue numbers ("fill-in"), red numbers ("cut-in"), and averages that spewed forth from Cuauhtémoc's pencil like hieroglyphics. Cuauhtémoc had tried this new method for a few of Manny's smaller projects since rejoining Morgan Smith. In the field, project managers raved to Manny that, with the latest instructions from Drafting and Design, the site was ready quicker than ever before, significantly below the projected budget. Preston Smith certainly liked the extra profits already in hand before he even put up a single building. Not long ago, Manny had boasted to a project manager pissing in the urinal next to his, "Instead of wasting our time fixing desmadres, we're getting precise like the Mayas, goddammit!"

"Oye, Cuau," Manny said as he glanced at the roll of plans on the drafting table. "This Fort Bliss project will be a government contract. With security checks y otras pendejadas. The military will eventually want to know who is working on the project. Every single person."

"Don't worry, I'm clean. I haven't killed anybody as far as I remember," Cuauhtémoc said.

"But we will have an issue. El viejo Smith also thinks so, but we can take care of it. You need to become an American citizen as soon as possible. Put in the paperwork this week if you can."

"Por que? I have permission to work here. I already own a house here. My family lives here. The kids go to school in Ysleta. That's the United States, isn't it?"

"I know that, Cuau. You don't have to convince me. It's these gringos and their competitive games. This is a huge contract, worth millions of dollars. The firms in town will be using everything and anything to win this contract from the Defense Department. And that includes dirty tricks and vicious rumors. We can either keep our fingers crossed and pray that our bid doesn't get thrown out for stupid reasons, or we can make damn sure we are the number one bid because of the quality of the work and the price. We can't let those cabrónes snatch away our business."

"Ándale pues, I'll become a gringo. But I don't even speak English very well."

Cuauhtémoc listened to Manny tell him the details of applying for American citizenship, and many thoughts flooded his mind. What mattered to the migra was that an employer sponsored you, that you had a job, that you paid your taxes and had stayed out of trouble. His children were already Americanos, but he and Pilar possessed only green cards. He wasn't about to return to Mexico. His old friend Hugo had regaled him with stories of movidas and corruption in Mexico City, of having to buy his boss a new car when Hugo was awarded a coveted job. Cuauhtémoc couldn't live like that. But he had never imagined he would have to become a citizen right away.

Cuauhtémoc was proud to be a Mexicano. The Americanos he had gotten to know in El Paso and Santa Ana often had no loyalty to family. It was always about money and status and putting other people down who did not look like you. His taste of poverty, his struggle, had bestowed on him another perspective, of feeling a kinship with the downtrodden, even negritos, rather than a disdain. George Washington and Thomas Jefferson had owned slaves. Some of these poor Mexican laborers scurrying across the border were not much better than slaves. Cuauhtémoc had even overheard nasty remarks from certain project managers about those illegales on the worksite. Americanos used these poor bastards to make a profit, and then wanted to discard them like yesterday's trash.

On the way home in the late afternoon, Cuauhtémoc glimpsed the Franklin Mountains through his rearview mirror. He peeked at the orange sunset as he glanced at the trunk of the Impala, which popped up and slammed down whenever he hit the slightest bump in the asphalt. The Impala's trunk was loaded with as many two-by-fours as he could stuff into it, a box of nails, a sack of cement, and another of yeso. The car was weighed down so much that the red flag taped at the end of the two-by-four bundle seemed to wipe the street behind him. A few idiots had honked at him. But he had just smiled angrily at them and confined himself to the slow lane. As soon as he was on Alameda past Delta, fewer cars tailgated him. Most simply roared past him without a comment or dirty look.

Cuauhtémoc slowly approached the rickety wooden bridge next to Mount Carmel and the old Ysleta Mission. As the Impala reached the top of the gravel incline, the front wheels suddenly jammed into a rut. The trunk flapped open, and half the two-by-four bundle spilled onto one side of the bridge with a series of sickening thumps. Cuauhtémoc lifted his foot off the gas pedal and allowed the Impala to roll forward from its own momentum over the bridge. The underside of the car scraped against the gravel with a languorous screech. At the other side, he stopped the car, jumped out, and started picking up the two-by-fours, like matchsticks, from the gravel road and the bridge. No cars were in sight, so he took his time picking up the last scattered pieces of wood.

"My God, your hands are bleeding!" Pilar exclaimed when he came home. "What happened?"

"Splinters from the wood. I loaded it at Cashway after work, and then some of it fell out at the bridge. Think I got them out."

Pilar handed him a pomada from Juárez and offered to pick out the splinters with a needle, but he said he was okay. Tonight for dinner they were having enchiladas, arroz, and frijoles. She said the phone company had finally sent someone to connect their phone. They had a new phone number, but it wouldn't work for a few days. While she finished setting the table, he would cart the wood and sacks of cement to the backyard. "Get those lepes to help you," she said.

He mentioned that the company wanted him to become a citizen, and explained why. Without missing a beat, Pilar asked him if she could, too. Wouldn't it bother her not to be a Mexicana anymore? he asked her. She would never return to Mexico, she said, with its crooks and the PRI, and mordidas to get a driver's license, to get married, to start a business. Their life was here, she said. Their life was better.

"Your own mother lived to see Villa. Aren't you proud of who you are?" he asked her.

"Course I am. But over there they don't pay you for your intelligence, for your hard work, for your ganas. They pay you if you're from the right family, if you do your boss favors, if you obey. How many times has Smith given you a raise without you even asking for one?"

"Every year."

Cuauhtémoc complained that he didn't want his children to become hippies. He didn't want his children growing up to hate their father or mother. What happened to decency, respect, and community in America? Did this country's values represent her own?

"No, but neither does Mexico," she said. At least in El Paso you could find your own way. Here you could have a choice to pick and choose what you wanted from both worlds.

~

"Julieta, come back here! Did you go to the bathroom?"

"Sí, Mamá."

"Francisco, Marcos?"

"Amá, I haven't."

"Go now, and come back quickly. We're late. Marquitos, pull your pants all the way down, and watch what you are doing!" Pilar said loudly at his back as the boy ran down the hallway. "I don't have time to change you again. Julieta, this is yours. Burritos de frijoles. Francisco, here."

"But I wanted a bologna sandwich."

"Tomorrow. Today it's burritos. I haven't gone to Big 8, but I will later today. After I drop you off at school."

"I hope I don't get 'The Penguin,'" Julia said, rolling up her bag lunch tightly in her hand. "I heard he's tough, and yells a lot."

"Who's 'The Penguin'?" Eight-year-old Francisco hiked up his pants over his belly and glanced at his sister nervously.

"He's a short teacher with a big head who looks like a penguin. In 4-1. You'll get Mrs. Vega. She's the best. She likes to dance in class on Fridays."

"Es muy simpática. Julieta had her last year," Pilar said, splashing water droplets on her hands and patting them onto Francisco's black hair to straighten it out. Francisco smiled tentatively, for the first time this morning. "Marcos, keep a tight grip on your lonche and put it where the teacher tells you, okay? Burritos and a cookie."

"Did I get a cookie too?"

"Yes, Julieta. Everybody got a cookie. Everybody ready? Vámonos."

Pilar and the four children scrambled out the front door. The kids yelled for Lobo, but Pilar hustled them through the chain-link gate and into the dirt street before the affectionate, slobbery German shepherd jumped on them. She held three-year-old Ismael's hand and strolled behind the other three kids, who were faster. As they made their way across the driveways of San Lorenzo Avenue, Pilar noticed two other children with their mothers also on their way to South Loop School.

"Julieta! Here. And Pancho. Don't lose your dime, or you won't have anything to drink at lunchtime."

"Mom, do I get a dime too?"

"No, Marquitos. They give you your milk in first grade. Now listen to me. I will be waiting at the school gate at 2:30, when you get out. I'll show you exactly where. Then we'll wait for Julieta and Pancho, who'll be out at 3:30." Julia and Francisco had sprinted about fifty feet in front of them, on San Lorenzo Avenue, stopping and starting a race against each other.

"Don't go!"

"Mayello."

"Don't go! Don't go! Don't go, Marquitos!"

"It's okay, Mayello. Marcos will be back. He's just going to school."

"No! No! No!"

"Mayellito, I'll bring you a rock from school," Marcos said kindly. He didn't seem as apprehensive as his older brother and sister had once been about their first day at South Loop. Julia and Francisco had been older when they had transferred from Santa Ana to South Loop last year. They had not been to the school, nor yet befriended any other children in Ysleta. What had immediately struck Pilar last year was that at least half the teachers at South Loop were Mexican American and everybody knew Spanish, even the güerito principal, Mr. MacIntosh. In California, Pilar had been treated as if she were an ignoramus because she could not communicate in English very well.

"Stop giving him rocks, Marcos. He's sucking the dirt off them and he's going to get sick," Pilar said, quickening her pace. It was a few minutes before eight in the morning, and they were approaching Southside Street. Over the small pedestrian bridge of the irrigation canal was Calavera, another neighborhood of adobe shacks, and South Loop School. "Watch out!"

A red Mustang veered suddenly onto Southside from Carranza Street, its chrome wheels spinning into the sand and gravel and unleashing a gigantic cloud of dust as it zoomed down the dirt road. Francisco had stepped back and waited at the corner, but where was Julieta? Pilar started to run frantically, pulling Ismael behind her, Marcos sprinting next to them. As Pilar glared at the malevolent red streak of the car disappearing behind a cloud of dust, she saw Julieta's white dress at the top of the bridge. Julia had dashed across the street. Pilar's heart was in her throat. She wanted to yell at Julia for her recklessness, but by the time Pilar met Francisco at the corner, with Marcos and Ismael in tow, she simply and silently thanked God for watching over them.

They crossed the street and met Julia at the top of the canal's embankment, at the bridge. The nine-year-old had been grinning triumphantly from ear to ear, until she saw her mother's ashen face. "Next time, Julieta, I want you to stop like Francisco and wait for the cars to go by. Is that understood, young lady?"

"Sí, señora," Julieta said, staring at her feet.

They walked across the narrow pedestrian bridge. Except for a trickle of water at the bottom, the canal was dry. The thick metal dam, about a quarter mile away and next to the Río Grande, was shut. In early September, the air was still hot even at dawn, but occasionally a gust of wind, like a stampede of ghost horses, galloped across the cotton fields in the Lower Valley. Not far behind were fall's thunderstorms.

When they were almost across the bridge, Pilar noticed the sweetly acrid smell of marijuana. Her eyes scanned the banks of the canal until she found them, under another, wider bridge less than a block away. She couldn't see their faces, which were shrouded in the shadows, but she spotted the momentary red glow of the cigarette. She saw a hand grab a metallic aerosol can on the canal's muddy floor. The silver mist sparkled like a cloud of silver bees.

When should she allow her children to walk home by themselves? Five-year-old Marcos she would have to pick up all year at the school gate. But Julieta and Francisco, after about a month, had already walked home together last year, with all of their friends from the neighborhood. Pilar had warned them about the marijuanos. The mothers at South Loop had banded together and promised to keep each other informed. Juanita Muñoz, who lived next to the canal on Southside Street, had said she always waited outside on her porch whenever she saw the kids coming home from school, to keep an eye on them. Nothing had ever happened, and the marijuanos had seemed less visible by the end of the school year, after many in the neighborhood complained to the sheriff and even la migra. But today, on the first day of school, those devils were back.

Where were the mothers of those miscreants? These lepes were probably at South Loop, in the older grades, or maybe they had already dropped out. Pilar had listened to stories of gang fights from the other mothers, "Barraca contra Calavera." Three months ago, she had overheard moaning in the canal behind their backyard chain-link fence, and for a moment she had imagined La Llorona. Pilar had sent

Cuauhtémoc to investigate. Next to tumbleweeds and cattails and empty beer bottles, he had come across un chavalo grande named "Joe," with his head bleeding from a rumble the night before. Cuauhtémoc had helped Joe to his home on Carranza Street. After that, Joe always waved enthusiastically at her from the street or the canal, as if her husband's act of kindness had somehow cemented a relationship between them. One day, through the blinds, she noticed Joe grabbing his ankle to adjust what appeared to be a shiny knife in his boot.

"Niños, listen to your teacher. Wait your turn when you want to talk, and don't just blurt out your question like some of those rude kids. Look your teacher in the eye when you are speaking to her. Pay attention in class, and do your work. If your friend is doing something he or she should not be doing, don't do the same thing. Would you eat a worm simply because your friend is eating a worm?"

"No!"

"Yuck!"

"Well, *think*. Just so you know, I signed forms from Mr. MacIntosh, giving him permission to spank you if you get in trouble."

"They spanked Freddy Pacheco last year, after he threw a rock in recess and broke a window in school. He couldn't sit down all day and he was crying," Julieta said with a smirk on her face.

"You know what Mr. MacIntosh told the parents at the final Open House last year? That the kids who came back with signed forms usually didn't need any spanking. But the kids whose parents wouldn't sign the forms were the kids who got into the most trouble. The lessons you learn at home, good or bad, you repeat in school. I know all of you will do just fine."

Mr. MacIntosh's secretary, Elvia Zaragoza, first walked Julia to her classroom, which was on the southern side of the enormous E that was South Loop School. Julieta gasped when she heard Elvia say she had Mr. Zubia (aka "El Penguino"). Pilar and the other children waited inside the principal's office, in front of Elvia's desk. Marcos nudged his older brother Francisco, and pointed with his big brown eyes at the large wooden paddle, lacquered and carved with the principal's name. The paddle hung on a piece of twine behind Mr. MacIntosh's desk. Elvia came back quickly and walked Marcos down the hallway immediately adjacent to the main office, the middle part of the E, where the youngest children had their classrooms. At a doorway down the hall, Marcos shook hands with what appeared to be a young, slender woman—Pilar could only see Mrs. Ryan's silhouette—and then waved at his mother at the other end of the hallway before stepping into the room.

"Panchito, it will be okay," Pilar said. Francisco, the eight-year-old, was crying silently as Elvia marched down the hall toward them. "Did you see how Marquitos didn't cry at all? And it's his very first day of school."

The eight-year-old boy, her shyest child, stared solemnly at her. Pilar wondered if his classmates would pick on Pancho because he was heavy. Pilar hugged Pancho as Elvia waited a few steps away. At least, Pilar thought, he will be with Mrs. Vega, who will prod him gently beyond his shyness. That señora was the most exuberant teacher Pilar had ever met.

Pilar walked from South Loop School toward Gonzales Street in Calavera. She felt at once liberated and sad after leaving her children in school for the first time this season. She glanced at Ismael, who gripped a black rock from the school playground in his tiny hand. His other hand held hers, but the three-year-old's eyes scoured Gonzales Street for more rocks. In about half an hour, at a comfortable pace for Mayello, they would be at Mount Carmel and Pilar could say a prayer before she and Mayello kept walking another half mile to the Big 8 and the Winn-Dixie.

The brown metal doors of Mount Carmel were closed, but unlocked, and Pilar tentatively walked into the foyer. She warned Mayello to be quiet while her eyes adjusted to the darkness. The oak confessional booths were to the right and left, their entrances draped in red velvet. Assorted doors and closets also lined the beige cinderblock walls, for the priest's vestments and supplies, for boxes of prayer- and hymnbooks, and a small marble shelf with a bowl of holy water. Beyond the foyer, above which was a small balcony, were rows and rows of oak pews. Three main aisles led to the marble altar and a life-size Christ on the Cross dangling from the ceiling above the altar. To the left of Jesus was an alcove with a statue of San José, who appeared mulatto. To the right was another alcove, with La Virgen María in malachite green and brownish gold. In front of the Virgin was a wrought-iron stand chock-full of flickering candles of different sizes, with ex-votos and a black metal collection box. Two old women, one near the front, another kneeling in the back, prayed quietly in the pews. Father Hernández strode from a closet near San José's alcove to the sacristy behind the marble altar. Pilar slid into a pew about halfway down the middle aisle, with Mayello next to her, and kneeled and prayed.

"Mayello, stop banging that rock on the seat, m'ijo," she whispered to her son. Ismael wiggled next to her, bored. He whacked the wooden pew a few times again, just to hear the loud, vibrating echo bounce off the beige cinderblock walls. Father Hernández paid him no mind, and Pilar shook her head at the child. When Mayello struck the pew again, Pilar grabbed the rock from his hand and continued praying with her eyes closed.

In a couple of seconds, Pilar heard what sounded like Mayello's voice in front of her, not next to her. She opened her eyes and found him sprinting down the middle aisle toward the altar! Underneath the bloody Jesus, Mayello jumped into the air, as if giving the Holy Ghost a high five. The boy stomped onto the stage in front of the marble altar and scurried behind it to hide. Pilar was horrified. Before she could reach Mayello, Father Hernández marched behind the marble altar, grabbed the three-year-old forcefully by the hand, and spanked him back to the middle aisle.

"Señora, we cannot have this in the House of God."

"I am sorry, Father. Please forgive my son."

"Señora, he is but a child, and does only what we teach him to do. But Jesus Christ is merciful and will show you how to teach your child."

"I am sorry, Father," Pilar repeated, deeply ashamed. She could barely look him in the eyes. "I will do my best to teach Ismael to respect this holy ground. Thank you." Mayello clung to her leg and sobbed. Pilar started to walk out the side door, about halfway up the rows of oak pews.

"Señora, are you new here?" The priest followed her outside. Mayello glared at him and at the huge wooden crucifix that swung from the priest's neck like a mallet. That crucifix had inadvertently smacked Mayello's skull when the priest had bent down to spank him.

"Yes, Father. We arrived in Ysleta from Juárez about a year ago. Pilar Martínez, para servirle," she said, and shook the priest's clammy hand. Father Hernández was older than Cuauhtémoc, but not as old as her father, don Pedro. The priest had wiry black-and-white hair, black plastic glasses, and seemed stocky under his thick brown Franciscan robe.

"Mucho gusto, señora Martínez. Padre Hernández de Zacatecas. Somos paisanos. Have you thought of enrolling your children in our Sunday school?" The slightest of smiles appeared across the priest's heavy lips.

"Father, nothing would make me happier. But we are still finishing our house in Ysleta, and we don't have the money to send them to Sunday school." Pilar tightened her grip on Mayello's hand.

"Señora, Sunday school is free. We only ask that parents contribute what they can, in food or volunteer work or money. Please let me know. I think all children would benefit from understanding the stories of the Bible, and from learning the moral lessons of Jesus Christ. I teach the class myself whenever I can." The priest forced a grin at Ismael, who stared at the yellow, crooked teeth.

"Thank you, Father, you are very generous. I will talk to my husband, but I know it would do these children so much good if they attended Sunday school. There are so many bad temptations in our neighborhood."

"May God be with you and your family."

"And also with you."

The Leaves of Rancho Seco
THE DAY BEFORE EASTER, 1970

Pilar Martínez was up before the sun. In front of their adobe house, the amber light of the newly installed streetlamp quivered in the darkness. Southside and Carl Longuemare roads were empty. She piled up her old blankets by the door for Cuauhtémoc to load and yanked out the wooden case of empty Coca-Cola and Fanta bottles from the alley for their first stop in Waterfil.

She first got the idea before Good Friday. Yet even on a day when she had done no heavy cleaning, her back ached. Pain had become a part of her body when she needed to get the children ready for school, when she cleaned the house yet again, when she helped Cuauhtémoc bring in more lumber, sacks of cement, and rebar for the patio/basketball court he envisioned in the backyard.

She was thirty-five years old, and she was getting old. Twelve-year-old Julieta was already as tall as she was. Pilar was always working, and Cuauhtémoc was stressed out with his new responsibilities as Manny's new official right-hand man. To her, this family seemed like leaves in the wind, from the same tree, yet floating to their own private destinies. So Pilar proposed Rancho Seco.

"Pilar," she heard from behind her, "what time did you get up?"

"About an hour ago. I've done the burritos, con frijoles y queso and strips of chile California. Packed all the fruit in the refrigerator into plastic bags. I'm gonna make peanut-butter-and-jelly sandwiches for Marcos and Mayello because they might not want burritos. But I need the cooler—can you get it for me?"

"You sure you want to go today?"

"Of course, it's going to be a gorgeous day. The metal folding chairs are also in the back. And I think the folding table will work if we can keep that leg from snapping shut. What else?"

"Well, let me think," Cuauhtémoc said, still in the white, sleeveless T-shirt he always slept in. "Coal and lighter fluid for la parilla."

"Got those at Big 8 yesterday. With T-bones, hamburger meat, cebollitas, a watermelon, napkins, plastic forks and knives, paper plates."

"Do the kids really want to go? Aren't you tired? Wouldn't it be better if we just took it easy this weekend, went out for an early dinner tomorrow, after Easter services?"

"Your sister Elvia's going. And Noni. And Seferina and her family."

"Ándale pues. Let me get myself ready and I'll get the cooler in the back."

"Oh, and música! Don't forget the radio! Make sure it has batteries, Cuauhtémoc," Pilar said loudly at the darkened hallway seconds after her husband had disappeared around the corner to return to their bedroom.

It was still cool and breezy when the yellow truck pulled out slowly from the driveway. Julia and Pancho and Marcos sat in the truck bed, their backs against the cab. Pancho held a baseball and a softball in each hand. Julia had her eyes tightly shut. Marcos was on one knee, trying to catch a glimpse of the road they left behind. Six-year-old Mayello, in between his parents in the cab of the yellow truck, reclined his small black head against his mother's shoulder, still half asleep. Nobody had truly wanted to go to Rancho Seco for the day, except Pilar. But once on the road they focused their collective attention on what lay ahead.

The air and the road seemed to change after their stop in Waterfil. The soda case was now filled with orange Fantas, red Sangrias, black Coca-Colas, and dark green 7 Ups clinking together like chimes. Every so often, the yellow truck would slow down almost to a halt to go over a boxy speed bump seemingly in the middle of nowhere. The giant cottonwoods, mulberrys, and desert pines were whitewashed with lime if they were near the two-lane, curbless highway. Dusty hamlets without paved streets appeared and disappeared next to cotton fields and giant swaths of alfalfa. The air was intermittently filled with the whiff of burning grass or wood, or the heavy sweet smell of irrigated alfalfa, or the stench of rotten eggs and shit, which prompted the children to groan, pinch their noses, and hold their breaths until they couldn't anymore.

Soon they abruptly turned off the highway and under a rusty wrought-iron open gate that led into a dusty lane aimed at the horizon. A Mexican compadre of Elvia's husband owned an immense farm without a sign, without a street number, an oasis of trees in the distance next to an irrigation canal. A farmhand waved them forward, with a dark red, almost maroon face under a brittle straw hat that sat athwart his sweaty head. Elvia's paneled station wagon was parked next to a shady clump of trees. Cuauhtémoc turned the truck toward it.

"Raquel! I'm so glad you came!" said Julieta.

"Of course," Raquel Hernández said, hugging Julia. They were each other's favorite cousins, both in the seventh grade at South Loop School, but in different homerooms. "You know, Noni will be here. And Rosa, and Becky."

"Oh, my God! My mother doesn't tell me anything. Just 'do this' and 'do that' and 'make sure your brothers are not getting into trouble.'"

"Speaking of that, señorita," Pilar said, "Julia, help me unload the truck, and set up over there under that tree. Pancho and Marcos, bring the cooler this way! Raquel, do me a favor and keep an eye on Mayello while I say hello to your mother. After you help me set up, Julieta, you can go with Raquel, okay?"

Julia rolled her eyes behind her mother's back, but Raquel just grinned.

"Your little brother's so cute! He looks like a little mummy with his eyes half-closed."

"He's not that cute. Don't let him bump into the truck, or he'll start cryin' and it will somehow be my fault. Oye, Raquel, do you know what Sylvia Rodríguez told me?" Julieta carried the blankets to the tree, keeping an eye on her mother.

"Sylvia Rodríguez?"

"You know, la gordita who's in the poetry magazine with Mrs. Nelson."

"I guess. You're the one who knows all the smarties in school."

"She told me Noni was kissing Julian Pacheco behind the portables last week. They were really going at it after school."

"Julian Pacheco? Yuck! He's really ugly."

"Whatever. I think Oscar Trujillo's kinda cute." Now fully awake, Mayello sprinted behind the giant cottonwood and was throwing rocks into a field.

"Oscar? You like Oscar?"

"He's cute. And he doesn't seem immature like most of the other seventh and eighth graders."

"He is serious and quiet. Is he on your quinceañera list?"

"My what?"

"Your quinceañera list. You know, for your court, six boys and six girls."

"But we're twelve years old! That's three years away!"

"It's just a list of boys I like, and my best friends, and who would go well with who. You know," Raquel said, blushing.

"Doesn't it change? How will you know who you want at your party three years from now?"

"It's just a list. I scratch people out all the time, and sometimes I add them back in."

"Am I on the list?"

"Of course. You've always been on the list. You've never been scratched out, not even once. But I might scratch out Noni if she starts going out with Julian Pacheco."

"I could never keep a list like that. Híjola, I don't think I'd pick a single bozo boy at South Loop, except maybe Oscar Trujillo. I'm hoping things change in high school. Better quality material," Julia said. Raquel giggled so hard she tripped on a rock.

"Let's get the blankets rolled out, and put the cooler and this other stuff on top of it, before my mother comes back and thinks of something else for me to do. Did you bring a radio? That 'Bridge over Troubled Water' is one of the most beautiful songs I've ever heard. You heard it?"

"The Beatles?"

"No, Simon Garfinkle, I think. The Beatles are dead."

In the late morning, the adults sat together in the shade, near the cabrito pit that Cuauhtémoc, Jorge—Elvia's husband—and Pancho had dug for the slabs of goat meat that would be their late lunch or early dinner. Marcos and Mayello had carried smooth rocks from in and around the canals for the bottom of the pit. Jorge had poured in a pile of red-hot coals around the rocks and topped it with mesquite. The goat meat was seasoned with salt, pepper, thyme, and rosemary, wrapped in thick foil along with scallions, carrots, potatoes, green peppers, and Spanish onions, then placed over the mesquite and covered with an old cookie sheet, a gunnysack, and a few choice branches. The delicious aroma from the pit, as well as the Mexican polkas and corridos that blasted from their radio—750 AM, "Radio KAMA!"—brought a calm to their picnic. Free of any more duties, the children split into groups. The girls claimed a faraway tree, with their own radio and blankets, and enough space to lie down and read magazines and gossip. The boys threw rocks, burned leaves, killed lizards, and targeted an old, gnarly cottonwood that seemed easy to climb and a good base to imagine a military campaign.

"The kids against the adults! We're gonna crush you!" eight-year-old Marcos screamed to no one in particular as he ran onto the field for a softball game in the afternoon. Everyone had finished eating cabrito, or peanut-butter-and-jelly sandwiches, or burritos, or a little bit of everything. Pancho walked slowly to second base and pointed Marcos to third base. Julieta, who thought softball stupid, stopped absentmindedly at first. The usually shy Pancho handed her the ball and told her she would be pitching. Raquel would be at first, and her older sister Noni would be catcher. Cousins Rosa and Becky would be in the outfield. Six-year-old Mayello, they agreed, would be on the adult team.

"Julieta, above the plate!"

"I'm trying. Why don't you pitch?"

"'Cause I need to get it, to throw them out!"

"Ay Dios mio!" Aunt Elvia said grinning, as one of Julia's pitches sailed just above her head. "This niña's throwin' fast and wild!" Tía Elvia was always ready for a dance, a good joke, or a baseball game. Her husband Jorge was her opposite: solemn, quiet, and, in front of his wife, happily obedient. "Right here. Put it right here, niña, so I can smack a Johnny Bench!"

Elvia hit a bouncy grounder to third base, and the softball trickled a few feet past Marcos, through his legs. "Throw it to first! Throw it, Marcos! Híjola!" The fat softball sailed over Raquel's head. Raquel ran after it as Aunt Elvia, waving her hands in the air as if swatting away flies from her head, rounded first and headed for second. By the time Raquel gripped the ball in her right hand, her mother was already rounding third, so she threw it to Noni at home plate. Aunt Elvia, backpedaling, headed to third base, but Pancho was already there, having pushed his younger brother away. Noni lobbed it to Pancho, who caught it with one hand. Even though Pancho was chubby, he easily caught up with his aunt, and touched her gently on the back for an out.

"You're out! You're out!" Marcos yelled, then glared at Pancho. "Tonto."

Jorge got on base with a fly that was dropped by Becky. Little Mayello bunted the ball after his father helped him hold the wooden bat just over home plate. Marcos yelled, "That's not fair! You can't help him! He's out! That's not fair!" While Marcos complained, Mayello immediately ran to third, and Elvia and Pilar hugged each other with laughter. Cuauhtémoc stopped Mayello and pointed him toward first. Noni was about to tag the small but speedy Mayello when she saw her father at second, and threw it hastily. The ball bounced where the shortstop would be, except nobody was between second and third base.

"Oh my God!"

"Run, Mayello, run!"

"Look at him! His pants are falling down! He looks like Cantinflas!"

"But he stopped at first base."

"Just look at that little face! Oh, he is so proud of himself!"

By the time the kids came up to bat, the adults were leading four to zero. Marcos hit a bloop single right over the pitcher. Noni, the oldest kid on the team, hit a hard grounder to third that almost knocked her mother off her feet. When Pancho came up to bat, the bases were loaded, and Pancho made them pay. Although he was fat, Pancho was extraordinarily strong, a fact his father Cuauhtémoc had always been proud of. When Pancho hit the softball, it sounded like a watermelon smashing into a concrete floor, a deep, heavy thump. The softball flew over the infield, over left center, and way above Uncle Jorge's head, like a dusty white comet, and landed in the next field.

"Wow! Panchito! That boy eats his frijoles!" said Elvia.

After Pancho smacked another home run on his next turn at bat, this one right over first base in right field, all the adults moved back warily whenever Panchito came to the plate.

The adults were up to bat, and the children were leading nineteen to seventeen. Like a gigantic blowtorch, the late March sun had scorched the dusty baseball diamond. When Marcos scratched the top of his head, he had been surprised by how hot it was. Everybody agreed to end the game after this final inning, in order to relax before the late afternoon became the early evening and they would have to return to Ysleta to prepare for Easter Sunday.

Pilar swung wildly at the softball, only to see it trickle toward third, far enough from Noni yet not fast enough so that Marcos could throw it in time to first base. Elvia hit a grounder between third and second base, and Marcos and Julia both ran after the ball. Players on both teams were shouting; everybody was running or jumping.

Running to second, Pilar saw that Julieta had scooped up the softball before Marcos. Pilar half-slid, half-stumbled toward the base, fell short of it, and her knee twisted awkwardly underneath her. She yelped and collapsed onto the ground.

Marcos yelled, "Mamá! Mamá! She's hurt! Papá!" His father sprinted toward second base. Julia tried to lift her mother up.

"Ya, ya, I'm okay," Pilar said, tears streaming down her face. She couldn't stand up, and there was a bloody gash on her knee. "Maybe we should stop for now." Cuauhtémoc lifted Pilar and carried her like a baby to the trees where the yellow truck was parked, and gently placed her on one of the blankets. Pilar winced. Jorge and Elvia walked quietly toward Cuauhtémoc and Pilar. Nobody had to tell the children to stay away.

Elvia brought Pilar ice wrapped in a rag, and Cuauhtémoc gently placed blankets under her knee and brought her a Coke from the cooler. Pilar offered them a tight smile. Pancho milled around the old yellow pickup, his brow furrowed, ignoring Mayello's pleas to go hunt for snakes in the canal.

An hour later, Cuauhtémoc talked solemnly with Jorge and Elvia. Pancho packed up their chairs and hauled their lime-green cooler back into the pickup's bed. Marcos found his mother in the pickup, her forearm across her sweaty temple, her eyes closed.

"Mamá, are we going?"

"Yes, m'ijo," Pilar said, straining to utter every word between short gasps.

Marcos glanced at her knee; it was unbelievably swollen, as if a grapefruit had been embedded under her skin. Around the edges, his mother's knee was black and blue. Blood was still dripping from the gash over the bone.

As the sun disappeared behind the Franklin Mountains, they drove through the cotton and alfalfa fields on the outskirts of eastern Juárez.

When they were back in the United States, instead of turning toward Ysleta, Cuauhtémoc kept driving on Zaragoza Road onto I-10, toward the hospital. The dark, furious wind whistled past their faces. Marcos, Julia, and Pancho gripped the sides of the truck as it roared along the freeway. The first stars peeked through the purple velvet sky.

Cuauhtémoc parked in the gloomy, nearly empty lot in front of the emergency room at Sierra Medical Center. He turned to the children and said, "Stay here until I come back." Their father helped their mother out of the truck and disappeared behind glass doors. Julia immediately jumped out of the truck bed and waited inside the cab with Mayello, who was asleep. Four other cars were scattered under the wan amber lights of the lot. For what seemed hours, no one else came in or out of the emergency room except a paramedic who yanked open the back of the ambulance, stepped quickly into it with what appeared to be a metallic toolbox, and stepped out and marched into the hospital again.

By the time their father returned to the truck, Julia and Mayello were both asleep, but Pancho and Marcos were guarding their belongings. The nearly full moon hovered above them. Marcos had wrapped himself in a dusty blanket, even though it hadn't been that cold.

"I'm sorry it took so long. Your mamá's fine. I'll pick her up tomorrow, after they put her leg in a cast."

"She's okay?" asked Pancho.

"Yes, they gave her medicine for her pain. They'll have to operate, but she should be home tomorrow. Vámonos." He settled into the truck and started the ignition as he repeated the news to Julia. Mayello was sound asleep on her lap. As he pulled out of the parking lot, Cuauhtémoc felt deeply relieved but also eerily burdened by the need to drive safely that night. Their home in Ysleta was still miles away.

As they drove east, no one said a word the entire ride home, and no one had to.

Four Children, Four Worlds
September 1974

Julia rummaged through the back of her closet and removed the cardboard boxes of old clothing her mother had kept. As secretary of the student council at Ysleta High School, she was part of the Homecoming skit aimed at roasting the Riverside Rangers that Friday. She knew the stupid cowgirl hat was in the closet, along with the cowgirl outfit with dangly leather fringes that her parents had bought for her seven years ago. Her voluptuous sixteen-year-old body wouldn't come close to fitting in the old skirt, but the ridiculously small cowgirl hat was perfect for the skit.

Julia ("Ju-lee-ah" or "Ju-lee," not "Hoo-lee-ah") had worn the cowgirl outfit only once. In fourth grade, Mr. Zubia, who had been such a hard-ass the entire year, remarked in a low, creaky voice how beautiful she looked while she was sitting alone at lunchtime. He gently touched the fringes of her skirt. Julia had been so startled to see his fingers so close to her knees that she recoiled, which prompted the Penguin to apologize profusely to her. He was extra nice to her for the last month of fourth grade. María Reynosa, a girl from Juárez who was two years older and more developed than the other girls, laughed at the Penguin's compliments and how he lovingly rubbed María's back as they worked on improving her English after school. Julia thought the Penguin was gross, but María reveled in the attention. Nine-year-old Julia had refused to wear the cowgirl outfit again. Pilar had scolded her for not appreciating the value of money and sacrifice, for not knowing what it was like to be a nine-year-old who couldn't afford shoes.

After a few minutes, Julia found the old, misshapen cowgirl hat at the bottom of the closet, and tried it on. It was perfect. With the small hat askew on her head, Julia applied a dark red, almost maroon lipstick on her lips, which her mother hated, but not as much as she hated the bright red one Julia used for Friday night home games, when she performed with the Ysleta Drum Corps. She had explained to her mother that Mr. Mellon wanted the girls to stand out under the stadium lights, which washed out their faces. What up close was extra-dark Egyptian eyeliner and painfully red lipstick, from the football stands appeared as normal makeup. Pilar said Julia looked like a payaso.

Many high school girls looked ridiculous with too much makeup and skin-tight skirts and low-cut blouses. But when Julia wore bright red lipstick, which she applied in the parking lot at school so her parents would not start a fight, she received dreamier, more solicitous looks from boys. Her friend Elena Rodríguez, who was a senior and editor of the *Pow Wow*, encouraged her to wear skirts. "Just look at how they stare at you. They're practically drooling, the little savages," Elena said. But boring high school boys had never gotten Julia excited.

"Mamá, does the car have any gas? I have to go to the print shop."

"I'll drive you. Just got a shipment from Avon on Thursday and I have to start delivering it today."

"Okay," Julieta said, standing by the doorway to her room. Of the four children, Julia was the only one with her own room, although it was right next to the kitchen. Her three brothers shared a room in the back, next to the new red basketball court her father had finished last year. The sacks of cement, the scattered wooden frame for the cement floor, the rolls of heavy metal wire for the foundation—this mess had finally been moved to the new apartments. Their backyard looked decent for once, and not like a perennial construction site. "Can you pick me up too? Around four or five?"

"Está bien. But I'm not going to sit waiting for you. You be ready, or take the bus home." Why was it she was always competing with Julieta to use the car?

"Mamá. I'll be ready. Elena made me responsible for proof-checking this issue of the *Pow Wow*. I think she and Mrs. Crouch want me to be editor next year."

"M'ija, you know how proud we are of you. Just make sure this Elena is not just giving you her work, and taking credit for it."

"Mamá, that's not how she is."

"At least she's smart like you. But those dresses she wears! Sometimes she looks like a prostitute. How can her mother allow her to wear that kind of clothing?"

"I don't think you should be insulting my friends, Mamá."

"I'm not insulting them; I'm telling you what I don't like about them. You should be encouraging her to be more modest. You should take Elena to Mount Carmel on Sundays—that's what you should be doing."

"I'll ask her," Julia said, rolling her eyes behind her mother's back, and imagining what Elena would say about a church invitation.

"One more thing, señorita. Your father and I have a surprise for you."

"A surprise? Am I going to have to go to los departamentos, to help Pancho and Marcos? I'm not doing that horrible work—I don't care. I do plenty of work around the house, cleaning the rooms of esos cochinos. Do you know I found dirty underwear stuck behind their bunk beds?"

"Don't criticize my babies," her mother said as she washed the morning dishes from Saturday's breakfast of huevos rancheros for her husband and Captain Crunch and Cheerios for Francisco, Marcos, and Mayello.

"They're not babies, Mamá."

"Everybody works hard in this family, not just you. Do you know how much I made selling Avon last month? Eighty-five dollars. My best month yet. I need to help your father—he is worried about his health. He won't tell you, but he is."

"Did they find anything else?"

"No, he just has to get used to taking that shot every day."

"He did look scared last week."

"It was a shock for him. He always thought of himself as invulnerable, but now he has diabetes. He'll be fine. In fact, your father's the one who told me to go ahead and do it."

"Do what?"

"Buy you the king-size bed and that matching vanity and dresser we saw the other day at Levitz," her mother said, smiling and looking ten years younger.

"No!"

"Yes. We're buying it today."

"Oh, Mamá! I can't believe it. Thank you so much! Are you sure we can afford it?" Julia had resigned herself to sleeping in Francisco's old twin bed forever, after her parents had bought the boys bunk beds. She hugged her mother from behind and kissed her cheek. "Thank you so much, Mamá."

"We're buying it after I'm finished with my deliveries. You can sleep on your new bed tonight. By the way, where are you and Elena going tonight? I don't want you coming in one minute after ten o'clock. Is that understood?"

"Yes, Mamá. Or you'll find me and drag me back home by my hair, I know, I know."

"It's because I love you, Julieta. If I didn't care, I would let you do whatever you want. Which is what worries me about your friend Elena. I wonder what kind of mother she has."

"Not as wonderful a mother as I have."

~

At Santiago's Print Shop near downtown El Paso, where Mrs. Crouch had haggled a reasonable price to print the *Pow Wow* for the school district—eight to twelve pages for a regular issue, but sixteen pages for the Homecoming issue—Julia had corrected countless misspellings and confusing headlines. Two feature pages on the Homecoming court had to be completely redone. She was not finished until five thirty, which had infuriated her mother who had arrived at four thirty. By the time they returned to Ysleta on the other side of town, it was six o'clock. In the driveway, Julia jumped out of the Volkswagen, finally free of her mother's endless harangue about how irresponsible and selfish she was. She found her father busily putting together the new bed in her room. The cream-colored vanity and the matching bureau were still wrapped in plastic and cardboard. Julia offered her father a gentle hug, noticing how much he was perspiring as he crouched over the metal frame and tightened the thick metal bolts of her bed. Suddenly Julia felt guilty because she had promised to pick Elena up at six, and was already late. Her father said, "That's okay. You get ready for the movies and I'll come back and finish after dinner. I need a glass of iced tea anyway."

Julia lurched out of the driveway in the Volkswagen, narrowly missing the black wrought-iron fence around their property. Every time she commandeered the Bug, she felt free of Ysleta, free of her household responsibilities, free of her mother and her suspicions and demands. Last year, Papá had taught her how to drive the stick shift of the Bug near the Río Grande, by the levee where many farm roads and fields lay desolate in the late afternoon. She had been a quick study, although at the beginning Papá would lose his temper and yell at her for mashing the gears without pumping the clutch properly, or for stalling the Bug for the fourth time in five minutes. With or without their permits or licenses, many kids in Ysleta already knew how to drive— Elena and her brothers had learned to drive when they were thirteen!— some because they were needed to help haul material to build their houses. There was little danger of getting caught. It was rare to see cops in Ysleta, even after El Paso had annexed the ramshackle neighborhood and forced it to be an official part of the city.

At her driving test, Julia had laughed nervously and grinned at the state trooper, who was blond and cute in his oh-so-tight uniform. In a soft, twangy voice, he had told her not to worry about parallel parking, that she was already an excellent driver and that parallel parking was simply a matter of practice and patience. They tried it a few times, and she finally did it right on her fourth try. Trooper Jeremy Johnson had attended Ysleta High too, about six years before, and had played middle linebacker for the football team. When Julia mentioned she was in the Drum Corps, the "Pride of the Lower Valley," he said matter-of-factly, "Once an Indian always an Indian," the school's motto. She had pranced out of the office with her new driver's permit clutched in her hand.

Julia picked up Elena in Pasodale and Verónica Aguirre in Eastwood, honking the Bug's shrill horn outside each house. Elena wasn't wearing a bra. Verónica gossiped about a girl they knew who had kissed the married Mr. Mellon in his office, and maybe more. Verónica, also a member of the Drum Corps, kept chatting excitedly as they drove to the new bar/discotheque El Milagro in Juárez.

Once inside El Milagro, the threesome scanned the tables for friends from other high schools—Trooperettes, Rangerettes, and Silver Foxes. Noni, Julia's cousin, had promised to make an appearance. In the large, cavernlike bar, with a black dance floor awash in flickering multicolored lights, the middle-aged bartenders did not card them when the girls ordered margaritas. Outside, the desert sky had just darkened, still early in the evening for a Saturday night. After a Mexican cumbia, "Jungle Boogie" reverberated from the humongous speakers attached to the ceiling. Half the dance floor pulsed with twisting bodies in tight bellbottom pants, miniskirts, and long cotton skirts in the wildest patterns. Elena nudged Julia as three boys, whom they later learned were at la Universidad de Juárez, strode confidently to their table and asked them to dance.

The prelude to Barry White's "You're the First, the Last, My Everything" began, and Elena sat down with her new friend, who wore too much jewelry and couldn't stop staring at Elena's bouncy breasts. The Mexican preppie in the corduroy jacket ordered appetizers and another round of drinks for the table. Elena rewarded him with a generous smile. Julia danced with her partner, "Chucho" or "Chico" or "Chato"—she wasn't sure. Julia danced nonstop, and after a few more songs even Elena's date stared at Julia, who was easily the best dancer of the group. During Stevie Wonder's "Superstition," "Chavo" realized his soulful stares and sleek moves had little to do with Julia's ecstasy. The boy metamorphosed from a solicitous, hormone-addled male into just another awkward spectator. Elena rubbed her niño papi's back to regain his attention, and laughed at his every word until he couldn't leave their table willingly. It was a good move, because the girls didn't have to pay for anything else that evening.

Like an expert lion tamer manipulating a dangerous cat, Elena skirted danger with her carefree caresses and come-hither looks, but she always had the boy under her control. Only once had Julia seen Elena misread the situation, when about two months ago an older man had grabbed her ass after a couple of dances. Elena had slapped him and marched away. Even Elena had her limits. But at El Milagro that evening, it was Verónica who disappeared mid-dance. Elena and Julia searched El Milagro's half-painted bathroom stalls and dark parking lots. Where the hell was Verónica? They found her in the backseat of a Buick with her beau, his hand lost in her blouse, his hips grinding against hers, and the panting Verónica in a hot, crazy sweat. Elena had rapped on the window with the back of her ringed fingers—*clack, clack, clack*—and yelled that they were leaving. In a few minutes, Verónica was happily in the Volkswagen as if nothing had happened. Elena and Julia glared at each other. It would be awhile before they invited Verónica to Juárez again.

The full moon glimmered on San Lorenzo Avenue's new pavement. Julia unlocked the black metal gate quietly. It was almost midnight. Lobo and Princey howled behind the chain-link fence that separated the back from the front yard. Luckily for Julia, their cacophony ceased just as suddenly as it had started. Julia quickly parked the car and pulled the black metal gate behind her. In the murky, bluish light, she fished out keys from her purse, but she couldn't find the right one. Julia tried another one, and this one turned the lock. The kitchen door seemed to creak even louder than the dogs' outburst. The hallway light suddenly flashed on the white stucco wall in the hallway. Her mother marched toward the kitchen door.

"Give me those keys, Julia," Pilar demanded, her face contorted with anger. Julia handed her the keys and stepped back. "When did I tell you to come in? When?"

"I know, Mamá, but the Volkswagen flooded, and I couldn't get it started."

"For two hours! Where were you?"

"We went to the movies, and the car stalled, and I couldn't get it started. So we waited in the parking lot until the gas dried."

"Don't lie to me, señorita, or I swear I'll smack you right where you stand."

"That's the truth, Mamá."

Her mother inched closer and sniffed the air.

"You've been drinking, haven't you? And I smell smoke on your clothes, you ingrata!" Pilar lunged at Julia's hair, giving it a hard yank. Julia shoved her mother's hand away and stepped toward her room next to the kitchen. "Come back here!" Pilar demanded. "Don't you turn your back on me, you stupid girl!"

"Are you crazy? Please calm down. Nothing happened, Mamá. I'm sorry I was late." Julia stood next to her doorway, shaking. For the first time in her life, Julia realized she was not only taller than her mother, but stronger, too.

"You've been smoking and getting drunk. Meanwhile your sick father is slaving away for you."

"Mamá, I'm not drunk and nothing happened. People were smoking in the lobby of the movie theatre."

"You're a liar!"

"Mamá, nothing happened."

"Have you been having sex? You disgusting creature! Is that what we've taught you? This is a house of God, not a brothel!"

"That didn't happen!"

"You're a liar, I know that!"

"Mamá, I'm sorry you were poor in Chihuahua. I'm sorry you didn't have shoes. And I'm sorry you never had a king-size bed. But it's not my fault how you grew up."

"You think I'm jealous of you? You know nothing. Just because you know English. Just because you have your little friends, and your makeup, and a car! Well, after I talk to your father you won't have them anymore. Maybe I'm just a poor, stupid Mexicana, but I never lied to my parents. And I never slept around with whatever tirilón winked at me."

"Mamá, I'm sorry I'm late," Julia said, her voice hoarse. She stared at her mother's dark brown eyes again, turned, and gently closed the door behind her. She waited. Julia imagined her mother bursting into her bedroom and viciously attacking her on her new bed. But after a minute, Pilar shuffled past the bedroom door, paused, and continued down the hallway. Only after Julia heard her parents' door close did she finally turn the lock on her own door as quietly as she could.

~

Francisco and Marcos knocked down the interior wall between the spider-infested living room and what had apparently once been a spacious kitchen and a bathroom. Their father had instructed them to unhinge the gigantic wooden doors between the rooms, and to avoid damaging the ornate fireplaces. "Take out the bathtub and sink and carry them outside to the front yard," he said in his idling truck in front of the Olive Street mansion, his arm dangling from the driver's window. "Save the doors in a pile in the basement. I'll be back after I go to Levitz, and we will go to the dump with whatever we can't sell for scrap."

Underneath where the collapsed porch had been last week, Francisco noticed black metal posts embedded in the brick and shaped like horse heads, with metal rings in their noses. His father said these had been used to tie horses to the front of this building one hundred years ago. Cuauhtémoc had also unearthed a small, rotted burlap bag with six oddly square rare coins.

"How long is this gonna take us? I don't want to be here all day," Marcos complained. He smashed the sledgehammer against skeletal wooden slats beneath the aqua wall, and finally punched a hole to the other side. Jets of fine dust exploded into the air. Streaks of sunlight captured tiny particles afloat in weirdly straight lines of light. Marcos was slim and athletic, with green eyes and straight brown hair. He was wearing an old pair of jeans his mother said he didn't really need anymore.

"It'll take us as long as it takes us. Get to work while I start hauling this junk to the front with la carrucha," Francisco ordered. His jeans were extremely tight at the waist and baggy around his legs. He dropped the metal knees of the wheelbarrow in the middle of the living room with a thud.

"We're working on Saturdays! My friends are playing baseball and basketball, and I'm doing construction! We should tell Papá to pay us! It's only fair!"

"You tell Apá to pay us," Francisco grinned mischievously. Sometimes he could get Marcos to do the most idiotic things, but not as easily as ten-year-old Ismael.

"Why isn't Julia here? She just prances around with her newspaper and her stupid friends. And we're slaves! Do you think it's fair?"

"Julia's a girl, and she's the oldest. You know how Apá treats her."

"Like a stupid queen."

"Know why?" Francisco huffed, stacking chunks of the plastered wall and the splintered wooden slats into the wheelbarrow.

"Why?"

"Because his mother died when he was ten."

"What does that have to do with us being slaves?"

"Apá sees girls the way he last saw his mother, as a ten-year-old niño. He thinks mujeres shouldn't do this kind of work."

"Somebody should tell him Julia is una mensa." With one powerful swing, Pancho knocked a two-by-four frame out of the wall. Bits of wooden slats and plaster and paint crashed onto the floor in front of them with a bang.

"That somebody could be you. Look, estos departamentos are for all of us. When we finish opening this space up, he's gonna get workers to construct apartments and then he'll rent them out. The old lady who owned this building sold it to Apá for almost nothing. We'll make money."

"Why doesn't he get workers to do this now?"

"Because we're cheap."

"Because we're pendejos."

At lunchtime, Francisco and Marcos trudged like weary, dirty soldiers to abuelita Josefina's apartment. Pancho's face was caked with dust and black grime, and his baggy jeans were smeared with dried mud. Marcos's nails were black, and his left forearm had a nasty scratch from the elbow to the wrist. He had ripped his jeans at one thigh when a wooden slat had jabbed him after he yanked it free from the wall. Their shoulders ached, their legs were twitchy with exhaustion, and their arms and hands were a patchwork of bruises, scratches, and splinters. Doña Pepita exclaimed "Ay, pobrecitos!" when she saw them like refugees at her screen door. She ordered them to wash up and rest. As a cool breeze meandered through the open windows, she served them chile rellenos, her famous frijoles and arroz, and cold Coca-Colas, which seemed to revive them.

Their father arrived at doña Josefina's about a half hour after they finished eating. All three of them drove the three blocks to the Olive apartments to load the old yellow Ford pickup with rubble. They loaded the chunks of wall, piles of splintered wood, mounds of paint and plaster first, for this would go to the dump last. On top they piled a rusty sink, a twisted mesh of pipes, rolls of electrical wiring, and a refrigerator door without a handle. The metal scrap they could sell for a few dollars at Beto's Yonke, near the garbage dump off Zaragoza Road in Ysleta.

The truck bed sank dangerously low to the ground, almost scraping the asphalt. Cuauhtémoc steered the yellow pickup gingerly down Texas Avenue, trying to stay in the right lane. A few cars honked at them, and Cuauhtémoc waved them forward. Two older teenagers in a white Mustang guffawed at the rusty yellow pickup, and zoomed past, screeching on a sharp turn at Yarborough. Francisco smiled embarrassedly and glanced at his stoic father. Marcos imagined flooring the pickup's accelerator, chasing the Mustang, and ramming it from behind.

~

"Apá said you need to help me sweep the truck out. I'm gonna drive it behind the house to the canal." Francisco threw their mother's straw broom into the truck's bed.

"You're gonna drive?" Marcos exclaimed.

"I know how to drive."

"Will you teach me?" Marcos reluctantly climbed into the truck again, and Francisco drove the truck to the canal behind their house.

"When Apá says you're ready, I'll teach you. It's not that hard." Suddenly they heard the distinctive buzz of the Volkswagen's motor. The Bug stopped in front of their driveway, and from the canal the boys saw their mother and Julia argue.

"Allá va la reyna. Looks like she's in trouble, finally."

After his brother drove the truck to the front of the house and parked it outside on San Lorenzo, Marcos noticed a group of boys on Carranza Street, a block away. Julio Mendoza and his brothers and a few others were choosing sides for a baseball game. He asked Pancho if he could borrow his mitt, and told him he was going to Carranza Street, in case their mother asked where he was. Francisco slapped the mitt onto Marcos's hand, and Marcos sprinted to his friends, reinvigorated by the chance of hitting a homer. When Marcos reached the group of boys, he glanced back to San Lorenzo Avenue, realizing he hadn't even asked Francisco if he wanted to join him. Panchito was pulling out the green garden hose and filling up a bucket of water, rags in hand, in order to wash their old Ford pickup.

The baseball game lasted two hours and seven innings, and his team won, 26 to 18. Marcos hit a couple of homers, although one would not have been a homer if Nacho Pacheco had not had to crawl under a red truck to retrieve the ball. The boys started a small fire in the empty lot and recounted the highlights of the game. Johnny Mijares suggested they play another game the next day, about the same time. Marcos said he'd be there.

Johnny, Julio, and Nacho complained bitterly about being suspended, or being caught smoking in the canal next to South Loop School, or having to attend summer school to make up failed classes. Marcos was a decent student, certainly better than Pancho, who struggled to get C's and B's, but not better than Julia, la pinchi reyna. Mayello was a freak and didn't count. Everybody knew Mayello was one of the smartest kids in school.

But one thing was certain. If Marcos got suspended for carrying a knife or smoking pot or ditching school, his parents would kill him.

After a few minutes, Marcos stood up, said good-bye to his friends, and walked home.

~

Although the youngest, Ismael had never been treated like the baby. Marcos called him "el maldito terco Turco," and occasionally punched him in the arm for no reason at all. Pancho mostly stayed away from Ismael. Pancho might trick him into doing or saying something Mayello regretted later, but that's about as much pain as Francisco inflicted on anybody. Julia, the eldest, discussed politics and the Vietnam War with Mayello, or would introduce her little brother to the early Beatles, Chicago, or Bread. At other times, Julia hated him for searching through her room when she wasn't there, or telling their mother about what he had overheard from the second phone in the house.

Mr. Harris, the homeroom teacher, noticed how Ismael completed every assignment in less than half the time it took the rest of the class. Mr. Harris started him early on algebra. Asking few questions, and once in a while making careless mistakes, Ismael completed chapter after chapter. Scowling, Ismael stared at the textbook. Then in a flurry of pencil strokes, he burst with answers. Mr. Smith, the Math Department head for seventh and eighth graders, and Mr. Harris decided to wait a year before asking Ismael to compete for the Number Sense Club. Too much pressure too soon could push this shy fifth-grader further into his self-imposed silence. In all his other subjects, Ismael scored straight A's.

Mayello obeyed his parents and teachers to be free of their demands. His brothers and sister were enemies who attempted to trick him. At times he could rely on his mother to defend him, but even she exhorted him to fight back. "One of these days," she told him, "when you hit Marcos as hard as he hits you, he'll think twice about bothering you." But fighting just meant wasting more time with a tonto. Mayello only wanted to be left alone with his thoughts.

With a shovel, Mayello flung dogshit over the fence in the backyard, to the banks of the canal. "The disgusting smell will keep the tirilónes away," his mother said. "Who is going to want to park their lowrider back there on Saturday night?" And she was right. El Muerto still parked his purple Chevelle Malibu behind Leticia Gamboa's house, to gulp beer with his buddies, or listen to his stereo with his girlfriend. But he stopped parking behind the Martínez house.

Mayello grabbed the black soap from Juárez with the powerful medicinal smell, turned on the water hose, and sprayed water first on Lobo, then on Princey. Soon the German shepherds were dripping wet. Before Lobo could shake himself dry or run away, Mayello grabbed him and soaped the dog's gray-and-black fur until the white suds covered Lobo like snowfall. The dog trembled even though it was hot for October. Mayello rinsed Lobo and released him. The animal sprinted to the other side of the backyard, rubbing his muzzle into the grass and wagging his tail wildly. Prince never bolted when it was his turn to get scrubbed, and was much more obedient than Lobo could ever be. Soon enough, Mayello announced to his mother that he was finished washing the dogs. She told him the rest of Saturday was his.

The ten-year-old pushed his three-speed bike out of the shed and pumped air into the rear tire, which had seemed low. He grabbed an old radio his father had given him, a beige portable with a large plastic dial. The radio's batteries were still strong. He strapped the radio to the handlebars with tape and rope. The boy ran into the house and grabbed a soda can from the refrigerator, a plastic bag from underneath the kitchen sink, and two dollars from his sock drawer in the bedroom. He searched his room until he found a paperback copy of *The Mystery of the Great Swamp*, which he had just bought from the Scholastic Book Club at South Loop School. As his bike rolled down the driveway and picked up speed on San Lorenzo Avenue, Mayello adjusted the plastic bag, which he had tied onto the bike between his legs, so that it wouldn't interfere with his legs pedaling. The radio blared one of his favorite songs, "Bennie and the Jets," from FM 92.5.

Under his favorite cottonwood, which sprang from the banks of an irrigation canal surrounded by acres and acres of pima cotton, Mayello imagined the boy in the book searching the swamp for the murderer of his father. Mysterious shadows lingered in the underbrush. Strange animal grunts and shrieks sliced through the air. Sudden splashes of water startled the boy. As he paddled through the swamp, waves in the river gently rocked his lone canoe. Mayello glanced from the book to the cotton fields. No one was around for miles. The boy in the mystery knew his father had been murdered by someone who had coveted their land. The father had resisted selling this land, so he could bequeath it to his children. The boy's father had not left his family much, but he did have the land. Oil had been discovered underneath it. After the father's gruesome murder, the family had lost their land. The boy had returned to reclaim it and decipher the mystery behind his father's death. In the book, the boy was in mortal danger, so close to repeating the fate of his father, so close to finding out the truth. Mayello closed the book and decided to finish the last chapters tonight, after his parents were asleep, when he could sneak into the storage shed in the backyard with his flashlight and Princey.

Mayello flicked open his pocketknife and whittled a fallen branch from the cottonwood into a spear-cane. He gripped the weapon and slowly descended into the irrigation canal, to the muddy bottom. At one end of the canal about a block away was a gigantic, corrugated metal tube. For a moment, he imagined a wild animal, maybe ravenous or rabid, bolting from the murky shadows straight at him. He imagined a wave of water suddenly rushing toward him, like a tsunami. Mayello tightened his hold on his weapon and pushed it inch by inch into the mud, flicked out a gob, and discovered a tadpole's slick tail wriggling in the sunlight.

He found a Styrofoam cup and jiggled the tadpole into it, along with a gob of mud and a spurt of water. Mayello stared at the tadpole. The eyes were shut, and yet he could discern its eyeballs. How did this animal live under the mud of the canal? Mayello noticed its dark army green, ridged back, and how the thick skin was covered with tiny, almost imperceptible bumps. Did this animal breathe through its skin? Did it have gills like a fish? What if the canal dried up? Would the tadpoles die, or would they become somehow dormant and await the next flood of water through the canal's banks? He placed the tadpole in the cup next to *The Mystery of the Great Swamp*.

Mayello walked closer to the other end of the canal, toward the ominous metal tube. A giant pool of greenish water surrounded the mouth of the tube. As he approached it, there was a splash. What had jumped into the water? Mayello stared at the water's depth and found a huge crayfish lurking at the bottom, trapped in a space inside the hollow of a broken cinderblock. If he could find a can, or something else to scoop the cangrejo out, he could capture it. Its claws were dangerous. One had pinched his finger in the canal behind his house and left a huge welt. Mayello was fascinated by these creatures, scorpionlike, armored, metallic green and brown, with giant claws for combat. The tail of a cangrejo was a massive, powerful propeller that the animal used to race underwater. But out of the water, in the hot ovenlike air of the desert, the animal quickly scurried over rocks on its spindly legs, yet not quick enough for a determined boy. Mayello couldn't find a can, but he did find a large piece of cardboard. He ripped the cardboard, and folded it to fashion a long scoop, just the right size to fit into the cinderblock hole.

With one quick heave of his cardboard scoop, he threw the crayfish, water, and globs of green algae onto the bank of the canal. The cangrejo tried to scurry back into the water, but Mayello immediately surrounded it with the wet cardboard, bending it into a miniature bullring around the creature. As the animal tested the walls of the cardboard for an opening, Mayello pinched its slimy green back with his fingers and carried the cangrejo up the bank. Next to his bicycle and his book and Styrofoam cup, he reorganized the miniature bullring and fortified it with rocks and dirt. In one hand dangled the cangrejo, flailing wildly in the hot air, its tail surprisingly potent. The hard antennae brushed against Mayello's fingers, but the claws would never reach his flesh as long as he pinched his fingers tightly around the lower back of the crayfish. After staring at the cangrejo inside the cardboard ring, Mayello dumped it in the plastic bag with his book and rode home in time for dinner. Before he walked inside, he grabbed the cangrejo and dropped it in the murky canal behind his house. Maybe, Mayello thought, he could grow his own private stash of mighty cangrejos and have them do battle in his backyard, a son against a father, brother against brother.

Thousands of Planets from Ysleta
LATE SUMMER 1978

Twenty-year-old Julia was glancing at the northern Italian countryside. The *International Herald Tribune,* which she had bought in Milan this morning, was still on her lap. Lisa Alvarez, her girlfriend from UTEP, sat next to her on the train to Rome, touching up her bright red lipstick. Pope Paul VI had died the day before, and the speculation about who would succeed the pontiff was the major news. The Italian newspapers, which she could more or less decipher with her Spanish, screamed in huge, 36- and even 54-point type: *Il Papa è morto!* Their backpacks were stashed in between their legs, and a duffel bag and a small rectangular suitcase were stowed above their heads. The train to Rome was packed with travelers, mostly Italians. A thirty- or forty-something-year-old man, unshaven, yet wearing stylish black slacks and a turquoise polo shirt, stared at them unabashedly.

"I don't know how fast they choose a pope, but wouldn't it be something if we could be there when they do," Julia said.

"I guess. Blanca was very nice. I like her."

"Too bad she couldn't come with us. Did you know she's the one who got me the summer job in Rhode Island with the nuns? It was one of the best things I've done in a long time."

Julia's friend Blanca Briano had met her German beau in Alamogordo, and now lived in Munich. Blanca, a Catholic activist, had mentioned the Warwick program to Julia one day. In exchange for free housing during the summer, Julia could be a translator for Spanish-speaking immigrants seeking refuge with the Sisters of Perpetual Charity. That summer Julia had helped the nuns in their health-care clinics and driven immigrants to their appointments from their work in the fields. Those pobrecitos, Julia had thought: they picked apples and corn and strawberries, and their children worked by their side. They lived in shacks, moving like nomads from region to region with the harvest and the weather. The migrant kids would go to school only a month here and there. What kind of education was that? The stupidities at UTEP seemed light years away. The nuns at Warwick had even helped Julia plan her trip to Europe, to the Vatican, Assisi, Fatima's shrine in Portugal. At religious shrines, the Sisters of Perpetual Charity knew contacts at convents and hospices, where they could stay inexpensively.

Lisa went back to applying her makeup. It had been Julia's idea to invite Lisa to Europe. It also made it easier for her parents to give her permission to go to Europe. Lisa had always been genial and easygoing, since they met freshman year in History of the Chicano Movement. But Julia wondered why Lisa had even enrolled in such a political class. She once blurted out, "My parents told me Chicanos are cholos. They're not?" In a way, Lisa reminded Julia of Pancho, and in a way she did not. Pancho was at least street savvy.

"Can I ask you a question?" Lisa asked, snapping shut her compact. "Do you think spending the summer with the nuns changed you? I mean, made you more religious?"

"Well, no. It's not like I want to go to church more often, although my mother would like that."

"So would mine." Lisa adjusted her long skirt.

"What the nuns were doing, that's what made an impression on me. They were helping people. Everybody's a Mexicano in El Paso, but in Rhode Island, they stuck out like sore thumbs. Away from the border, they're treated like animals."

"That's really a shame. Isn't it funny how here we're American girls? It's so different from El Paso, like we're Spanish somehow."

What an idiot, Julia thought. Her first years at UTEP exposed her to new ideas, to the clashes between Anglos and Mexicanos, and their perceptions and misperceptions of each other. Yet her experience at Warwick changed her more deeply than she would admit. Reading about the life of St. Francis of Assisi had sent a thundershock to Julia's psyche. St. Francis had turned against his status-conscious parents and their wealth. He had challenged the then-pope and the corrupt Catholic Church and vowed a life of service to the downtrodden and dispossessed. His story was one of the reasons Julia had wanted to go on this pilgrimage to Europe.

Julia went back to her newspaper, intermittently staring out the window as the train rolled past the hilly Italian countryside. They would be in Rome in a few hours, and then they'd have to search for the convent recommended by Sister Theresa. Suddenly Julia heard Lisa talking to the man in front of them.

Lisa crossed her legs and told "Fernando" or "Fernandes," an Italian Argentine or an Argentine Italian, who they were, and that they were traveling in Europe for the first time. He said he had recognized their Spanish and knew Spanish and Italian and "a little Anglaise." He lived in Rome and would be glad to show them the most important sights . . .

~

Julia Martínez sat alone in the medieval square in front of Assisi's church, consumed by a white cloud of anger. Lisa had abandoned her, to gallivant with that old Italian Argentine pendejo. They'd catch up with Julia back in Rome, Lisa had giggled to her, already holding hands with Fernando.

In the basilica, Julia shook her head. St. Francis had chastised the Catholic Church for being materialistic, yet here was this grand basilica with the intricate art and sculpture from the fourteenth and fifteenth centuries, in honor of the friar. Had the Catholic Church turned him into a saint to save itself? The visit to the basilica left Julia strangely empty, and yet it was hard for her to leave.

Julia knelt in one of the dark wooden pews, her eyes closed. She imagined being back in Ysleta, in the little church with the simple relics of the Virgin Mary, St. Joseph, and the crucified Jesus hanging between them, its paint somewhat chipped, the eyes a bit askew. Julia imagined dirt in between her toes, a body that ached for no reason at all, and the sooty faces of poor children from Juárez. She opened her eyes and refocused on the expertly carved figurines, the well-dressed matrons milling at the front, and the gold behind the marble altar.

This doesn't have to be me, Julia thought. *I don't have to be Lisa, la tonta. And I don't have to be my mother either. I don't have to be a tourist, staring at baubles. I can find my own way.*

~

"Sit down, Carlos. Hombre, it's so good to spend some time with you, even if it's just two days," Cuauhtémoc said, grinning. They plopped themselves on the sofa in the living room, while Pilar and Lucha, Carlos's wife, washed the dishes. Carlos and Lucha's daughters, Marisa and Liliana, were clearing the table and asking where to store the leftover brisket, mashed potatoes, and green beans. Fourteen-year-old Mayello stared briefly at the blond Liliana, who was a few months older than him, and quickly tied up the trash bag and hauled it to the trash cans in the driveway. The Ortegas had been staying with the Martínez family in Ysleta for the weekend, as they made their way back to Chihuahua, after a two-week summer trip to Arkansas to visit Carlos's brother and his family. Two weeks ago, the four Ortegas had stayed one night in Ysleta, and this time they'd stay two.

"Oye, thank you, Cuau. You and Pilar have been more than generous," Carlos said, his eyes staring timidly at his cowboy boots. He was a heavyset man, with a sunburnt face, tight denim jeans, and a western shirt with marblelike buttons. Cuauhtémoc's red-and-white pickup pulled into the driveway.

"Oh, here comes Panchito and Marcos. They were working at los departamentos today, helping clean one that became unoccupied." Cuauhtémoc reached over and turned on their big-screen television. "Let's hear the news. Pilar, will you bring me un cafecito?"

"So you make good money with your apartments?"

"Seguro que sí. And the boys do most of the work. I don't owe a penny on them, and so every rent's profit. Here, boys. You remember our friend Carlos from Chihuahua?" Pancho grinned shyly, shook Carlos's hand with a firm grip, and sat down next to his father. Marcos also shook Carlos's hand, but kept standing, quiet. "We used to call him 'Carlitos,'" Cuauhtémoc explained.

"Well, now it should be Carlotes," Carlos said, slapping himself on his protruding stomach. "But maybe these boys are hungry."

"In a minute. They can stay a bit and chat with us." He turned on the television. "Mira, that's where Julieta is right now, in the Vatican. One of these days they'll choose a Mexican pope."

"I'll be right back. Con permiso," sixteen-year-old Marcos said, and strode into the kitchen. He said hello to Marisa and Liliana with a half-grin, kissed his mother, and shook hands with Lucha. Then he sat down and poured himself a cup of coffee.

"How long will she be there? She went by herself?" asked Carlos.

"About three weeks. I think she's just about to fly back to New York. She went with a friend from UTEP, the university here. Una buena muchachita."

"I don't know if I would have let my Marisa or Liliana go so far by themselves. Maybe I'm just too old fashioned. But your Julia is two years older than Marisa, right?"

"Seguro que sí. And Julieta's very responsible. Your niñas are also very responsible. Muy ayudadoras, I can see that. It's good to teach them good values, right Panchito?" Pancho grinned perfunctorily. "But it's also good to make them responsible for themselves. To give them a little freedom, as long as they know what to do with it."

"You're right. You are absolutely right."

"You know, I have marveled at your Marisa and Liliana, how well mannered they are. Muy Mexicanas, but Mexicanas from el rancho. That's how children should be. Here you have sinvergüenzas, smoking pot, mujeres too, in cars with boys."

"No lo creas, Cuau. It happens in Mexico too. It happens everywhere."

"Oye, Panchito. So how's los departamentos? Everything okay?"

"Oh, yes. We cleaned the stove, mopped the floors. Marcos painted the living room, and we started the bedroom, but we ran out of the lime green paint. I'll get more tomorrow at Cashway or Benjamin's," Francisco said, looking shyly to one side as he spoke to his father.

"Your niños are real trabajadores! You should be proud of them, Cuauhtémoc."

"They're good boys," Cuauhtémoc said, smiling broadly, and patting his oldest son on his dusty knee. "Panchito, did you know what Carlitos used to do for money at La Agricultura, when we were about your age? Play the guitar. Oh, he had a wonderful voice, like Javier Solis's."

"Ay traigo una. My brother gave me one in Arkansas, from Spain."

"Pilar! Carlos brought a guitar!" Cuauhtémoc shouted excitedly toward the kitchen. "Oye, Carlos play for us, won't you? Did you know, Panchito, that when your mother and I were nóvios, I got Carlos to serenade your mother on my behalf? Oh, those were the best of times. Kids don't do that anymore. It's a shame."

That evening, Pilar and Cuauhtémoc, with Lucha and Carlos, gathered in the living room, sipping coffee and chatting about old friends and old times. As soon as Carlos settled the guitar in his hands, Cuauhtémoc turned off the TV. Carlos began to strum "Anillo de Compromiso." Cuauhtémoc grabbed Pilar's hand, and all three stared at the romantic balladeer who sang about love's promise, in the slow, carefully measured words of a rich baritone. Marisa, the oldest of the Ortega children, listened to her father's first few songs, then excused herself to Julieta's old room, to watch television. Liliana and Marcos and Mayello, in the boys' room, watched an episode of *Charlie's Angels*.

Late in the evening, when cars stopped cruising on San Lorenzo Avenue and dogs stopped barking, the adults went to sleep. Mayello lay in his bed, pretending to be asleep, but really masturbating slowly to the image of Liliana, who he had thought flirted with him the first time the girls had stayed with them two weeks ago. She had laughed at his sarcasm, and even touched his shoulder, smiling sweetly in his face. Liliana's impromptu caress, just a touch with an exclamation about how much bigger El Paso was than Chihuahua City, had sent a shiver through Mayello's body. Liliana was a Mexican blond who looked like many of the teenagers at Ysleta High, yet spoke only a mellifluous Spanish, with ivory-white breasts that peeked out at the right moments from her blouse. In the dark, Mayello imagined undoing that blouse and . . .

He heard whispers through the air-conditioning duct.

Mayello slowly lifted himself out of bed in the darkness. When he stepped into the hallway he could not hear the voices anymore. He remained still, standing in between the bedrooms, waiting. Nothing. His steps were silent on the linoleum floor. In the kitchen, only the neon blue numbers of the microwave pierced the black night. Outside, the wan amber streetlight bathed Carlos Ortega's pickup in an eerie light, almost making it appear like a shimmering mirage.

As he walked back through the hallway, Mayello heard a high-pitched purr. A woman's moan. Pleading, her pleading. A deeper voice. Marcos's voice. Behind a bathroom door. Liliana's voice, moaning. Whispers. "Ay, Dios de mi vida, así, así, ay Dios mio, eres precioso. Eres absolutamente precioso, mi rey."

Mayello hurried back to his bedroom, closed the door as quietly as he could, and slinked into bed without a sound. After what seemed hours without moving a muscle, Ismael turned to face the blackness of the ceiling. His head was pounding. In a while, his mind went numb, and he tumbled into the black abyss of a merciful sleep.

Little Napoleon
April 1982

They parked next to the cottonwood in the shadows of the industrial park that had arisen from the cotton fields. Ismael believed his favorite cottonwood had been saved by its spot next to the irrigation canal. The steamy black asphalt for the parking lot, like a slow moving wave of lava, had cooled and halted a few feet from the canal. On this cool Sunday night in early April of his senior year, the cottonwood made him feel safe. He turned off the lights of the Bug and reached over and kissed Cyndi Lucero.

"Izzy, my love, I can't stay out too late tonight," Cyndi said. "I have band practice tomorrow morning."

"I know. Can I?" he asked, unbuttoning her blouse. She smiled, gently rubbing him with her small delicate hands. Ismael unsnapped her bra from the front and slowly cupped her small white breasts with one hand while he stroked her cheek with the other. Though both were seniors, he and Cyndi were somewhat of an odd couple at Ysleta High School. Ismael was slightly over six feet tall, with straight black hair, dark brown eyes, his mother's light complexion, and a permanent scowl on his face. Cyndi was short, slim, and pretty, with long auburn hair, big green eyes, and freckles that Ismael relished on her cheeks and even her breasts. Once, one of the hairy Led Zeppelin losers who loitered around Kawliga, the life-size Indian mascot in front of the principal's office, asked Ismael if he hurt his small girlfriend when they made love. Surprised, Ismael ignored him, then shot him a smile and a wink as he kept marching to Publications.

Ismael and Cyndi had other important differences. Ismael was fluent in Spanish and comfortable being a Mexicano—not a Chicano, Mexican American, or God forbid, a Hispanic. He was editor in chief of the school newspaper and in the top ten of his graduating class. Although smart enough, Cyndi was not in Ismael's league. But she was feisty, which Ismael appreciated. Cyndi was a Features editor on the newspaper and a saxophonist in the Ysleta Indians Marching Band. She didn't know Spanish very well, but when provoked blurted out a curse word in an awkward accent. Her father was a Chicano from El Paso, and her mother was Irish, with a hard, humorless personality. Her parents had divorced years ago, and because Cyndi had ended up with her mother, she did not speak Spanish at home. Her two younger brothers had richly dark skin the color of chocolate, like Mexicanos with a heavy dollop of Indian blood, yet they did not know a word of Spanish and even less about their Mexican heritage. In many ways, Cyndi saw a bit of her father in Ismael, and reconnected with this distant, elusive, and moody parent through her boyfriend. For Ismael, Cyndi was the girl from the slightly better side of town, with an exotic sparkle of Anglo whiteness and yet still Latina. Cyndi had also happily ushered Ismael to many teenage firsts, and he was grateful.

"Can we get in the back? There's more room."

They each stepped outside immediately—they knew the drill—and shoved the VW's black seats forward all the way, onto the dashboard. The shadows from the factory walls enveloped them in a blacker darkness than the surrounding desert night. Cyndi had already slipped off her shoes, and removed her blouse and bra, draping them over the VW's seat.

"What am I going to do when you leave me?" Cyndi asked, kissing him on the lips as she positioned herself on top of him.

"Where am I going?"

"Stanford. Yale. Harvard. You know you'll get in. Everybody knows."

"What are you talking about? My SATs are not great. My parents don't have the money. Maybe I shouldn't have listened to Mrs. Sanchez. My father almost fainted when I told him how much I needed just for the application fees. Maybe I'll go to UTEP."

"You're not going to UTEP! You have a shot, Izzy. Nobody at Ysleta has ever gone to the Ivy League."

"I'm not sure I want to leave home. New Jersey was great last summer, but it was nerve-racking. The kids smoked pot, and spoke much better than I do. I don't know; I felt like I didn't belong. Like a stupid Mexican. I don't think I said more than three sentences in class all summer."

"You're one of the smartest kids at Ysleta. You were in the *El Paso Times*! Who from Ysleta or Socorro or Riverside ever won the Gannett scholarship for the Blair Summer School for Journalism? You did. Stop putting yourself down, Izzy. It's a bad habit."

"Cyndi, I don't want to leave you either."

"If you get into Stanford, then you better goddamn go."

"But aren't you going to miss me?"

"Sweetie, I'll miss you every day. Lemme show you how much I'm going to miss you." She unzipped his pants, kissed his chest, and gently rubbed him. Her lips, a nude, glossy color, slowly fluttered over his skin and teased him into a delirium.

Ismael's head pressed against the rear side window, which had fogged up. He felt warm, dizzy, and drunk. He massaged Cyndi's back, slowly working his hands to her hips, and pushed down her jeans. She kept pulling her hair back behind her neck, rubbing him until his mind was blissfully blank. When he felt he couldn't hold back any longer, he stroked her cheeks, and carefully pulled her away from him. Cyndi kissed him on the lips and groaned. Ismael touched and rubbed her, torturing her until her hips became insistent.

"Come here," she said.

Ismael held his breath, and Cyndi gasped. Back and forth, the VW's backseat creaked and groaned gently with their rhythm. With every movement, she welcomed him. Her hair fell across her face, and her eyes alternatively shut tightly and opened wide in wonder. Their slow pace quickened, and the slightest shifts of their bodies released new green and red explosions of sensation.

Their first time together had been clumsy. He had been shocked by how he had felt, as if he were being pleasantly consumed, and he did not know what was hers and what was his. This small girl, half his size and weight, held him utterly vulnerable to her will.

The second and third times, he watched her, how she reacted to each move, and understood the power of timing and being gentle. If he waited, and encouraged and pleased her, he would be so thrilled by what he had accomplished that he would also lose himself for a few precious moments. What began as an endurance test had transformed into waiting, listening, and coaxing. When he gave her what she wanted, she would be depleted and exhausted. For an hour afterward, she would refuse to release her grip around his body. She caressed him and promised she would be his forever.

Ismael drove to Ysleta alone, having dropped off Cyndi in Pasodale. He knew what she meant. Whatever happened, these memories would somehow help them through an uncertain future. He snuck in through the black metal gate, patted old Princey on the head, quickly opened the backyard door, and stepped into his bedroom.

~

The next day at the breakfast table, Ismael drank coffee and glanced at sloppily typed copy from the *Pow Wow*'s editorial page. His mother, in her new pale yellow bathrobe, stirred his avena at the stove while Francisco ate huevos rancheros with frijoles.

"Is that the last issue?"

"That's it. And I'm done, thank God."

"And? What's it about? Anything good?"

"Well, somebody in Student Council, or someone who handles their finances, stole money raised from the car washes and candy sales and whatever else they've done this year. There's a shortfall, and nobody knows what happened."

"Mr. N," Francisco said, snickering.

Francisco shifted his heavy body in the tall swivel seat next to the kitchen table. He had always been overweight. But after he had graduated from high school and started a degree at UTEP part-time, his weight had exploded. In the late afternoon, Pancho spent most days helping his father at los departamentos, with plumbing jobs, or lugging Sheetrock and cinderblocks and lumber to the site, or checking on Moises (aka "Mo-ee"), an undocumented worker from Juárez who was an excellent, albeit slow, carpenter and general handyman. Cuauhtémoc and Francisco were thinking of buying another old apartment building four blocks away from Olive Street, where abuelita Josefina had occupied apartment #1 free of charge for years. All the tenants respectfully waved hello to "doña Pepita" whenever they spotted her casually smoking a cigarette inside her screened porch.

"El amigo de Pancho, Mamá. He stole their money, I think."

"Callate," Francisco said. "You're the one who knows him so well."

"Who's this Mr. N?" Pilar asked, still methodically stirring the oatmeal. "A teacher?"

"He's the Student Council advisor. Uno que le gusta Juan Gabriel," Ismael said, grinning mischievously, referring to a Mexican crooner who was openly gay and despised by Pilar.

"Ápoco this Mr. N is a joto?" She turned suddenly to face Ismael with a steamy bowl of oatmeal cradled in her hands.

"That's what they say. Ask Pancho; he was Mr. N's buddy."

Francisco almost choked on his huevos. "I think he's Mayello's advisor at the *Pow Wow*, Mamá. Why do you think he's always so busy with his newspaper?"

"Not true! Mrs. Crouch is my advisor."

She set the bowl in front of Ismael. "I'm sure you are both wrong. The school district would've kicked him out."

"It's not a rumor, Mamá," Ismael continued, half-laughing. "Este Mr. N goes dancing around the hallways of Ysleta singing, 'Arriba Juárez!' Ysleta's full of jotos, Mamá." Francisco sniggered loudly, almost spilling his plate on the linoleum floor.

"Ay, Mayello. Mira como éres. That's your school you're talking about. It's one of the best schools in El Paso." Pilar poured herself a cup of coffee, then looked at her cup for a moment before pouring in condensed milk. Streaks of gray now interrupted the shine of her black hair.

"No tiene respeto éste muchacho, Mamá," Francisco said. "You know how he is. A payaso."

"I'm the one who should get respect around here," Ismael said. "When they show me respect, I'll *think* about showing them respect. Primero que se hinquen. Right, Mamá?"

"Mira mira. Quien te crees? Look at our little Napoleon. He thinks he's muy muy," Pilar said. "Just remember I'm the one who changed your diapers and wiped your mocos before you could even walk. You'll always be my babies." She kissed Ismael and Francisco on top of their heads.

"Oye, Panchito, the brakes on the Bug seem kinda low to me," Ismael said.

"And? How's that my problem?"

"Pancho, don't be that way. I don't know how to fix them and you do."

"How low?"

"Well, when I put the clutch in I have to press the brakes almost to the floor to stop the car. Does it need new brake pads?"

"Probably. But I'm meeting Papá to buy the materials for the roof of the new bedroom and bathroom. He wants to start right away. Can't do it today." Francisco, after years of rooming together with his brothers in Ysleta, was finally getting his own room and a private bathroom.

"Pancho, he shouldn't be driving that car if the brakes are low. He'll have an accident," their mother said as she filled a bowl of oatmeal for herself.

"Que se ponga trucha. Why did he wait so long? That car's so old, I'm surprised the motor hasn't fallen out."

"Mamá, one or two days won't hurt. I'll pull the emergency brake if something happens. I'll be careful," Ismael said, realizing he should have waited to have this conversation with his brother when the two were alone. Ismael didn't want to lose his car. He needed it every day this week, for the *Pow Wow*, the print shop, to go downtown to visit his abuelita, for Cyndi.

"Mayello, you can't drive it on the freeway."

"Okay, I won't." He was lying.

"Ándale pues, tomorrow," Francisco said, after glancing at his mother, who was staring at him with a worried look in her eyes. "I'll get the brake pads today after class. Let me take a peek at the Bug right now, to make sure that's the problem. But mañana you have to help me after school. Mo-ee is coming here to start the roof, and Papá wants me to help him get it done quickly so he can go back to los departamentos."

"Ándale pues. It's a deal."

"What would you do without such a good older brother like Panchito? Gracias, m'ijo. Thank you for everything you do for this family." His mother beamed and kissed the top of Pancho's twenty-three-year-old head again.

"Thank you, Panchito," Ismael repeated sarcastically. "When I'm president of the United States, you won't have to kneel, okay?"

~

In blue jeans and Converse sneakers, Ismael walked through the long beige hallways of Ysleta High. He said quick hellos to those he knew and avoided conversations. He was in a hurry to get to Publications. Rueben Quintero suddenly patted the taller Ismael on the back and said, "Ese, Mayello," for no reason, and kept on strutting down the hallway. Rueben was also a senior and from his neighborhood, but

Ismael had not exchanged more than three words with him since childhood. Ismael grinned and opened his locker, thinking about what books and notebooks he would need this morning.

Rueben had been a hotshot in grade school—a fast runner and a champion of schoolyard scuffles. In huddles next to the cotton fields, he had proudly displayed glossy pictures of naked women that he carried in his back pocket. In contrast, in their last year at South Loop, pudgy and painfully shy Ismael Martínez had been declared valedictorian. These antipodes of the schoolyard, the jock and the nerd, entered Ysleta High on different trajectories. Ismael continued his meteoric rise in high school, to the editorship of the school newspaper, and achieved nearly straight A's, except for Typing and Pre-Calculus. Ismael also grew taller—some would even say lanky except for a slight jiggle to his stomach—and metamorphosed into an outspoken teenager admired by fellow students and hated by autocratic teachers. He won writing and newspaper awards from the University Interscholastic League in Austin. Ismael's picture had appeared in the *El Paso Times*. Meanwhile, Rueben did not survive the junior varsity tryouts for football. He lingered in the school's doorways waiting for who knew what, ogling the honeys, and cackling with friends. Over the years, Rueben and Ismael had occasionally crossed each other's paths in the hallways, Ismael always in a hurry to meet another deadline. To Ismael, Rueben became part of the formless crowd who would barely finish high school and never consider attending college. Rueben reminded Ismael of his brother Francisco, except that Francisco was more decent and dutiful, and the opposite of street tough. But both Rueben and Francisco were happy in Ysleta and El Paso. Ismael was not.

In Ismael's mind, ignorance was like rot. This "I don't care that Mexicanos can't get elected for mayor or city council." That "me-vále that the neighborhood was poor, and what mattered was only familia and that everybody had enough chorizo to eat." This "why do I need to learn anything else para qué?" Ismael couldn't stand it. What was wrong with these people?

Ismael knew Anglos as well as Mexicanos in El Paso possessed this I-don't-care attitude. He saw it in the eyes of burned-out teachers, somnolent janitors, petty administrators, and mannered adults like his father. But in New Jersey at the Blair Summer School for Journalism, Ismael met students from a potpourri of ethnic, religious, and geographic backgrounds who were so much more articulate and confident than he was. The Blair kids argued as if their lives depended on it, standing and addressing a crowd at a moment's notice. He felt uncomfortable and even embarrassed because of his accent. His entire wardrobe consisted of only jeans and T-shirts. Why didn't anyone warn him about how to dress? Ismael was practically mute in class most of the summer. But by the end of July, just before he returned to El Paso, Ismael had gotten to second base with Mary Olezeki, a perky and athletic blond from Trenton, New Jersey. Also, he had penned a good article on environmental pollution for the final issue of the Blair student newspaper.

Mrs. Crouch had arranged for Ismael's first period to be in Publications, so her editor in chief could run errands to the print shop every morning. Second period was his regular newspaper period with the entire staff of the *Pow Wow*, so it was a while before he had a real class. He sat down in front of a gray Smith Corona manual typewriter and retyped the final lead editorial of the year, by Nora Aguirre, a junior who would be next year's editor in chief. It wasn't a bad piece; Nora just couldn't type. If Ismael gave it to the printer as is, the old man was liable to add even more mistakes of his own and create a monumental mess Ismael would have to clean up in final galleys.

These page editors and photographers and writers had no standards, Ismael thought. Photographs were out of focus; captions were often fragments, or subjects inexplicably had no names; and no one seemed to know basic grammar or spelling. Rarely did the "story" reveal what happened or when it happened or why it should matter.

Shortly after Ismael began as editor in chief, the staff began calling him "the Dictator." But then his article on the inequity of state funding for poor school districts won a UIL award from Austin—only the third time in the forty-year history of the *Pow Wow*. When he won again for his editorials on the causes of low SAT scores among Mexican-American students, the staffers called him "the Dictator," but to his face and with a smile. The distribution of the *Pow Wow* became an event in the classroom, the newspaper a focus of intrigue, controversy, and attention.

"Why are you here so early?" He heard a young woman's high-pitched voice behind him.

"Hi, Michelle. Last issue, and I'm typing up some final copy. Your page ready?"

"But of course, sweetheart," she said, sitting down in front of another typewriter. "I'm always ready, you know that. Don't you dare touch my copy, okay? I showed it to Mrs. Crouch, and she okayed it." Michelle Acosta had often rankled him, frequently going over his head to Mrs. Crouch. She was one of the few students who wasn't afraid of Ismael, and the only one who routinely challenged him. Ismael glanced at her as she typed furiously, much faster than he ever could. Michelle's svelte figure was neatly and stylishly attired in black slacks, a cream-colored blouse, and a black vest embroidered with flowers. Her skin was like white porcelain, her coiffed hair brunette, her deep brown eyes small and quick. She was the editorial editor, the president of the Kiowa sorority, vice president of the student council, and Homecoming queen.

"Are you running the Harrison letter?" Ismael said quickly, finishing Nora's piece on the typewriter.

"Yes. With your response, of course."

"I don't understand why you decided to run it. He doesn't know what he's talking about."

"He turned it in, and it's in response to your editorial about student rights. Isn't that the point of letters to the editor? To respond to the editor? Anyway, Mrs. Crouch said it's unusual to print an editor's response to a letter to the editor."

"Print as many of his letters as you want, but he's still wrong. 'Students and teachers are not equal.' The Supreme Court does not agree with him. Students have equal rights with teachers. Anybody should be allowed to park wherever they want, first come first serve. Why should the teachers have the better parking spaces?"

"Ismael, teachers have materials and supplies to carry. They're the leaders and authorities of this school. Doesn't that matter?"

"That's BS, and you know it."

"I told you not to talk to me like that."

"Okay, I'm sorry. But students also carry books, and some come from far away. It's not an 'option' or 'luxury' for many of them to bring a car. Harrison doesn't know what he's talking about. He just wants to have us under his boot."

"Why do you hate him so much? I have him for Government, and he's a good teacher. Tough, but usually fair."

"I don't like being told what to do."

Michelle stared right into his eyes for a long moment, as if challenging him or coming on to him, he was never sure. Ismael could smell her sweet, delicate perfume waft over the ink from his typewriter. She smiled disarmingly. "You let Cyndi tell you what to do."

"Well," Ismael said, flustered. "I like what she tells me to do most of the time."

"Oh, really? And what is that?" Michelle abruptly took the seat next to him, laying the copy she had been typing on top of his typewriter. They were alone in Publications. Michelle crossed her legs tightly and waited. He bowed his head as he searched for a pencil that had rolled on the floor. Ismael glanced at her legs, her smooth and muscular thighs. "What exactly does your girlfriend want you to do with her, Ismael?" she repeated with a grin.

"All sorts of things."

"Wonderful things?"

"Yes, of course, deliciously wonderful things. So I don't mind doing them."

"A gentleman never kisses and tells."

"And I never do. But the point is, Michelle, that Harrison is full of you-know-what. Do you boss Danny around? Do you force him to do what he doesn't want to do?"

"Course I do. He's my sweetie. I have him tied around my little pinkie, but that's between you and me," she laughed.

"Understood. But Harrison isn't into any reciprocal relationship. He wants to dominate the students."

"But Ismael, don't you respect any authority? You listen to your father and mother, don't you? Don't you do things simply 'cause they ask you to, without questioning every single detail?"

"Sure I do. But they don't boss me around. Yes, they tell me what to do, but they explain things, in a way they didn't before, say, when I was a little boy. Harrison doesn't explain anything. He wants obedience. These 'authority figures' don't deserve any respect; they deserve my questions. And they should answer them."

"Ismael, don't you get tired of asking questions all the time? It pushes people away, it intimidates them. Don't you sometimes just want to get along? You didn't join Chieftains, did you?"

"I'm not into fraternities. I don't like hanging around pep rallies, or after football games, or doing Navarette's grunt work painting the Y on the stadium."

"Those aren't the only things we do. Many of the things we do are outside of school. Kiowa helps collect food for poor kids, and we have clothing drives for the local churches."

"I'm a poor kid. Kiowa should drop a box of food at my house."

"Ay, Ismael. You are so mean. You know everybody in this school respects you. The teachers are constantly talking about you. How proud they are. Even the ones who don't particularly like you. But you should also join a service organization like the Chieftains. You know Jerry, Javier, and Troy—they're really nice guys. It would get you out of the little world you're always in. It's good not to be selfish."

"Selfish? I break my back for this newspaper. I clean up everybody's messes. How is that selfish?"

"Well, I didn't say you were completely selfish. You have your qualities. And Cyndi is a nice girl, so she must see something in you!"

"You betcha she's a nice girl. *Very* nice."

"Híjola, Ismael!"

"That's a good Spanish word. Don't forget that one."

"Maybe the right word for you is not 'selfish' but 'mean.'"

"Si me picas te pico."

"What does that mean?"

"If you push me, I'll push you back."

"That's a wonderful philosophy. Please be nice and call Jerry. The Chieftains are a great fraternity, and you'll love them." Michelle stood up and smoothed out her black velvet vest. The bell rang for second period. In three seconds, the hallways were packed with students chatting and laughing. "And don't touch my copy. See ya!"

Ismael watched Michelle Acosta walk out the door, and stared at her cute, tight behind as she turned into the hallway's chaos.

~

Pilar opened her mailbox and retrieved the El Paso Electric Company bill, the Southwestern Bell phone bill, and the El Paso Water Utility bills for their home and their apartments on Olive Street. At the bottom was a crumpled, thick letter, in a smudged white envelope with a San Antonio postmark. For a second, she imagined a letter notifying them that their daughter had unfortunately and mysteriously been killed in a jungle in Central America.

Pilar opened the envelope and sat down on the edge of a low, flat brick wall Cuauhtémoc had built for the flower bed in front of the kitchen's picture window. It was mid-April, and already the spring's gentle heat and rains had coaxed waxy green leaves from the branches of the three mulberry trees in their front yard. The letter read:

Queridos Papá y Mamá:

God be with you, and may His justice be served in this world and the next, to those who suffer innocently, and to those who oppress the poor to satisfy their greed. I am fine. I have been very happy with the Sisters of the Holy Trinity. I spent my first month mostly traveling with a group from MACC, the Mexican-American Cultural Center in San Antonio, where Father Ariel teaches a seminar. You remember Padre Ariel from Santa Lucia? He says hello, and wonders how Santa Lucia is. Are you still going to mass at Mount Carmel? If you visit Santa Lucia, which has a much better mass anyway, tell Padre Ignacio we made it to Nicaragua, and that we are with Sister Rosaelba and Sister Alicia, and that everyone is fine.

Papá y Mamá, the things I have seen have changed my life. I hope you are not too worried about me, and I know you did not want me to go on this trip with MACC. But I love you and I wanted to tell you how much I appreciated that you respected my decision. The people of Nicaragua are filled with the Holy Spirit. A revolutionary Holy Spirit. I have never been to a country where even the poorest have this hope, this light, because the American puppet dictator has finally been defeated, because finally the people can create their own destiny. Around campfires, on street corners, people sing and recite poetry, la gente dance to this new beginning they finally have won with their blood. The criminal American president, Ronald Reagan, is trying to take it all back. He is sending money to contrarevolucionarios to defeat the victory of the Sandinistas. If you have not heard about this, in those American newspapers that are so trusting of the imperialistic American government, you soon will. If one day you hear I have died, shot by a group of thugs as we travel to help poor people—we are doing the real work of Jesús, Mamá y Papá—you can blame Reagan for my death. I never felt like I had a sense of purpose until now.

Yesterday we went to an orphanage in Managua, where there are dozens of children who have lost parents in the war against Somoza. We brought them food, and books, and paper to draw and write. I taught a class in personal hygiene to a group of girls, and talked about what role women will have in this new society. One of them told me she wanted to become a nun because she believed God had finally saved them from oppression. Her parents have been missing for a year, and I'm afraid they are not coming back. So many poor people have died simply because they wanted a better life, because they fought against the evil dictator supported by the American government. We have heard rumors of atrocities, in Nicaragua and beyond. Something terrible happened recently in El Mozote, in El Salvador. Apparently thousands of people died, an entire village wiped out by the Salvadoran army and its supporters. We have sent emissaries to document what happened, but it is still dangerous. Many groups fight each other in El Salvador, and the army rapes and murders whoever they think might be helping the rebels who fight for the poor. Above all, we must bear witness, and give voice to those who never had one.

Mamá y Papá, do not be surprised if this letter has been read by someone in the post office in Ysleta or even by the FBI or the CIA. I have a missionary friend who was returning to San Antonio, Michael, take it out of Nicaragua. I told him to mail it from San Antonio, to prevent suspicions. But the evil of the Reagan government is beyond measure, and so even these precautions might not be enough. I am sure Michael is being watched, so you never know. While we were preparing for our trip in MACC, we were constantly harassed by the police. During a peaceful protest in San Antonio against the U.S. government, we were beaten for "disorderly conduct." There is no free speech in the United States, only its pretense. So many Americans are being brainwashed by the government that even if their mouths are "free" to say anything, they are mental prisoners to a culture that does not see the destructive policies their government supports in poor countries.

Papá y Mamá, I will return to finish college in San Antonio. Don't worry—I am only on leave until September, and I plan to be back in Texas sometime this summer. I know how much you value education, and I value it too. But what I was learning at the university was simply theoretical. What I am learning here is practical, purposeful. So this is part of my education too. The sisters have been carefully guiding me, and I am not taking any chances or doing anything dangerous. I know I have probably not been the best daughter, sometimes too immersed in the superficial American culture I embraced when I was younger. But San Antonio, and MACC, and Nicaragua have opened my eyes and changed me forever. That can only be good, right? You have allowed me to find my way, and for that I will always be grateful.

Papá and Mamá, I have one last favor to ask of you. I need about $300, or if you can, $500, to travel and stay in Nicaragua as long as I want to. The sisters do not ask me for any money, but I know their convent needs it, and I want to contribute what I can while I am here. $500 will last me for months here, because Nicaragua is so poor. No tienen nada, solo el amor de Dios. Michael's address is at the bottom of this letter. If you send him a money order made out to him, he will cash it and bring the money to me when he returns to Managua in about three weeks. Gracias, and may God be with you always.

Con cariño,
Your daughter, Julia

P.S. Por favor say hello to the boys for me, and to Abuelita and Abuelito.

Pilar folded the letter back into its ripped envelope and walked into the house. She immediately turned on the burner for the deep fryer for the chile rellenos, and started stuffing the chile California with Muenster cheese while the oil heated on the stove. Her egg batter was ready. Soon Cuauhtémoc and Francisco would be home for dinner.

Her rice, with tomate and garlic and onions, was already cooling in the tightly enclosed pressure cooker, to prevent it from drying out.

Esa muchacha no tiene vergüenza, Pilar thought. After Julieta had ignored their pleas not to go to Nicaragua, after Julieta had lectured them about how two years of college, on scholarship, had left her "bored and brainwashed," she had the gall to ask them for more money. What had Julieta done with the money they had sent her for the beginning of her third year, before she quit to join MACC full-time and the Catholic radicals in Nicaragua? Wasn't MACC in reality the one brainwashing their daughter?

Pilar imagined burning the letter that lay on the dining room table, before Cuauhtémoc arrived and read it. She was absolutely certain that tomorrow morning her husband would take the money out of the bank and rush a money order to his precious daughter. Even after she defied them. Even after she berated them about how their version of Catholicism was "ignorant" and "oppressive" and "materialistic." Pilar wondered how many of the nuns in San Antonio or Managua knew the immoral life Julieta had led in Ysleta, before her miraculous political conversion in college.

It was also her own fault, Pilar thought. She had allowed Cuauhtémoc to spoil Julieta, instead of putting her to work like the boys, because Pilar had been so poor in Chihuahua. Why was Julieta halfway around the world fighting for the poor when her own family was poor in Ysleta? The only reason they had any money in the bank was because she and Cuauhtémoc and the boys had nearly broken their backs working. Their thriftiness, Cuauhtémoc's steady work, and her extra income from Avon had become their investment in the Olive apartments, a financial godsend. These opportunities had come to them only because they lived in America. And now Julieta was calling the American government criminal.

Pilar heard the wheezy, metallic drone of Cuauhtémoc's pickup as it pulled into the driveway. Francisco sat next to his father, holding a scuffed Samsonite briefcase and a yellow plastic Safeway bag containing the good clothes he had worn in school. It always seemed strange to see Pancho carrying that briefcase, with his old black pants streaked with dust or dried cement, his baggy T-shirt with a gash ripped into its lower left side. She watched her son quietly shut the metal gate to their driveway and shuffle heavily toward the house. Francisco was now taller and heavier than his father.

"Cómo está mi señora?" Cuauhtémoc said as he gently kissed Pilar.

"Dinner will be ready in a few minutes," she said, still thinking about the letter on the dining room table, which was covered in plastic and only used for big get-togethers or visitors.

"Señora Big," Francisco said playfully as he bent down so his mother could kiss him on top of his head. He turned immediately to the six chile rellenos cooling atop layers of paper towels on a plate.

"Panchito, please clean up. Dinner will be ready in a few minutes."

"Okay, Mamá."

Pilar set the kitchen table, putting Cuauhtémoc's plate in front of the swivel chair next to the wall and Panchito's plate at the round end of the elongated Formica half-oval that separated the kitchen from the dining room. She placed an iced tea in front of each plate, spoons and forks on top of white paper napkins. A few chile rellenos awaited under a pan lid for Mayello's return from the print shop.

"Y el correo?" Cuauhtémoc said as he sat in his chair and took a sip of tea. Panchito walked in, sat down, and ate as if the house were on fire.

"It's on the table. Nos escribió Julieta," Pilar said matter-of-factly.

"Is she okay?" Panchito stopped chewing.

"Yes, she's fine, m'ijo. Having the time of her life in Nicaragua." Pancho sighed and picked up his fork.

"What do you think?" Cuauhtémoc asked when he had finished the letter.

"Send her the money, if you want. She won't starve, but I don't want her begging the nuns for money and whatnot."

"Thank you, mi amor."

"Julia wants money? For what?" Pancho asked.

"She wants to stay in Nicaragua until the end of summer."

"Why doesn't she get a job?"

"That's a very good question, m'ijo. But that's not how your sister is. She wants to save the world, but she wants us to pay for it. Read the letter. You'll get a lesson in hypocrisy."

"Pilar, you are being too harsh."

"Am I? Why did you let her drop out of UTEP, and now out of that university in San Antonio? A few courses here, a few more there, and where's her degree? Tell me that! Julieta is twenty-four years old!"

"Yes, you're right, she is twenty-four, and I don't control her. She's an adult. She told us she will finish her degree. We won't keep sending her money forever. Give her time."

"Time? For what? To travel to the other side of the world to get herself shot? To come back and tell us how ignorant we are and how smart she is? When she was here, it was like pulling teeth to get her to help me clean this house. Look at my Panchito. Every day, UTEP and los departamentos. Works and works and works, and never complains."

"We hit the lottery with Pancho," Cuauhtémoc said, turning to his eldest son with an appreciative glance. "I don't know what we would do without him."

"Marcos will finish his degree in Albuquerque. Before Julieta I might add. And Mayello has done so well at Ysleta. Everybody is doing what they're supposed to, except Julieta."

"I don't like that she's in Nicaragua, and when she returns I'll tell her she has to finish her degree in two years, or else. She actually got good grades at UTEP. So let's not exaggerate. And don't you like that she's with the church?"

"El Papa Juan Pablo Segundo condemned those liberation theologians. Didn't you ever look at the books she was reading at UTEP? Blasphemy and lies. They use God for their own political purposes, to justify murders and wars. The Sandinistas are a bunch of communists just like in Poland and the Soviet Union. But when they need the people to help them, they're quick to use the church and God for their purposes."

Cuauhtémoc folded the letter and slid it to twenty-three-year-old Francisco, who left it untouched while he finished inhaling his food. A piece of butter dropped onto the envelope, smearing it with a yellowish stain.

"Gracias, Mamá." Francisco stood up and carried his plate to the kitchen sink. "I have to do some homework."

"Cómo te va en la escuela?"

"Bien. I like my class in business," he said curtly. Panchito never liked to talk much about school.

"If you want a cup of yerbabuena tea later, I'll make you one."

"Gracias, Señora Big."

Pilar waited until Francisco had walked down the hallway and into the boys' old room. "Look at him. He never asks for anything, and he's always there for us. Forget los departamentos for a while and get Panchito's room finished. Is Mo-ee going to finish the roof soon?"

"Yes, this weekend. Pancho and Mayello will help. Where is Mayello anyway? When we were loading the two-by-sixes, he took off in el carrito and didn't help us at all."

"He's at the printers, and should be here soon. You want to turn all your sons into laborers?"

"He has to learn to work hard. That's what a man does."

"And you think I'm just sitting here scratching my belly button all day? Today I yanked out the weeds in the backyard, I polished the furniture, I swept the carpet, went shopping for food, and finished the laundry, all in time to get dinner ready before you arrived. Look at my hands, Cuauhtémoc. My skin is cracked and bleeding."

"No one ever questions how hard you work."

"Fine, I'm just tired. It's been a long day."

"You are the best wife any man could have. I'll make you chocolate caliente tonight. I think there's a Cantinflas movie on later."

"Ándale pues."

~

Later that evening, after Pilar finished washing the dishes, Cuauhtémoc brought two cups of hot Mexican chocolate to the living room. As they settled into the couch in front of their TV, they heard the buzzing motor of the Volkswagen Beetle over the opening credits of *El Patrullero 777*. Then the sound of the door opening.

"Mayello, is that you?"

"Si, Mamá," Ismael said, walking over to the living room.

"Are you finished?"

"I'm done, Papá. Last issue finally printed."

"Que bien. You mind helping me unload the truck when you finish dinner?"

"Of course not. Why don't you finish your movie, and I'll get started in a few minutes, okay?"

"Just put the lumber inside Pancho's new room, and stack it against one of the walls so they have room to move while they're working on the roof this weekend."

"Ándale pues."

"M'ijo, I left you chile rellenos next to the stove. Hay frijoles and arroz también. Get a pair of gloves before you unload the wood in the truck, so you don't get splinters."

"He doesn't need gloves."

"Why not? Mayello tiene manos de pianista!"

"Mamá, I'm okay. Don't worry."

As Pilar watched the movie, she saw Mayello pick up the stack of mail, sit at the kitchen table, and slowly eat his chile rellenos. After a few minutes, he stood up and walked toward the glazed rock wall that Cuauhtémoc had fashioned years ago as a showpiece for their living room, before their adobe house had a finished roof.

"Mamá, Papá. I got into Harvard."

"What? Cuauhtémoc, turn that thing off!"

"What? You got in where?"

"Into Harvard, Papá. Where the Kennedys went. They gave me money and everything."

"Harvard! Harvard, Cuauhtémoc!" Pilar shouted and jumped up and hugged her son. Tears streamed down her face. "Bendito sea Dios!"

"We are so proud of you, son," Cuauhtémoc said quietly, his eyes wet. "You see what kind of sons we have? Where exactly is Harvard?"

"Somewhere near Boston."

"It's the most famous university in the United States. The absolute best," Pilar said, suddenly somber. "You're going to leave us too, m'ijo."

~

"Don't go. What are you going to do so far away from your familia?" doña Josefina said with a catch in her throat.

"It's the best school in the country, Abuelita. I have to go. I *want* to go." In the small living room that faced the red-brick tenements across the street, don Pedro soaked his feet and dropped tablets of salt into the hot water. The old man wiggled his toes, grinned into the warm night air, and gently closed his eyes. Doña Josefina heated a quesadilla oozing with Muenster cheese on her skillet on the stove, while Ismael slowly munched on a quesadilla quarter at the table.

"You don't know anybody in Bo-ston. By the time you come back, your grandfather and I will be buried in the hot sand. Stay in El Paso and go to college here, like Panchito."

"Abuelita, did you know that President Kennedy went to that school? Senators and presidents and very famous people have gone to Harvard. It costs more than ten thousand dollars per year to go to this school."

"Jesús, María, y José! Puros malditos ricachones. You'll be poor and alone if you go there."

They sat down on her porch, just outside the living room. In the darkness, doña Josefina's face was momentarily lit when she struck a match to light her cigarette. She hunched over and stared at the concrete floor. The hump on her back was almost as high as her head.

"They're giving me una beca. Abuelita, this school will change my life."

"What do I know about these things, Mayello? I'm just a poor Mexicana with nothing but this viejo in the living room with his stinky feet. What are your parents going to do without you? First Marcos, then Julieta, and now you. I know we don't count for anything, but I say don't go."

"I'll miss everybody too. But I'll be back for Christmas, and for the summer. Abuelita, it's the best school in the United States."

"You'll come back a different person. Worse, you won't want to come back after you see everything out there. Why would you want to come back to this horrible nada?"

"Abuelita, that's not true. I'll be back. I'll call you every week, on the weekends when it's cheaper. I'll learn so much. Nobody at Ysleta has ever been to Harvard, at least no one the teachers can remember."

"It's a great honor, m'ijo. We know that. I'm sure everyone in Ysleta is proud of you. But this is who you are," she said, for a moment scanning the dark night air and the empty street. A cricket chirped in the darkness. "God help you when you go to this 'Havid.' You will be so far away from us, from everything you know. You will be alone. What if something happens to you? Who's going to help you? But you always wanted to be alone; you were always so independent, so stubborn."

"Like you."

"Ay, Dios. Just remember your familia, Mayello. Go, but come back," doña Josefina said sadly, taking a quesadilla quarter from the plate on the ground. She handed the rest to Ismael. She stared at the screen door for a moment, her lazy eye ablaze in a red light as she inhaled her cigarette. "Pedro! Get up and wash the dishes! This hombre is unbelievable. He will sleep all day if I let him. Get up before I go in there with a broomstick and smash it on your head! Viejo apestoso."

"Oiga, señora," a raspy voice proclaimed on the other side of the screen door. "Don't you know you're talking to one of the kings of 'Havid'?"

"Ahora veras, cabrón. They'd throw you in the trash at 'Havid,' that I know!"

Something to Hold on To

January 1984

Ismael rolled under his mother's thick crocheted blanket in his room at Claverly Hall. The wind howled outside his floor-to-ceiling convex window overlooking the spires of Adams House. Mounds of snow piled atop the cobblestone sidewalks of Cambridge. He squinted to decipher the quality of the sunlight, whether it was lunchtime or near evening. Ismael heard no noises in the other rooms and hallways of this cavernous annex of Quincy House, except for a weird, sharp creaking somewhere above his head. He vaguely remembered that Jonathan and Colin had each mentioned they would return home after finals, the first to the Bronx and the latter to Newton, a suburb of Boston. Perhaps they had left and he was already alone.

This was Ismael's second day of sleep. Strangely, he felt sore and weak and barely alive. He had finished his finals early, since his four classes had luckily (and unluckily) crammed their exams into the first three days of Harvard's two-week exam period. Much of his Christmas vacation in El Paso had been spent sneaking into the main reading room of the UTEP library. Like all his friends, he hated Harvard's practice of giving first-semester final exams after the holidays. It was a wicked way of ruining any trip home.

Jonathan had invited him to New York after exams, but Ismael had declined, hoping to see Samantha. After his last exam at Mem Hall, he had dragged himself through the merciless winter winds of Harvard Yard, slipping badly on the cobblestone sidewalks of Mass Ave and injuring his knee and elbow. After a quick dinner, he had finally collapsed on his single bed. Ismael had ten days to rest, to return the piles of books stacked on his dusty floor to Widener and Lamont libraries. Ten days to discard the empty bags of Cheetos and the greasy brown paper bags of Elsie Burgers. During this hiatus, he could also read for pleasure, browse the shelves of Harvard Book Store and the Starr Book Shop, and decide on his classes for the spring semester of his second year. He needed to buy new notebooks at the Harvard Coop and stash this semester's ratty notebooks in the wooden lettuce crate at the bottom of his closet. Maybe he could even work a few extra hours, copying papers and running errands, at his work-study job in the Office for Sponsored Research on Mount Auburn.

Ismael hoped he would earn at least a B in all his classes, which was a decent grade at Harvard. At times he even fervently prayed for another A or A-, for more proof that he deserved to be here. His roommate Jonathan was an excellent student, and already knew he wanted to study psychology in graduate school. Colin openly struggled, and had a townie's perspective of Harvard. He hated its snobbery while he admired its wealth. Ismael knew he most likely had done better than Colin, but not as well as Jonathan. In any case, they all worked to the point of exhaustion and were good, if distant friends. Michael, the arrogant blond-haired asshole from Long Beach, who had been Ismael's roommate freshman year, had been exiled to the Quad.

In Hollis Hall last year, Jonathan had been in a shadowy room across a dingy hallway, and Collin one floor above. None had remotely liked their assigned roommates. The threesome had enjoyed eating together in the Freshman Commons, and so they had applied for Quincy House as a group. Three freshmen, alone, found that they could be comrades along the Charles. At the end of freshman year, when Ismael had received an A- in Expository Writing (his first one at Harvard), he had felt redeemed. Maybe Harvard had not made a mistake accepting him. During the summer after freshman year, when he worked in El Paso as a stockboy at the downtown J. C. Penney, Ismael had jogged after work alongside the Border Highway to get in better shape for next year. That A- had lifted his spirits. Ismael had taken a chance and written Samantha a few letters. She had written back immediately and even sent her picture. At the El Paso Public Library, he had read Hobbes and Machiavelli and Locke for his sophomore year's required course in political philosophy, with Harvey "C-minus" Mansfield.

The fall semester of his sophomore year, Ismael declared his major as government, imagining that might be the best way to law school. But what was law school? Ismael had no clue. That's what the incredibly impressive students in his classes wanted to do, and he was certain he couldn't get the grades to be pre-med, or an econ major. At Harvard, time was always short. Most students were effusively confident. Decisions, especially for the terrified outsiders of this new world, were chaotic and instinctual.

For Ismael, another revelation freshman year had been that he was a Chicano, brown against a white background. Many students at first had imagined he was Greek or Italian. Samantha—who was a freshman at the University of Maine, with a friend at Hollis Hall—had kissed him slowly on the mouth one evening, despite discovering he was Mexican American. For some reason, this had shocked him.

Every semester he was taken aback when students noted his lispy accent. He marveled at how others quickly joined (or had been invited to join) student clubs, how they casually walked up to professors after class to chat, and how so many partied on Saturdays while they bragged about how easy their classes were. Ismael felt he was barely surviving, studying night and day just to make a B+. He hadn't even owned a winter coat that first year. On one of the coldest days of the year, he bought one from a wooden bin at Keezer's.

By the time he was a sophomore, he desperately wanted to know more about Mexico and El Paso. Ismael had grown up less than a mile from the Mexican-American border, and yet he knew next to nothing about his family's history. School textbooks in Texas treated Mexico as an afterthought, and Mexican Americans as unimportant and invisible. In Cambridge, however, activist students urged him to protest the

Reagan administration's policies for Latin America. Ismael read about the favelas in Brazil, and saw Harvard RAZA's posters with Mexicanos picking lettuce or grapes. He had known they were talking about people like him and his family, yet those causes seemed so distant from Harvard Square. Many who protested so vociferously for these causes knew next to nothing about being poor.

Being Mexicano had bestowed upon him one great advantage: he could read research articles and books in Spanish. When Professor Karl, who taught Political Economy of Latin America, had stunned him by giving him an A on his final paper on Mexico, Ismael had discovered his niche at Harvard. He had stumbled upon a way to thrive in this alien world.

In bed, Ismael stared at the huge black J. C. Penney speakers that he had suspended from the ceiling with chains and a warped wooden plank he had found on the sidewalks of Cambridge. After midterms in October, he did something strange: he stopped praying each night. He imagined the speakers crashing down onto his skull. He imagined this punishment from God for his impudence. But in the darkness nothing happened.

Despite his mother and father's ideas, Ismael believed God probably did not exist. After attending years of church services at Mount Carmel, he thought God was something you created to help you when you were weak or vulnerable. In a peculiar way, God existed in Ysleta, but not at Harvard.

Ismael had read Marx, Rousseau, and Voltaire for Political Philosophy. For hours in the Quincy House dining hall, students like Adam Colisiano, who was a gay atheist, a fellow sophomore, and gov major, loudly argued their positions against God and the Catholic Church. Ismael had met Jews, Baptists, Buddhists, and agnostics, which made El Paso seem a quaint, tidy, and arbitrary corner in the world of religions. But what most emboldened his loss of faith was that the biggest assholes at Harvard were often the most successful students. You did whatever it took to attain that A, to win that argument in a seminar class, to bed that winsome, leggy Brazilian blonde in the ridiculously short black shirt in the front row of Comparative Perspectives on Latin America's Political Economy. At Harvard, the strong and savvy and confident thrived, while the nice or shy or quaintly moral were just bit players. In Ysleta, you believed in God because you were poor and needed something to hold on to. At Harvard, you believed in your good or bad luck, in all-nighters, in your political savvy.

Ismael stood and picked up the garbage in his room. He made his bed, glanced out the window at the menacing, shiny ice on the sidewalks, and decided to return the library books after dinner. An awful, sickly sweet scent, a mixture of perspiration and dust, forced him to open his window with a hard tug. Gusts of cold air rushed into the room like a swirl of ghosts. Slipping on a pair of shorts, he carried the garbage to the hallway's trash room. Claverly's ornate, cavernous halls were mausoleum quiet. The cracked INS-green paint on the walls, for once, did not revolt him. He was free, and he was finished with exams.

When Ismael walked back into his suite, he noticed that the answering machine's neon red light was blinking. He played Jonathan's message, which said he'd see both of them in February, when classes resumed. Samantha's message confirmed she'd be at Harvard Square on Saturday, for a one-day stay before she returned to Maine. Ismael stepped behind Colin's bamboo partition; his bedcovers were on the floor, econ books were propped open on every surface of his desk, and his calculator and mechanical pencils were scattered next to the books. Most likely Colin was in the middle of one of his finals right now. Ismael gently pushed open the door to Jonathan's room, which was organized and empty. By tomorrow, Ismael would have the place to himself for his get-together with Samantha.

He deleted both messages, then walked into the restroom and shut the door. For a few minutes, he imagined seducing Samantha in his room, and pulling off her sweater, then her tight jeans. He imagined making love to her until her curly, thick brown hair was matted with perspiration. This was the first time Samantha had agreed not only to visit him, but to stay with him. His heart throbbed inside his chest. The first few minutes in Harvard Square would tell him if she had changed her mind, or if she wanted to get into bed and stay there with him all weekend. Ismael showered in water so hot his skin turned bright pink. The deadness on his skin finally washed away.

Shortly before dinner, Ismael said good-bye to Colin, who had decided to drive with friends to Newton for the week before the start of the next semester. Ismael was alone in his Claverly suite. He wrapped a dusty black scarf around his neck and buttoned up his dark brown wool overcoat from Keezer's, which released a faint whiff of mothballs. Ismael skipped over the slate steps outside the Quincy House dining hall and pushed open the heavy glass doors. Nobody was at the pinball machines in the lobby as he climbed the twisty inner staircase to the dining room. No line of students lingered in front of the trays of hamburgers, toasted buns, astonishingly green green beans, mashed potatoes, and steamed baby carrots. In the dining room, a few students, like apparitions with Alzheimer's, glanced distractedly into the air at no one in particular. Their books, notebooks, and coffee cups were piled around them like mini fortresses. A group of loud girls argued and laughed about a ski trip to Vermont. Ismael slumped into a seat overlooking Tommy's Lunch on Mount Auburn. He slowly ate his cheeseburger and sipped a Diet Coke. Only a few hours ago, the blood-red sun had sunk behind the business school on the other side of the Charles River. His body and the world were on different tracks of time.

Back at Claverly, Ismael shoved open the thick door to his suite, threw his empty blue backpack on the floor, and ran to pick up the phone in the darkness.

"Hello, hello?"

"Ay, ah . . . espérate! May aye speak to Iz-mai-el?"

"Mamá, soy yo, Mayello. Your English is very good señora, don't worry," he laughed.

"Mayello, I'm so glad it's you. How do I know who's going to answer your phone? You already sound exactly like your roommates. We've been calling you for the last hour, and nobody except your machina picks up. Where were you?"

"In the library, returning books. Hace un friaso aquí."

"Ten mucho cuidado. Oye, te llamamos para decirte algo muy triste. Your abuelita died this morning."

"What?"

"Sí, se murió mi mamá," his mother sniffled. "Your grandfather couldn't wake her up this morning, and he called us, and we went over there as quickly as possible. The ambulance was already there by the time we arrived. They said she must've died in her sleep. She looked peaceful."

"She was fine when I saw her a few weeks ago. I brought her asaderos from Licon's. What happened?"

"M'ijo, she was eighty-three years old. God was ready for her."

"It's a bit shocking to all of us, I know," his father said on the other phone line. "I always thought she was as strong as an ox. But she lived a good life, and she had family around her. She didn't suffer. Don Pedro is very sad, but he'll be okay. He'll be staying with us for a few days."

"Mayello, she was so proud of you," his mother blurted out.

"Ay, Mamá. Who cares about that?" Ismael said almost angrily. "I can't believe Abuelita's dead. Everybody knows? Pancho, Marcos, Julia? How are they doing?"

"We haven't told Julia yet; we can't get ahold of her in Minnesota. But we'll keep trying," his father said. "Panchito is making all the arrangements at Mount Carmel."

"Give me the number and I'll call Julia, if you want. You have so much to worry about already."

As his mother searched for Julia's number in Minnesota, Ismael could not help thinking of his grandfather Pedro. He was the one who lived for the moment, who had lifted doña Josefina's spirits when she had teetered close to despair or even violence. What had made him find a song in even the darkest moments? What, or who, would keep him from his abyss?

"We know you can't come to the funeral," his mother said tentatively. "It's so far. We know, m'ijo."

"Ay, Mamá. I can postpone my exams. I know Harvard will let me do it." Ismael suddenly felt his stomach twist into an awful knot as he heard his own lie.

"Your abuelita knew you loved her, and that's what matters," said his mother.

"The family will take care of things over here. We know how hard it is. Doña Josefina would have wanted you to do well. I know my suegra. She was always bragging about you to her neighbors."

"She didn't brag, Cuauhtémoc. She wanted Ismael to come back home when he was done. She was so happy to see you over Christmas."

"She was proud, m'ijo, as we all are. Focus on your work, and we'll call you and tell you what's happening."

Just before he hung up the phone, Ismael promised his mother he would light a candle for his abuelita at Saint Paul Catholic Church in Harvard Square. But the pain in Ismael's stomach did not disappear. He lay quietly in bed, envisioning his abuelita's face the last time he saw her, her slightly watery eyes, the one eye askew and white with cataract, the pale brown-spotted skin on her soft face. When she had said her final farewell to him, she had stood at her porch in the Olive apartments, almost in midstep forward. Her wrinkled face and her frail body had been ready for something, ready to yell at his abuelito, ready for Ismael to ask for just one more cup of coffee. She wore her favorite coffee-brown loose slacks, and a blouse with a shimmering blue and white marblelike pattern. Ismael remembered how she smelled when he hugged her good-bye, of talcum powder, sweet perspiration, and onions. Why had he lied to his parents? Why hadn't he told them he was finished with his exams? What would be the point of returning home for the funeral when only her body was left? Her kindness, her toughness, her spirit, her ganas were gone.

After an hour, the pain in his stomach receded, and he undressed himself. In bed, he drifted into an uneasy sleep. Deep into the night, Ismael dreamed about Samantha Pearson, her auburn hair across his face, her long, athletic legs wrapped insistently around his. Ismael dreamed Samantha and he were inside his room, but afloat in Ysleta. Like possessed dice, the speakers dangled dangerously above them. He dreamed the earth below was a desert, canals and ditches and cotton fields, with a darkness thickened by the smell of alfalfa and wet dirt, a black landscape that harbored an amorphous pain just beyond their island of a bed.

~

Pancho trudged around the empty apartment, trying to guess how many gallons of paint he'd need from the Benjamin Moore store on Texas Avenue. Next to the door of his abuelito's old apartment were three cardboard boxes with pots and pans and a few last items from the dresser and the bathroom. The dresser itself, with its broken drawers in pieces, he'd throw out at the yonke on his way home. Pancho's heavy footsteps echoed loudly as he walked to the bathroom to check how many tiles needed to be replaced, and in what color.

Don Pedro was already in Ysleta, in the little apartment his father had constructed in the backyard with its own shower and bathroom. Abuelito had not protested the move. He didn't want to live alone, and everybody had noticed how deeply depressed he was after doña Josefina died. Don Pedro's new twin bed was moved into the backyard apartment, and Pancho dragged Ismael's old dresser to his abuelito's new bedroom. After that, don Pedro seemed almost back to normal. The old man's mental wanderings seemed to lessen. He took up smoking quietly in his bedroom, or sitting gingerly on the low brick wall of the flower beds in the backyard, under the pomegranate tree, sometimes patting one of the dogs in the sun. After a while, around midmorning, don Pedro shuffled slowly into the kitchen and poured himself a cup of coffee and read the newspaper. Sometimes Pancho walked in from UTEP or from working at los departamentos, and he would find his grandfather asleep in the living room, snoring loudly, his foot stretched out under the round marble table. Don Pedro seemed happy to belong somewhere again.

At least now their old apartment on Olive Street could be rented for money. It was the best apartment in the building, with a screened-in porch, a spacious living room, and an ornate turn-of-the-century fireplace. Cuauhtémoc had stripped decades of old paint and returned the façade and pillars of the fireplace to its elegant wooden splendor. In all the apartments, the restored fireplaces, with carved wreaths around pillars, were showpieces that astonished the viejitos and viejitas in los departamentos.

It was Pancho's job to get an empty apartment ready to show prospective tenants. He had already plastered the holes in the wall in his abuelitos' old kitchen. He needed to inspect and repair the walls in the bedroom, living room, and bathroom before he could paint. Pancho would finish the plastering today, sand down the white yeso once it was dry, until a swipe of his palm could not distinguish the wall from where the hole had been. Then he would apply the first coat of oyster white with a paint roller. After work, his father would do the edges with a brush. To Pancho, each paint job revealed a room of innumerable edges. They'd have to replace the stove, since it was old and would probably start leaking gas soon, a disaster they definitely wanted to avoid. He and his father would decide about the expenses of the stove together, after work, when they had agreed to meet at the Olive apartments. They could also stick masking tape around the edges of the fireplaces to make sure the paint rollers didn't destroy the painstaking work they had achieved with these beautifully varnished fireplace mantels.

"Panchito, I saw your truck on the street, so I came over to say hello."

Francisco finished dropping the boxes into the truck's bed and returned the greeting. "Buenas tardes, señora Olivas, how are you? How's your back?"

"Dios Nuestro Señor has answered my prayers, my son. It's not hurting me anymore after el doctor gave me some pastillas. The doctor recommended I take a hot bath, but when I turned on the hot water only cold water came out."

"Oh, it might be the boiler. The pilot light might be out. Let me go over and check it now, if that's okay."

"Panchito, you are an angel of mercy. Your father doesn't know how lucky he is to have you. One of these days I hope he gives you these apartments, as payment for your years of hard work and sacrifice."

"It's no problem, señora Olivas. I'm ready whenever you are." Pancho followed the old woman, who walked at a painstakingly slow pace on the brick path that led to the apartment entrances in the backyard. Panchito stared at her gently shuffling blue slippers, which caught a few times on the edges of the red brick, and worried she would tumble forward and break her hip. But each time doña Lupe righted herself at the last moment.

"Oye, Panchito, I don't see your brothers around here anymore. Why don't they help you?"

"Well, Ismael is in Boston," Pancho said, as he jarred open the decorative hallway door to the boiler in her apartment, kneeled heavily, and lay down to get a better look inside the small blue metal door that he had pried open at the bottom of the tank. He checked the valves and gauges, and didn't smell any gas.

"Boston? What's he doing over there?"

"I don't know if you remember, señora, but he's in college."

"I'm sorry, m'ijo. I even forget my name sometimes. That's what happens when you get old. Don't get old, Panchito. Why doesn't he study here? Aren't the schools here any good?" Señora Olivas warbled in a creaky, high-pitched voice that Francisco had always found endearing.

"Well, the one Ismael goes to is a very famous school. Presidents have gone there. Do you have a match, señora? And Marcos is in Albuquerque, also at a university there."

"Here you go. Hope these still work. I don't think it's fair that your brothers have abandoned your parents in Ysleta and have left you here to do all the work. But your father is a smart man. If I see him today, I'll make sure to remind him how much you help me. He may be the owner, Panchito, but we count on you."

"You don't have to do that, señora. I'm at the university too, at UTEP on Mesa Street." On his first try, Pancho held the match with his fingertips, but it blew out before he brought it close enough to the pilot light. His chest and stomach were cold against the linoleum floor. He had scratched an index finger against a sharp metal edge inside the boiler.

"Well, that's good. Don't let those brothers come back and think they're muy muy. You are as good as they are. You're smart, and better than that, you are a good man. That's what matters in the eyes of God."

"Thank you, señora. Your pilot was out, and I just turned it on again. Give it about thirty minutes or so to heat up the water in the tank—the burner just turned on, did you hear it?—and then try the hot water again. If it doesn't work, I should be here later and I'll look at it again. But it should be fine. Hasta luego, señora."

"Panchito, say hello to your mother for me. Here, take her this bag of bizcochos I made yesterday, with extra sugar and cinnamon. I've put in a few more just for you. Gracias, m'ijo. Drive safely. There are so many locos on the road nowadays. They hardly wait for us to cross the street before they screech through the intersection like sons of the Devil."

It was not until six in the evening that Pancho returned home, the yellow truck carefully following his father's Buick for fifteen miles on the Border Highway. Before his father left work at Morgan Smith Building Associates, Pancho had already purchased the oyster white paint, rollers, roller pans, and brushes, and had prepped the walls and fireplaces. Pancho had also stopped by the Magoffin apartments and picked up the rents from doña María, the sprightly widow in apartment #2. She collected the rents from the tenants, and gave Pancho or his father a heads-up whenever a pipe burst or un atrasado was loading furniture at midnight. Doña María, in return, received the lowest rent at the Magoffin apartments. It had taken Pancho and his father but a few minutes to take a quick detour to the dump and toss the old dresser into a junk pile in the middle of the desert. This weekend they'd buy a new Amana or Magic Chef, and the apartment would be ready to show next week.

As soon as he dropped his old Samsonite briefcase on his bed and washed his grimy hands, Pancho ate flautas with his parents, then said he would rest in his room. He was exhausted and needed to finish a problem set for Business Economics, which was due by the end of the week. He shut the door and turned off the lights, except for the golden desk lamp next to the curtained window to the backyard. Through the air conditioning vents, Pancho could hear fragments of his father's and mother's discussion about what movie they might screen tonight. He heard his grandfather's sudden, loud guffaw.

In the dim light, Pancho pored over the Dallas Cowboys official newsletter. The Raiders had beaten the Washington Redskins in the Super Bowl a few weeks before, providing him some consolation after an excellent Cowboys season (12–4) had ended dismally in a first-round playoff loss to the Rams. If the Redskins, the archrival of his Cowboys in the NFC East, had won Super Bowl XVIII, he might have cried. Pancho's room had four different Cowboys pennants tacked to the walls. The old yellow truck his father had given him had a giant Cowboys sunscreen affixed to the back window and a Cowboys sticker on its rusty bumper. An extra Cowboys sticker, with a five-pointed navy blue star, graced one side of his Samsonite briefcase, for his papers and assignments for his two courses at UTEP. A shiny blue Cowboys jacket was in his closet, two Cowboys plastic drinking cups were in the kitchen cupboard, there were Cowboys pencils on his desk and in his briefcase, and his keys hung on a Cowboys keychain. Without a doubt, Francisco Martínez was the biggest Cowboys fan on San Lorenzo Avenue. Whenever the Cowboys lost a game, the fat twenty-five-year-old, who had the appearance of a kind, somewhat frightened giant, would become deeply depressed and almost physically ill. He would decline to come out of his room for hours. On those unfortunate Sundays, his parents knew to leave him alone and not even offer him dinner.

Groggy and tired from squinting to read the small font of the newsletter, Pancho closed his eyes and imagined traveling to Texas Stadium in Dallas to watch a live game. After a few minutes, his rotund stomach slowly and rhythmically rose and fell under his sheer white T-shirt, and his breathing wheezed. Pancho was asleep on his sister's old king-size bed. The Cowboys newsletter was draped across his chest. The massive headboard, with gaudy red velour and a gold, flowery wooden trim, he had long ago unscrewed from the bed frame and jammed into the supply closet next to his grandfather's bedroom in the back. When Julia finally left home for good, Francisco did not want to waste the most comfortable, ample bed in the house.

The incessant ringing of the telephone woke Pancho up. Why didn't his parents answer it? He glanced at his red LED watch and saw it was ten at night.

"Hello," Pancho said in a deep, croaky voice.

"Oye, Panchito. How are you?" said Marcos.

"What's up? Why are you calling me so late?"

"Were you asleep? Sorry, ese. But I'm glad you picked up. Figured you would anyway."

"How's school? Everything fine?"

"Oh, yeah. Everything's great. Papá y Mamá?"

"Everybody's fine over here." There was a long pause. When Ismael called from Harvard, often on a Sunday when the rates were cheaper, he wanted to hear a familiar voice. But when Pancho's brothers called at an odd hour, or in the middle of the week, they usually wanted more money.

"Oye, I have a favor to ask. Something important, Panchito."

"What?"

"I'm changing apartments, ese. Next week, and I need your help moving."

"Y?"

"Well, can you come up here and help me, with your trokita?"

"All the way to Alba-fucking-querque? That's five hours, at least! Five hours, and back."

"I know, I know. But Panchito, I'll save money. The rent's cheaper. It's better for me. No seas gacho."

"It's a long drive, and I have a problem set due this week. Get one of your friends to help you."

"I asked them already, but they either don't have cars or they have these tiny ranflas that can't carry shit. Look, you can do your work here, stay overnight one night, and then drive back home on Sunday. If I save on rent, I don't have to keep begging you for more money. I need your help, bro."

After a long pause, Pancho said, "Ándale pues." The trip would be a good excuse not to work at los departamentos for the weekend. He would love to drive through the starkly beautiful countryside of New Mexico, its chile farms and razor-sharp mountains. La gente humilde there reminded him of what he liked best about Ysleta. And maybe, truly, his brother wouldn't be asking for more money every other week. "Okay, pero I have to talk to Mom and Dad. Have to get the truck greased, change the oil, check the tires and brakes. Maybe I'll have to take it in for a complete tune-up. It's about time anyway. Getting a little sick of El Paso."

"Ese, Panchito, I won't forget it. We'll take you out to dinner and show you a good time. Thank you, bro. You want me to talk to them?"

"Nah, it's all right. I'll talk to them tomorrow morning. Mamá will probably want to make you a box of flautas, and burritos for me for the trip."

~

On Saturday morning, Pancho drove his old yellow pickup alongside the Sandia Mountains, relaxing as his mind soared with "Venus and Mars" from Paul McCartney and Wings. The rugged beauty of the mountains in layers of shadow and light, alongside the prehistoric sea that was now a vast desert, swelled Pancho's heart with happiness. These few hours of tranquility were worth the sacrifice of his weekend to help Marcos.

After a long while, Pancho pulled up to the old adobe apartments next to one of the main drags of the University of New Mexico. Last year he had moved Marcos into these apartments, which he had thought were dumpy compared to their Olive and Magoffin apartments in El Paso. As a landlord, Francisco had never rented to college students. Viejitos on Social Security were plentiful in El Segundo Barrio, usually on time with their rents, and rarely destructive of the property. Families with children were the worst tenants. Marcos pushed open the screen door without a screen and hugged Pancho. In a few minutes, the brothers were loading the yellow pickup with boxes of books, a bed frame, chairs, and a kitchen table with shiny silver legs. Pancho had brought Marcos an old green sofa a tenant from Magoffin had abandoned. It was the best piece of furniture in the back of the pickup.

"So you think three or four trips?" Marcos asked as he climbed into the passenger's seat and slammed the creaky yellow door with a bang.

"Yeah, just about. You got a lot of junk. Why don't you get rid of some of it?"

"May have to. Thanks, bro. I owe you one."

"Vámonos. Left or right?" Pancho asked as he pulled out from the driveway. After a few more turns, and in about fifteen minutes, they were cruising through a tree-lined neighborhood in Albuquerque. They stopped at a tidy little ranch house, white with aqua-green trim, a porch, a backyard, and an old maroon Volvo in front of the garage. "Here?" Pancho said, puzzled.

"Yeah, nice, huh?"

Pancho hoisted himself off the front seat, aired out his sticky pants with a shy glance around the quiet neighborhood, and yanked open the gate to the pickup's bed. He started to stack the boxes on the sidewalk to make room to drag the sofa out. "How's this cheaper than where you live now?"

"Well, ese, Sylvia and I will share the expenses."

"Sylvia? Who's Sylvia?"

"My girlfriend, ese. She'll be out in a second."

"Órale," Pancho murmured. A loud metallic door slammed shut behind him. He turned to see an athletic brunette bounding toward them in tight jeans, bright red sneakers, and a navy blue T-shirt tied at the waist. Her curls dangled around her head like small snakes. Sylvia shook his hand firmly and immediately lifted an armful of boxes with a cheeky wide smile. Pancho noticed the muscles on Sylvia's arms and shoulders, and how she stared adoringly at every move his brother made.

Sylvia, Pancho found out, was a second-year law student, three years older than Marcos, and from California. She also possessed a boisterous laugh, which Marcos loved to tease out of her with political or sexually tinged jokes. Sylvia was quick, decisive, and confident. When the three sat down to eat at a booth at Rosita's, Sylvia bounced into the seat next to Marcos, lightly jabbed him in the ribs, kissed him on the cheek, and squeezed his thigh. She almost seemed a different species from their mother, Pilar. Their mother had always prized a demure nature and thought it unseemly to say what you meant even if it was true.

Sylvia encouraged Marcos's edgier side, and made him laugh as Pancho had never seen his brother laugh before, in an earsplitting, devilish crescendo that turned every head in the restaurant toward their table. They chatted about her pro bono work for an immigrant rights group, about Rudolfo Anaya and a speech on Chicano literature he had given the week before. They were participating in a march next week. Sylvia was hilarious, and even a fanatic about baseball and football. After a few beers, Marcos's green eyes became glassy, yet the mischievous grin never left his face. Sylvia drove them home, and made sure Pancho had a good pillow and enough blankets on the pull-out sofa bed in the living room. When Marcos poked his head from their bedroom to check if Pancho needed anything else, he seemed to have sobered up. He closed the door behind him with a grin.

Pancho lay quietly on the sofa bed. It wasn't comfortable because his weight pushed the thin mattress onto the metal frame and jammed a bar against his backbone. He wondered how Marcos would keep Papá and Mamá from finding out about Sylvia. Their parents rarely called Ismael or Marcos or Julia, because the children called home about once a week. But it was bound to happen. A phone call from Ysleta out of the blue. A strange, assertive female voice answering Marcos's phone. Questions. Then outrage.

Pancho shifted his weight and tried pushing a pillow into the space atop the metal bar against his back. In the absolute darkness, he heard murmurs behind the bedroom door, then soft pleas, sudden gasps, and occasional, languorous moans. The noises grew louder until Pancho felt he was in the same room with the two lovers. Pancho lay absolutely still so they would not overhear the creak of the sofa bed. Pancho imagined what it would be like to be with a woman. He imagined he wasn't overweight and under-confident. He imagined somebody would like him for who he was. Sylvia reminded him of a certain Dallas Cowboys cheerleader. He was happy for his brother, happy that Marcos had stepped out of the shadows of Ismael and Julia at Ysleta High, happy that he was loved by such a beautiful and impressive woman. And yet, here Pancho was, still incapable of looking a woman straight in the eyes for more than a second. Here was Pancho, alone and marooned.

~

In Saint Paul, the University of Minnesota had shut down because of a nasty blizzard that had so far dumped three feet of snow onto the streets. The wind howled outside Julia's small apartment. At times the window glass shook with a savage fury. For curtains, she had nailed to the wall hemmed sections of a bedsheet with pale yellow flowers. Only two pieces of furniture interrupted the flat open space, two chairs, on top of which were a wobbly stack of books, reams of paper, and utility bills. Over the tan carpet in every room she had spread blood-red Persian rugs that her friend Zahara had brought for her from Iran. In one corner of her bedroom floor were blankets, including a sarape from El Mercado Juárez, which Julia had nostalgically kept since her days in San Antonio and El Paso. A black reading lamp hung over her bedding. Next to her pillow were copies of the Bible and the Koran. A blue Smith Corona electric typewriter, still in its grainy brown plastic case, lay next to the lamp. Julia stood over the stove in the kitchen, Mexican rice on one burner, a lamb kebab simmering on another. A frying pan with hot oil, for buñuelos, cooled atop a back burner. Next to the pan, a large yellow bowl was stacked with square fritters lightly dusted with sugar and cinnamon, Zahara's favorite Mexican dish.

Julia thought about her fateful decision, one that she would today reveal to her best friend Zahara. It had been almost a year and a half since Julia had left San Antonio and enrolled at the University of Minnesota. She had traveled with Zahara to Minnesota, first to a conference to debate the imperialist tactics of the United States in Latin America and the Middle East, and then permanently, after Zahara had chosen to transfer to Minnesota and had encouraged Julia to follow her. Zahara and her friends understood Julia, how she wanted to fight American imperialism abroad, and how she wanted to fight the American cultural oppression that had consumed her as a teenager.

Zahara had marched with Julia when they had been beaten by the police in San Antonio for disturbing the peace during a protest against the Reagan administration's policies in Nicaragua and Iran. Zahara had nervously accompanied Julia when they had been followed for miles by a black sedan in Minneapolis, after a meeting of political activists to plan yet another protest and conference in the spring. Zahara had introduced her, first in San Antonio and then in Minneapolis, to

Muslim friends who embraced Julia and her activism. Julia particularly admired Zahara's Iranian friends for Iran's stunning success in taking American hostages at the U.S. embassy in 1979. For once, the "Great Satan" had been humiliated.

After Julia arrived in Minnesota, she realized more than ever that her Catholic background had oppressed her in many ways. The Catholicism she had accepted as her birthright in Ysleta had systematically undermined her activism, she thought. It blocked the Mexican-American community from creating a life, in the here and now, that honestly followed God. The Catholic Church—which in the time of Luther had forced financial payments from its followers for a guaranteed pass to heaven—was not much different now. How was the opulence of the Vatican and its churches consistent with Jesus' life as a pauper? Why had the church never apologized for the genocide and forced conversion of the native peoples of Mexico? Why had the pope repeatedly become an ally of rich nations against the Third World? After years of trying to find her place within her faith, of focusing on the most progressive elements within the Catholic Church, Julia concluded this power-obsessed institution would never change. For a long time, she did not know what to do and prayed entire weekends without leaving her apartment. Last weekend, in a moment of exhaustion and ecstasy, a revelation came as Julia prayed to an image of Our Lady of Fatima. The Virgin's holy site in Portugal had been the highlight of Julia's pilgrimage to Europe five years before. For the first time in a long time Julia's heart was filled with a giddy joy.

~

"Bueno? Ay, Dios mio," Pilar said, followed by what sounded like the sharp plastic clatter of the phone hitting the floor.

"Mamá, es Julia. Sorry to call you so early in the morning. Maybe I should've waited until later."

"No, m'ija. Everything okay? Espérate, your father's also getting out of bed. Here take this phone," she said to Cuauhtémoc, "and I'll go to the kitchen. It's Julia."

"Julia, is everything all right?" her father said in a raspy voice. "It's three in the morning, m'ija."

"I'm sorry. I have to talk to you; it's something very important. Papá, Mamá, I've made a decision, and I wanted to share it with you. I've decided to convert to the Muslim religion."

"What?" Pilar screamed. "Are you out of your mind?"

"Julia, what are you saying?"

"I want to be a Muslim. I've even chosen a new Muslim name, Aliyah."

"Julia, are you drunk?"

"No, Papá, I'm not drunk. I've thought about this for a very long time. I think it's the right thing for me, a way to follow God."

"Are you crazy? Has someone brainwashed you?"

"No, of course not. This isn't something I'm just calling about today and changing my mind next week. I've really thought about it and prayed to the Virgin de Fatima. Did you know 'Fatima' is a Muslim name?"

"Julia, what kind of ridiculous nonsense is this?"

"Pilar, let's just hear what she has to say."

"Please, Mamá. I've been very dissatisfied with the Iglesia Católica, and I want to follow the path of God, the true path, and I want to have children. Did you know Jesús and María and José are in the Koran? Muslims consider Jesus a prophet."

"You are abandoning us! You are betraying what the holiest of churches believes, what our church believes! Cuauhtémoc, I told you something like this would happen, but you let her go to Central America, you let her go to Minnesota, and now look at the results!"

"Mamá, please. I'm not betraying anybody, I'm just trying to find what's best for me."

"This is your answer? A betrayal of our Lord Jesus Christ? Of everything we believe in? You've ignored us, you've made fun of us, as if we were ignorant peasants. But you're the one who's wrong, that I know."

"Pilar, please hear her out. She's an adult, it's her life. Give her time to consider what she's about to do."

"That's your response? To encourage her to do this? She's betraying us! And for what? For religious zealots who hate America, for a crazy culture that glorifies dying!"

"Mamá, that's not true. Muslims are not like that. They pray every day, they follow the Koran, they love their families. They don't build golden temples for Allah. They want to create a life here on earth that follows the word of God."

"Julia, is this about a boy? Did you fall in love with a Muslim man? Is he asking you to convert for him?"

"No, Papá. Nobody is asking me to do anything. This is one thing I am sure about."

"At least your abuelita's dead and will never hear your blasphemy. If you do this, Julia, you will be dead to me. You will no longer be my daughter."

"Mamá, how can you say that?"

"Cuauhtémoc, you have always justified whatever she does, you send her money for whatever she wants. She skips around the United States from college to college, one protest after another, and you're twenty-five, señorita. Nothing to show for it. Look at Marcos—he's four years younger and he's about to finish college. Look at Mayello at Harvard, working on weekends until midnight. Panchito, doing the best he can at UTEP. He never asks for anything and he helps us with los departamentos. And you? You were always the selfish child. Always "I need this" and "give me that." Your arrogance! You're probably sleeping with some Muslim idiot and you're about to marry him. Will that be the next call in the middle of the night? And now you're calling us to congratulate you on abandoning our religion? You are dead to me."

"Pilar, please, don't make this worse."

"Don't you see! She's a traitor!"

"Mamá, please. I can't control what you think. But there is no man, Mamá. I know you are hurt, but I don't mean to hurt you, Mamá. I want you to understand."

"Understand what? That you abandoned us long ago? That you despise us and what we believe? That you are spitting on our God? I think I understand only too well."

"Mamá, I didn't tell my best friend Zahara until a few minutes ago."

"Julia, do you think we're stupid? That we don't know people? I'm sure this little friend of yours has been giving you books to defame the Catholic Church, to promote her religion. You go follow her. See if that religion of hers is as perfect as she makes it out to be. See if you can close your eyes to what those Muslim radicals have done against the holy land of Israel, against the United States. Your friends the Iranians and the Iraqis are slaughtering each other by the thousands in an idiotic war. You must be out of your mind."

"Pilar, please. What can we do? Julia, please think this through. This is not something you should do without thinking about what it means not only to you, but to all of us. M'ija, we love you. No one can expect any religion to be perfect. This is how you grew up. This is who you are. If you become Muslim, who will you be? Come home. I will send you the money and you can come home. Isn't that right, Pilar? Pilar? I think she hung up the phone. Julia, she's very upset."

"Papá, I have thought about it. I'm happy with what I am doing. But I will call you again and tell you what's happening."

"M'ija, please think it over carefully. I know you are an adult. But you need to know becoming a Muslim won't just be accepted by us. You are sacrificing your family in Ysleta. This is a shock to all of us. I remember meeting this friend of yours—Zaha, Zahar?—what's her name, again?"

"Zahara."

"Wasn't she in San Antonio too?"

"Yes, we drove to El Paso one Thanksgiving."

"You know, m'ija, I'll tell you this maybe because it doesn't matter anymore. But I thought you were becoming a lesbian. That's what I feared the most."

"Ay, Papá! How can you say that? She's like my sister, Papá."

"I don't know what's worse, becoming a lesbian or becoming a Muslim. Why do you have to change your name? You know, I can hear your mother sobbing in the living room. I have to go talk to her."

"Papá, my Muslim name will be Aliyah. Please try to talk to her, and tell her that I love her."

"Julia, call me back in a couple of days. Let me talk to your mother and calm her down. Call back and consider what you are doing carefully. You are leaving everything you were in Ysleta. Your mother has always been a much more devout Catholic than I ever was. But I am still a Mexicano. That is my heritage and I am proud of it. Are you rejecting that too? I know you are an adult and are responsible for your own decisions now. But please, think this over. We love you too, Julia."

"I'll call you back in a few days."

"Hasta luego, m'ija."

"Adios, Papá."

Each an Island Adrift

JUNE 1986

As he drove down the Border Highway, Cuauhtémoc remembered the day when his oldest, Julia, had been born. An expressive, intelligent baby girl, Julia reminded him of his mother: they possessed the same brown-black eyes. Those eyes had practically healed the wound of his mother's early death when he was ten years old. That Julia was not "Julia" anymore, but "Aliyah," did not diminish that she had recently given birth to her own daughter. "Zahira" meant "luminous in the eyes of God."

Cuauhtémoc lifted his foot off the truck's accelerator as he saw a group of Mexicanos sprinting across the highway. He glanced around: the migra was nowhere in sight, thank goodness. These poor bastards scurrying into the Ascarate neighborhood to evade the migra weren't that different from whom he had been thirty years ago.

Cuauhtémoc remembered the day Francisco had been born, how proud he had been that the Martínez name would continue, that he would have a son to help him. What if caring for these children had taken Pilar away from him and his needs? Wasn't having a family fulfilling his destiny as a human being too? There were more pressures with a family, and more expenses, but also more joys, and Pilar had been a good mother.

When Marcos graduated from the University of New Mexico two years ago, Cuauhtémoc could see the end in sight. Panchito needed another year, but was only going to UTEP part-time, which wasn't that expensive. Julia was still attending classes in Maryland. Cuauhtémoc wasn't sure when she would finish her undergraduate degree, but she was not his responsibility anymore. Two weeks ago, at Ismael's graduation, Cuauhtémoc was rapturous, not only because his youngest had graduated from the school of the Roosevelts and the Kennedys, but also because Mayello was finished with school.

He and Pilar had painstakingly calculated their expenses over the past six months, in anticipation of Mayello's graduation and their trip to Cambridge and the East Coast, and they knew they had enough. Sure, expenses would pop up. A new roof for the house. A replacement stove or refrigerator for a newly vacated apartment. Another "emergency loan" to Julia. Maybe even graduate school for his children. But at fifty-one years old, Cuauhtémoc would tell his bosses he was retiring today. His heart was tired, but he was elated.

Cuauhtémoc told Manny Ramirez first. Manny didn't seem terribly surprised and graciously congratulated Cuauhtémoc. "Well, viejo," Manny said as he closed his office door, "you're probably doing it the right way, before you start pissing in your pants. Look what happened to El Serio. Dead on his drafting stool. Never got to enjoy a day in the sun of his retirement. Nada. I heard his wife took up with a neighbor within the year. Pobre pendejo."

"I just want to spend time with Pilar and I can do that now. I'm more or less healthy. My kids are out of the house, except for Panchito. I have the money. We want to travel." They had already been to Europe twice, which had astonished their neighbors in Barraca. In October, they would go to la Costa del Sol in Spain, and the following year perhaps to Israel and Egypt. Pilar wanted to see the Holy Land before she died.

"How's your diabetes?"

"It's under control. I take my insulin shots. I think in a way it made me think about the years I have left. A few quality years, maybe ten or so, and then who knows. Right now my family has everything they need. I don't owe anybody anything. Why keep killing yourself? Mas y mas y mas. I'm not a gringo in that way."

"Este pobre Preston Smith, he will die on his swivel chair," Manny said, pointing with his eyes at the cofounder and principal owner of Morgan Smith and Sons, ensconced in a corner office of wall-windows composed of tiny, nearly invisible grid lines like transparent graph paper. "Doing one more deal. Making one more million. That's how he is, and how he always will be. You should tell him yourself, just for the hell of it."

"Ándale pues."

"The cabrón is going to miss you, but don't expect him to cry for you, Cuau. He's going to miss all the money he made from your hard work, ese."

"He was always fair with me and I have no complaints."

"If another big project comes along, you interested in contract work? These young pendejos are not always reliable. Contract work pays better than what you get now, but without the benefits."

"Sure, why not. Once in a while. Just give me a call."

Manny reminded Cuauhtémoc to talk to Jeannie about how to disburse his 401(k). He had been putting money into the plan for years. With Ismael's help, he had chosen investments that had ballooned his total to more than he could have ever imagined. One day Manny had seen Cuauhtémoc's statement on his drafting table and said, "You're rich, cabrón. You've got more money than I do!"

Cuauhtémoc waited a few minutes before going to Mr. Smith's office. He had rarely spoken to the old man beyond a quick hello. Manny had always acted as a buffer. The longest conversation Cuauhtémoc had ever had with Mr. Preston Smith happened when Mr. Smith stopped him in the hallway and told him he had heard from Manny that Ismael had been accepted to Harvard. For the first and last time, Mr. Smith complained about how his own granddaughter's application to Harvard was rejected, and how his son Dylan wasn't reliable as a father or a construction manager. That year Cuauhtémoc received his biggest raise ever. It was also the year Dylan moved to Bisbee, Arizona, to run his own firm. Cuauhtémoc later heard from

Manny that Dylan's company had gone bankrupt. The old man had refused to bail the son out again. Dylan's older brother, Eric, on the other hand, was a graduate of Wharton Business School, and was destined to take over Morgan Smith one day.

"Cuauhtémoc, how have you been? Please come in," Mr. Smith said when he heard the soft knock at his door. The old man, with shockingly white hair above his ears, rarely wore a tie to work, and dressed in only dark gray slacks and a crisp blue oxford shirt. "How can I help you?"

"Well, señor Smith, I have come to tell you I'm retiring. In two weeks, I am leaving Morgan Smith."

"Oh, Cuauhtémoc. Are you sure? This seems so sudden. You have been with us for decades, one of our best draftsmen."

"Thank you, señor. But I thought about it for a long time, and I want to spend time with my wife Pilar, and maybe travel with her. I've saved enough money, and I have my departamentos, as you know. My children are done with school. It's a good time for me to go."

"Well, Cuauhtémoc, I know many here will be sad to see you go. You have been a wonderful employee. I wish some of these younger people would follow your example. Sometimes I think you and I are from another world that doesn't exist anymore. Manny, I'm sure, asked you if you would be willing to do contract work. We might have a few big projects coming into the pipeline soon."

"He did, and I told him I would."

"Well, that's wonderful. That certainly makes it much easier for us. How's your boy, the one who graduated from Harvard last month? I'm sorry, but I forgot his name."

"Ismael. He's fine. Trying to figure out what his next step is. He is very smart, and a hard worker. He might go to law school; he was accepted at the University of California, in Berkeley. I'm very proud of him."

"A chip off the old block. You should be proud of him. Sometimes I wish I had paid more attention to my own family. Maybe I spent too much time with this company, but at a certain point they have to sink or swim, don't you think?"

"Yes, I think you are right, señor."

"Anything we can do, Cuauhtémoc, just let me know."

"Thank you, señor Smith. I appreciate that."

Cuauhtémoc walked out of Mr. Smith's office feeling a sense of relief. Inside that glass box, he had felt trapped and claustrophobic, as if he had walked into a vacuum. Maybe his blood sugar levels were too low.

~

The house was quiet. Under the achingly bright light of the kitchen skylight, Pilar meticulously scrubbed the dishes smeared with eggs. Cuauhtémoc had left for work in downtown El Paso. Pancho was at UTEP and would meet his father at los departamentos after work to install an air conditioner in apartment #6. Marcos was en route to Clint High School, to clean up his classroom and prepare for next year. Pilar frowned as she used her fingernails to scrape off the stubborn bits of egg stuck between the fork prongs. Julia was in Maryland, married to a Muslim and caring for Zahira, their first child, while Ismael had decided to work in New Haven, Connecticut, of all places.

When the children attended South Loop School two blocks away, Pilar had relished the silence in the morning. That had been her time to exhale as she swept the floors and polished her furniture and pruned her roses. If she finished her work early, she might have turned on the TV and exercised with la Denise Austin or Jack LaLanne, or she might have called la señora Tapia and asked her if she wanted to join her for a one- or two-mile walk along the canals of Americas Avenue. She never imagined she would one day dread the silence. She never imagined she could think of the silence as a condemnation from God of what was missing, instead of what had been accomplished.

Before beginning her housework, Pilar found her tattered prayer book in her dresser, a gift from Father Hernandez at Mount

Carmel, and knelt before her bed and prayed. She prayed to God that Cuauhtémoc and she would not want for anything after his retirement. She prayed that they could meet all their emergency expenses with the money they had saved in the bank. Los departamentos would provide more than enough income to live on. They had no debts, and even owned three small empty lots in Ysleta and Socorro. But for at least ten years, they would be without health insurance, until they qualified for Medicare in their sixties. Ismael had warned them that a serious illness could devastate them financially. Pilar joked to the children, "If I get sick and die, just throw me in the canal with the frogs and lizards. It'll be a cheap funeral, and at least I'll be next to you forever."

Pilar was sick of the arguments with her husband and how he made her feel guilty about being a housewife. He had worked hard and had endured pressures and responsibilities she could only imagine. Yet her husband also ruled their household. If he preferred a new Ford truck for their next car, for carting escombro and bricks and lumber to and from los departamentos, then that's what they bought. Luckily, Cuauhtémoc could often be persuaded to her point of view. That's how she eventually bought her Camry, and why they decided on Spain and Portugal for their first trip, instead of Mexico. Eventually, she would have a clothes dryer. They had the money, and even the space (after don Pedro died last year), for a new washer and dryer. But the scorching Ysleta sun was free, and putting their clean, wet clothes on the clothesline was quick and easy. The dogs, as they had gotten older, had stopped dragging the underwear and socks through the dirt.

In the afternoon, Pilar collected her Avon money as she delivered packages of perfumes and powders and soaps to three ladies who lived in the neighborhood just above Alameda, next to where the old bus stop had once been. For years, she had marched from their home on San Lorenzo Avenue to the bus stop about one mile away, with four small ornery children in tow. These interminable journeys walking through dust and heat and sitting in a bus without air-conditioning as it rumbled downtown had been shortened to a few blissful minutes in her Camry.

Pilar decided to fry corn tortillas lightly, for entomatadas. Cuauhtémoc couldn't eat enchiladas anymore, as his stomach became upset from the spicy red New Mexico chile Pilar bought by the sackful at La Feria. She grated the Muenster cheese and chopped a couple of small white onions finely, and dipped the tortillas in her fresh tomato sauce after she plucked them from the frying pan. Pilar stacked them, like pancakes, with a layer of cheese and onions in between each tomatoey tortilla until she had four plates and a few extras. The high-pitched whine of their red Buick station wagon announced Marcos's return. She had paid for the Buick with her own money from Avon. Although she loved her Camry for its reliability, sleekness, and sophisticated color of rosé wine, the Buick represented what she could accomplish by herself.

"How are you, señora Big?"

"Marquitos, you have a good day in school?" He dropped a stack of thick, colorful posters on a chair, the first of which was of the space shuttle *Challenger,* with its ill-fated crew and Christa McAuliffe smiling broadly just before they blasted off to the heavens. Twenty-four-year-old Marcos kissed his mother's hair and hugged her shoulders. He towered over her, an athlete with green eyes that had always reminded Pilar of a cat. Immediately he stepped around her and washed his hands at the kitchen sink.

"Oh, fine. I have big news. They want me to be the JV soccer coach."

"Instead of teaching?"

"No, in addition. For more money. It's a big job, but after school. The principal asked me today."

"But can you do that and teach your class next September?"

"Think so. It'll be a lot more work, but also more money, more responsibility. I was finishing cleaning out my classroom when el señor Sanchez called me to his office. He told me how much the students respected me, and how well I had done my first year of teaching English at Clint High School. He knew I loved playing soccer. He told me the JV coach had told him he would be leaving Clint for another job."

Indeed, the principal had asked the other coaches about a replacement, and Marcos's name kept coming up. He had never taught soccer before, but Principal Sanchez said he could take a coaching clinic at UTEP this summer, and start with the basics. The school would pay for everything, and even start paying Marcos more next month as he got ready for next year.

"M'ijo, you are already working so hard. And now coaching soccer?"

"Mamá, many of the kids are from Juárez. These kids are in ESL classes, and because they don't speak English well they're set aside, even ignored or made fun of. But in soccer, when they win, they suddenly belong and become part of the school. We had a pep rally this year dedicated to the winning season of our soccer team. That's the first time we've done that. Without soccer, these Juárez kids wouldn't go back to school."

"Well, what do I know? The only one who knows if you can do it is you. The principal would not have asked you if he didn't think you could do it. Have you written to Mayello to congratulate him on graduating from Harvard? It was such a beautiful ceremony, m'ijo. I don't know why you couldn't take one day off from work. It was a shame not to have you there, and Julia, but I never expected much from her. Even Mrs. Vega attended his graduation. Can you believe that?"

"Well, I couldn't go," Marcos said, chewing his entomatadas slowly.

"Dios Nuestro Señor washed the feet of his enemies. He didn't hold any jealousies," Pilar said, placing a glass of milk in front of Marcos.

"I'm not jealous of Mayello. Why should I be?"

"I'm not saying you are. We're very proud of what you have accomplished. You graduated with honors from New Mexico University."

"The University of New Mexico, Mamá."

"I'm sorry. You're in the Army Reserve. Now you're going to be a soccer coach. You don't ask us for much, and you pay your own way. Do you know how proud we are of you?"

"Thank you, Mamá. I appreciate it."

"Look at José Alfredo across the street. According to la señora Tapia, he got arrested for smoking marijuana, and then punched the policeman who arrested him. Can you believe that? What a disgrace! None of my children would ever do that because we raised you right."

Pilar stirred a pan with yerbabuena on the stove. For a moment, she stared into space. "Marcos, please write to your brother. Congratulate him on graduating from college. Mayello's all by himself up there in New Haven, and I know he's lonely. You know how he is. Siempre quiere lo que no puede. Ningún hombre es una isla."

"Ándale pues, I'll do it tonight. I have to go to Walgreens anyway. I'll get a card there."

In the evening, after Cuauhtémoc and Panchito had eaten entomatadas, Panchito locked himself in the back bedroom to finish homework. Cuauhtémoc turned on the television in the living room and sat on the sofa in the dark, flipping channels. Marcos left for Walgreens in the station wagon. Pilar sipped her spearmint tea by herself in the kitchen, until she heard the phone ring and picked it up. After about fifteen minutes, she walked into the flickering darkness of the living room and sat down next to Cuauhtémoc.

"That was Julieta," Pilar said. The Mexican news channel was reporting on a nuclear disaster in Russia two months ago, the details of which were only now trickling out to the world.

"Oh, how is she?"

"She wants to come to El Paso in two weeks, stay for a month or two, with Zahira."

"That's wonderful. Two weeks, huh?"

Pilar glared at her husband who stared at the TV like a zombie. She waited a few seconds for any other reaction, and gave up. Why couldn't he see what their daughter wanted to do? Julieta would leave little

Zahira with them while she spent the time visiting her radical amiguitas in Juárez. The last time Julieta visited, she had left them a one-hundred-and-fifty-six-dollar phone bill. But yes, she was saving the world and plotting God knows what in Juárez with her friends, all on their dime.

Pilar knew Mohammed could not afford to keep Julieta in Maryland for the summer. He was going back to Iran to finish research for his doctorate. Why didn't Julieta go with him? The last time Julieta and Mohammed had been in Ysleta, it had taken all of Pilar's strength not to respond harshly to their casual attacks against the United States. "The United States is the house of the devil. The United States kills innocents in Palestine, as an agent of the Jews. America oppresses Latin America and creates puppet regimes." These most hateful words were all said with gentle smiles and great arrogance.

And yet, Pilar had thought, Julieta treated her own mother like a servant. And yet Mohammed himself was being educated in the United States, and bragged about the scholarships he received in Maryland. When Pilar had dared to contradict them, they didn't even bother to give her arguments much thought. Instead they answered her with polite smiles, as if to say to each other, 'It's too bad this poor Mexicana doesn't have a clue.' Jesus Christ was a Jew, that much Pilar knew. She also knew despite whatever purity or superiority Mohammed and Julieta-Aliyah assumed, they did not treat their own family with decency. They did not like to be contradicted. They did not take responsibility for what they did.

Julieta had not been brainwashed. She had embraced the Muslim religion and ese maldito viejo Khomeini. She had become one of them.

Pilar peered through the picture window next to the living room, the one with dozens of diamond-shaped glass panes each about a foot tall. She saw the red Buick station wagon roaring up the driveway. Some souls in her family had been lost, and she hoped they would return. Some had never left, but seemed estranged in the neighborhood. Others had abandoned Ysleta, and Pilar had no desire to have them back. But at least Marcos was finally home.

~

A few minutes past one in the morning, Ismael arrived in a rental van at the corner of Orange and Pearl Streets in New Haven. The tree-lined streets were deserted. Danger seemed to lurk behind every hedge. His new landlord, Dr. Marcus D'Angelo, a neurologist at Yale Medical School, had mentioned that most of the students who rented from him would be absent for the summer. That was one reason Ismael was paying such cheap rent for his apartment; another was that D'Angelo, a jittery man with tiny eyeglasses, wanted someone to watch the building. For sweeping the floors once a week, Ismael would receive another discount on his rent. The neighborhood, boasted D'Angelo, was the best in the otherwise poor, gritty, and at times violent city. Ismael looked nervously at the silhouettes cast by the mysterious Italianate and Queen Anne homes. As he lugged his suitcases up the narrow stairway, he felt a tearing at his heart.

His girlfriend, Lilah Kantor, who had graduated from Harvard with him earlier this month, had begged him to find a job in Boston. But from New Haven he could still see Lilah every weekend. Ismael's new job, as an ESL instructor for the English Language Institute at Yale, was just twenty hours per week. It wasn't the kind of job his ambitious Harvard friends had accepted, but Ismael could easily abandon it in a year if he chose to act on his deferral to Berkeley's Boalt Law School. The job offered full-time benefits without full-time commitments. It was a respite to gather himself after four intense and fatiguing years at Harvard.

Lilah had volunteered to go back to El Paso with him. She liked his family, and at Thanksgiving his father and mother had been stunned when they heard this nice Jewish girl from Boston speak a tentative, yet fluent Spanish. But it wasn't El Paso, or a lack of El Paso, that plagued him. Ismael did not belong anywhere anymore. In a strange way, Harvard had ruined him. After graduation, he was thrust into finding a job, leaping into a career, and marrying a nice girl. It should have been a pleasant start to his adult life, but when Ismael surveyed the future he suddenly couldn't breathe.

Ismael's mind, his success at Harvard, and a certain lack of time had trapped him. In the world of books, Ismael had scored A's and A-'s by focusing on courses in Latin American politics, by using his Spanish to stand out from his undergraduate competitors in the gov department. Good grades had bolstered his shaky confidence. Moreover, whenever Anglo, African-American, and Asian beauties found him exotic and attractive, he was secretly surprised. What had Isabel, Yvette, and Joaniko seen in him? Whenever a girl casually invited him to explore her body after a Quincy House party, or slid deliciously closer to him during an impromptu sip of cognac on her couch, he imagined she had made a mistake. But when her eyes shined with an unmistakable ache, Ismael felt a quiver scurry up his spine. Indeed, books and sex helped Ismael overcome the psychological storm at Harvard.

Ismael met Lilah his senior year at a Mexico seminar, after he received high honors for his thesis on the Mexican "bureaucratic authoritarian" state. He had applied to law schools, yet retreated into a state of panic. His own choices had trapped him. Ismael had studied Villa and the battle of Juárez, Obregón and Carranza, and the disastrous miscalculations at the Battle of Celaya. Yet all this knowledge seemed not a search for himself anymore, but academic makework. What had begun as a way to learn about who he was had become another game of power and self-alienation. One reader of his thesis praised the original research in Spanish, in Mexican archives not yet unearthed by Harvard professors, but lamented the writing "from someone whose native language is obviously not English." Yet Ismael's language was not Spanish either. He was in between languages, using one to succeed in the other, yet not quite an heir to either. How could he escape yet another exile? Where did he belong? Above all, Ismael wanted desperately to find his voice.

For Ismael, books were permanent. Literature was perhaps a place he could make a home. He had only to crack the code, in

English, a language his and not his. Nietzsche's *Beyond Good and Evil*, Dostoyevsky's *Crime and Punishment*, and Faulkner's *Light in August* tantalized him. It was simultaneously literature and philosophy. But his time to think and to improve his skills seemed abruptly at an end. The mantra Ismael heard senior year, in whispers and shouts, was "Why don't you become good at something useful? It's time to stop dreaming and start doing." Facing this wall—on one side the glimmers of his self, on the other side the incessant demands of the practical world—Ismael chose to stop the madness and confusion. He chose to keep these pressures at bay. He needed to give himself time to write. New Haven was a retreat, away but not too far away from Lilah. Going to New Haven was going toward nothing, to make the space to create himself again, to breathe.

Ismael carted his last box of books into his new apartment and closed the door. He plucked out Fowler's *Modern English Usage* and a textbook entitled *Modern English*. As his body crumpled onto his foam mattress on the scuffed linoleum floor, Ismael dropped the books next to his bed and fell asleep, weak with exhaustion.

The next night Ismael sat at his new kitchen table, a heavy square Formica top that he had lugged on his shoulders, block by block, from a Livingston Street tag sale. The submarine-gray dust cover of *Modern English Usage* was jammed in between pages 156 and 157. *Modern English* had a yellow No. 2 pencil inserted in the chapter covering absolute constructions and other noun phrases. Ismael rubbed his eyes and turned off the overhead kitchen lights and sat in the darkness for a few minutes. Out the window next to the table was a sea of asphalt roofs disappearing into the moonlit night. Above them, the branches of giant elm trees darkened the sky. Only a bleak light, the color of urine, seeped into his kitchen floor from underneath the door to the hallway. Ismael was the only person living at 512 Orange Street.

He turned off the bedroom lights and slipped into the sky-blue covers of his mattress, a bed atop cinderblocks and plywood. Tomorrow morning he would get up and finish what he had started today. It was a story about his abuelita doña Josefina, an old woman face-to-face with the last moments of her life.

New Worlds

APRIL–MAY 1989

They had returned to Lilah's apartment. After she served him a small shot glass of Grand Marnier, they kissed on the sofa (her roommate was out for the evening), and she locked her bedroom door. Yet he wondered whether the car alarm he heard in the distance was from his rental. Soon Ismael and Lilah were in bed together, and the world around them fell away into the darkness. Only then did his car cease to exist in his mind. After Ismael woke up and made hazelnut coffee for both of them, he slipped on his jogging shorts. He ran toward the Charles River and passed Pembroke Street and a few broken beer bottles on the sidewalk. Hallelujah! His Dodge Colt appeared untouched.

"So who's going to be there?" asked Ismael as he steered the car onto a windy, tree-lined road dotted with New England Colonials. He stopped in front of the Wellesley town square, with a red-brick church on a hillside. Its blindingly white steeple pierced the sky like a needle.

"Turn right and just follow Lexington for a while. My sisters, maybe Danny, Becky's boyfriend, and maybe one or two of Deborah's friends from Harvard. My parents, of course."

"You sure what I'm wearing is fine?"

"Sure."

"How long do we have to stay?"

"Until after the meal. I haven't seen them for a while. I've been so busy at work. My mother invited us to stay over," Lilah said, her blue eyes staring straight ahead.

He glanced at her. "I don't know. Maybe."

"Why don't you like my parents?"

"Why do you say that? I'm going, aren't I?"

"Did you send your parents an Easter card? It's this Sunday, isn't it?"

"Yeah, I'll do it tomorrow."

"We could send them Easter lilies. Wouldn't your mother love that?"

"She would. When are you coming back to El Paso with me?"

"Whenever you want. Take the next right and just follow the road until you get to my house. You remember, don't you?"

"More or less. I didn't pay much attention when your father picked us up at the train station." The houses were nestled inside a suburban forest. The meandering driveways and hedges seemed trimmed with a plumb line. Lilah's gray and white house was behind a row of trees and a low grayish rock wall. The two-acre property sloped downward toward a line of trees at the entrance of a preservation land trust that was the Kantors' backyard. He and Lilah had hiked for hours in this forest of labyrinthine paths. Lilah knew them by heart. The picture windows of Lilah's house felt to Ismael like giant eyes following their every move.

Lilah's mother opened the door. People milled about in the spacious living room, in the kitchen, and around the long, diligently arranged table with a Haggadah in front of each seat. He smiled, shook hands, and introduced himself, saying as little as possible. Ismael knew how to work this kind of crowd. As an undergraduate, he would have been intimidated by the wall-to-wall picture windows overlooking the woods, the fine white-and-gray china on the table, and the bifurcated etching of an orchestra conductor on the wall. The baritone of Lilah's father reverberated in the background as he lectured Danny in medicalese. Mrs. Kantor (or Jenny, as Ismael had not yet dared call her) hugged him awkwardly, and stared at him for a second too long as if to say, "Well, here you are again. How nice."

Lilah's blue eyes widened as she hugged her sisters, embraced her mother, and kissed her father. She ushered Ismael in to present him to the guests and to show him his seat at the Passover table with a quick step and verve that radiated her joy at coming home. They took turns reading the story about the slavery of the Jewish people in Egypt and their miraculous escape from the decree to slaughter their firstborns. When it was Lilah's turn and she read the passage, "And the mountains skipped like lambs, the hills like rams," she snorted loudly. Everybody knew those had been her favorite lines as a child. Ismael was secretly pleased to see Lilah's eyes sparkle at the sight of her family. That made the trip worth it. He dug into the matzo ball soup, his favorite dish at previous Passover meals. That soup always warmed the pit of his stomach.

"Ismael, are you applying to law school again? You can't be thinking of staying another year in New Haven, can you?" Mrs. Kantor said, squeezing herself into her seat. Lilah's mother possessed lively blue-gray eyes, jowly cheeks, and a body twice the size of any of her daughters. She had just brought two more bowls of matzo ball soup, one of which she placed in front of Ismael's first bowl.

"Well, I don't know. I might apply to graduate school. Haven't decided."

"Would they take you back at Berkeley if you applied again?"

"I suppose so. My job in New Haven is great."

"Great? Isn't it only a part-time job?"

"It is, but I enjoy it. It gives me time to do other work."

"Other work?"

"He's writing stories, Mom. His first one's been accepted at the *Blue Mesa Review*. Isn't that wonderful?"

"Do they pay you?"

"Not really. I get five copies of the review."

"That's a shame. Don't you think you need to do something practical, like going to law school or business school, even if you do write? Marion's daughter—remember her, Lilah?—just published a novel and she's a real-estate lawyer."

"Mom, Jessica wrote a romance. That's not exactly real literature." Lilah smiled nervously at Ismael.

"But she got a $10,000 advance and is on a book tour in the Northeast. She was on the radio in Boston last week. She's really talented. They just bought a house in Newton. Her husband's an intern at Mass General. She has a three-year-old girl and another one on the way," Mrs. Kantor said excitedly. A drop of perspiration trickled over her thick makeup, down her pinkish white temple.

"Good for her. Have you heard anything about Elise? I haven't seen her in years."

"Marion told me she's at Harvard Business School, her second year. She'll probably get a job in New York, in finance or derivatives. Elise interned at First Boston last summer."

"Jenny, do you even know what derivatives are?" bellowed Dr. Kantor from the head of the table. Everyone fell silent. All eyes turned to Mrs. Kantor. The Haggadah on Ismael's lap fell to the floor with a soft thud.

"Well, they're some sort of financial product," she stammered. "Derivatives make money for a bank, that's all I know. Elise is a very smart girl."

"It's okay, Mom. I don't know what derivatives are either, and I really don't care." Lilah picked up her mother's and Ismael's soup bowls and marched into the kitchen.

"A derivative security, according to Black, and certainly not Fowler, is a financial contract whose value depends on, and is derived from, the value of an underlying asset, like gold or oil or pork bellies," Dr. Kantor proclaimed to no one in particular. Only Danny Cohan, a student at Harvard Medical School, Becky's boyfriend and Dr. Kantor's biggest fan, seemed to pay attention.

"Elise is moving to New York?" Becky said quickly, standing up to pick up her father's and Danny's soup bowls. "Did you hear what happened in Central Park?"

"Oh, what an awful story! Is that woman still alive?" Mrs. Kantor exclaimed, on the edge of her seat. "The *New York Times* said she was small and blond, and left to die."

"They brutalized and raped her."

"And Elise is a jogger too. Didn't she run a marathon last year?"

"I read it in the *Globe*. Her skull was bashed in."

"Lilah, you don't jog by yourself in the Fens, do you?"

"A gang of four or five black men. They attacked her like animals," somebody else chimed in.

"No, I only run on Beacon, or with Ismael on the Charles. But there are spots, under the bridges, where no one's around."

"Did you hear Reverend Al on CNN?" piped in Dr. Kantor, who pushed his chair from the table. "'Let's not taint an entire community! These boys are not a pack of wolves!' Of course they're wolves. They're worse than wolves. Did you know that studies on intelligence have shown blacks have lower IQs than just about any other racial group?"

"This is about some kids who attacked a jogger. What does that have to do with intelligence studies?" Lilah said, looking at Ismael.

"This is what they do. Why, Nancy's purse got stolen and she got knocked down by a black man in the middle of the afternoon last week, right in front of the John Hancock Building," Mrs. Kantor said, passing the tsimmes to Lilah. "The poor dear needed four stitches on her forehead."

"Lilah, you don't see a pack of Jewish boys, yamulkes flapping, beating up and raping a girl, do you? That's the difference."

"Imagine a different kind of Mitzvah tank. When that van's a rockin' don't come a knockin'!"

"Those Hasids are all a bit creepy."

"Look, Lilah, the fact is blacks have never scored above the average in analytical problem-solving, logic, or mental mathematics tests. Neurologists and statisticians have pointed this out, and of course have argued that society, racism, have played crucial roles in these results," Lilah's father said.

"Those kids don't represent anybody but themselves and their families. How do you explain when a poor kid doesn't join a wolf pack? Doesn't do what his friends are doing?"

"Lilah, of course that would be an interesting, aberrant case. But over the years these statistical results of intelligence studies show that, even when controlled for income, or the education of their parents, blacks never do as well as Asians, or Jews."

"Ismael, you grew up poor, yet you went to Harvard," Mrs. Kantor said, turning to him.

"And you never raped anybody."

"Deborah!"

"What I mean, Lilah, is simply that we have a good example right here." Mrs. Kantor's eyes tried to calm down her daughter, who glared at her.

"Just leave the poor guy alone. Gosh, Mom, can't we stop talking about this?" Deborah got up and passed the asparagus to her side of the table.

"It's okay. I did, I mean I do, have great parents," Ismael said smiling and shifting in his seat. "And my parents were tough on us. We lived in a neighborhood with drugs, gangs. Everyone was poor, everybody was from Mexico. Some families did well, others didn't. But my parents never allowed us to get involved with cholos. They put us to work, and encouraged us to be tough and independent. To think for ourselves."

"We were encouraged to kvetch and feel special."

"What's a 'sholo'?"

"It worked, didn't it? I remember I used the techniques I learned from training monkeys in my lab on you children. They're actually quite effective."

"It's 'cholo,' and it means something like 'hoodlum,' right?" Lilah said, turning to Ismael.

"Monkeys? You trained us like monkeys? What does that mean exactly?"

Ismael picked up his near-empty plate, squeezed Lilah's shoulder, and picked up her plate as well. He walked into the kitchen, away from the Passover table and the Kantors and Wellesley. He lingered in the kitchen, pretending to open and close the refrigerator to search for something and hoping dinner would end soon and they could return to Lilah's apartment. He knew they had accepted him, if begrudgingly, or ignored him, or in the case of Deborah, Lilah's younger sister, genuinely befriended him. He wasn't trying to fit in anymore. He just wanted to survive the evening. He wanted to make Lilah happy.

Ismael remembered the first few dinners he had with Lilah's parents. He did not know about liberal Massachusetts politics, or the Democratic Party, and did not care one way or another. But they did, and vehemently so. He was not familiar with medicine, or medical politics. He did not know about statistics, or the history of Harvard (Mrs. Kantor had been Class of '58). Ismael couldn't play a musical instrument, and did not know what bass or treble clef was, or adagio molto, or who George Solti was, for that matter. He was not interested in how to shoot a chipmunk with a pump-action pellet gun and how to trap a squirrel persistently attacking a bird feeder. Ismael did not care about the state of American medical care, HMOs and their war against doctors, pharmaceutical companies and their price gouging, and how Dr. Kantor could pontificate on these and other topics in ninety-minute lectures, even if his audience turned glassy-eyed. Indeed, at the dinner table Ismael felt like the gray squirrel in the Have-a-Heart trap under the oak tree. Ismael had first hated himself for his ignorance. Then he had hated himself for his silence. Finally Ismael stopped hating himself when he realized the Kantors had little control over Lilah and Lilah loved him.

He walked to the hallway, studying the grandfather clock that did and did not work, the picture of Dr. Kantor shaking hands with George H. W. Bush, and a glass sculpture of a dolphin leaping into the air. Pictures of the Kantor family were arranged on bookshelves. There was one of Lilah with straight, long brown hair and braces. She was in between the split trunk of a tree, about twelve or thirteen years old. It was Ismael's favorite picture. He imagined stealing it one day. Lilah looked like a young granny, her smile so genuine. She wasn't exactly pretty, and she must've endured so many taunts from the gorgeous girls in high school. How could this family raise such a good person? He hated the Kantors, yet he also wanted to be like them. He hated himself for not having what he wanted, and for not even knowing what he wanted anymore. Ismael was from Ysleta. But he had also left Ysleta forever.

"Bear, what are you doing here?"

"Looking at you with your cute braces."

"You really like that picture, don't you? It's called that awkward young-adult phase."

"You look beautiful to me."

"Ismael, can we stay here tonight? I really miss my parents. Deborah is staying over, too."

"Okay, fine."

"Thank you so much. It means a lot to me. I know you kinda hate it," she said, and rubbed his back gently. She kissed him slowly and deliciously on the mouth, and he imagined what could happen tonight. Her fingers traced the outline of his spine, and a shiver raced up to his neck and down to his back.

"We'll just keep this between the two of us."

~

"Come in, come in." Lori, a blond-haired woman with hazel eyes, hugged her new in-laws, Pilar and Cuauhtémoc Martínez.

"Ay, Lori, I love that palma you planted in your front lawn. It's so beeyou-tee-ful," Pilar said in her heavily accented English. "How are you feeling?"

"My morning sickness seems to have migrated to the afternoon! But I'm fine."

"Maybe you shouldn't be working in your garden anymore, m'ija. You work too hard."

"Oh, no! School's over and I'm used to being busy. Please sit down. Marcos told me the fight will start in a few minutes. Cuauhtémoc, can I get you something to drink? I made guacamole and bought tamales at Pepe's."

"Iced tea, if you have it, or just a glass of water. Thank you." Cuauhtémoc smiled. He didn't like Lori's guacamole, which was almost creamy, not naturally lumpy like Pilar's.

"M'ijo, your house is looking beautiful!" Pilar said, and kissed Marcos's forehead in the kitchen.

"Mamá, Papá, cómo están? Let me show you the gazebo we're finishing in the backyard. It's almost done."

"Ay, you have done so much in such a short time. Are you sure you're not overextending yourself?" The foursome walked into the backyard of the new house on George Dieter, only a few miles north from Ysleta. A tapered and perfectly shaped rock wall surrounded the backyard. Other new homes were either under construction or newly inhabited. The neighborhood was a planned community, solidly middle class, with expensive barbeque grills in the backyards, new or nearly new Camrys or Ford Explorers in the driveways, landscaped front- and backyards, bay windows, brass door knockers, and palm trees.

"Has he told you he's enrolled in a master's program at UTEP?" Marcos had also reenrolled in the Army Reserve.

"What's this about a master's program?" Pilar asked worriedly. They walked around the new white gazebo. The mid-May heat lingered in the air. The gazebo, which could fit a small band inside of it, was a perfectly proportioned hexagon, with a new pink-brick walkway that meandered through the backyard and to the backdoor of Marcos and Lori's new home.

"Well, I don't want to be a teacher forever. I want to move up to administration, maybe as an assistant principal or a principal. I'm starting this summer."

"But with the baby coming in five months, and this new house . . ."

"We raised a trabajador, Pilar, you know that. I'm proud of you, m'ijo. Your workers are doing a good job on this gazebo. You see the two-by-sixes they're using on the roof?"

"The fight starts in a few minutes, so let's go back in. Let's see how Chávez does against this Mayweather. It should be a good fight."

"You know, if Julio César wins, this will be his third world title," Cuauhtémoc said, as he and Marcos walked back toward the house. Marcos held the cream-colored wrought-iron screen door for his father.

"I'll show you the new carpeting in the baby's room," Lori said to Pilar, and they followed the men into the house.

As soon as they were alone in front of the wide-screen TV, Cuauhtémoc sipped his iced tea and said, "Will you be able to afford your house, the baby, and school without Lori working at Clint High School anymore? You know, if you need anything, let us know."

"We're okay, Papá," Marcos said and turned up the volume to hear Larry Merchant comment on the tactics Julio César Chávez would need to keep Roger Mayweather from beating him to the punch.

Marcos, still slim and athletic at twenty-seven years old, jumped up from his sofa, fetched rust-colored matching bowls of guacamole and tortilla chips, and placed them in front of his father. He returned to the kitchen and grabbed a Corona Light for himself from the stainless steel double-door refrigerator. His father was allergic to beer, so he didn't offer him one. As Marcos settled into the couch again and clips from the 1985 Chávez-Mayweather fight flashed on the TV screen, he studied his father's haggard brown face. Cuauhtémoc had shuffled slowly across the backyard, as if nursing a pain in his back or leg.

"I thought you were going to quit the Army Reserve, m'ijo."

"I like the exercise, and they make it easy for me at Fort Bliss. I only have to go once a month on a weekend, and I get paid to train."

"There's nothing wrong with that. You know, in México every man has to commit to one year of government service after high school. Some of the sinvergüenzas in Ysleta could use a little of that, instead of just scratching their belly buttons and smoking marijuana in the canal all the time. Americanos are too easy on their children."

"Apatzingan, right?"

"Apatzingan, Michoacán. That's where I went when I was nineteen years old. Work and discipline build character. Why do you think Chávez is such a great fighter? Probably the best boxer México has ever produced. They say that once he did not visit his children for six months, while training for a title fight. You have to sacrifice for what you want. You're doing that, too. Where are they sending you for your two weeks this year?"

"The Mojavé Desert."

"In California?"

"No, Arizona. Desert training exercises, they call it."

"Well, if Lori needs anything she can count on us. Look, they're finally ready to start the fight."

As Chávez and Mayweather touched gloves on the TV screen, Marcos watched his father. Cuauhtémoc commented excitedly that Chávez was wearing the colors of Mexico, red, white, and green. Mayweather was beating Chávez to the punch in the early rounds. Marcos noticed how his father seemed outraged every time Mayweather hit the Mexican fighter below the belt. His father also nervously commented on the shortness of Mexican fighters, worried perhaps that Chávez had made a mistake moving up in weight for this fight. Why did his father care so much about Chávez and Mexico? Why Mexican boxers? Where did this undying pride come from? Why didn't it dissipate at some point to just seeing things the way they were? Marcos did not understand it.

Mexico had been his father's home, but hadn't Cuauhtémoc left Mexico to pursue a better life in the United States? That had been decades ago. Part of the problem, Marcos thought, was that El Paso allowed you to live as if you lived in Mexico, but without many of its problems. The people spoke Spanish on the streets, from the poor to the rich, and still had quinceañeras, bodas, cenas with the abuelitos, and dias de campo on Easter. You could even spend your time listening to the news from Juárez TV and radio stations, as his parents did. You could shop in J-town for jarampiñados, chiles, sodas, and attend mass at la catedral dedicated to the Virgin de Guadalupe in the Juárez zócalo. The proximity of Mexico, its constant presence, the renewal of Mexicans either visiting El Paso or coming here forever, allowed Mexicanos like his father and mother to leave their country, but not really.

For Marcos, on the other hand, Juárez meant mordidas to surly cops, and crowded, badly paved streets, and too much traffic. Shopping in Juárez meant no recourse, if you did not like the merchandise, even with a receipt. It meant regateando, haggling for prices, for anything from a cheesy sarape at El Mercado Juárez to parking in a lot with an "attendant" who did or did not work at the lot, but who would "take care of you" for a few pesos. Without the payoff, this new friend might be the one who damaged or stole your car. Mexico was exciting and frustrating, a land not of laws but of ever-shifting, murky relationships. South of the border the status and power to inflict official and unofficial pain were much more important than in El Paso, Texas. Marcos did not feel he owed Juárez or Mexico anything. It was where his parents were from. It was a place he visited warily. When Marcos crossed the international bridge, he just wanted to come back in one piece.

As Mayweather taunted Chávez after the Mexican fighter clocked him with a left hook, Cuauhtémoc exclaimed, "This Mayweather, qué payaso. He's just pretending it was nothing. But he did get hurt." But Marcos knew Chávez was losing on points. The fighter's corner had probably told him to pick up the pace, or lose the fight. Lori was in the kitchen, getting two plates of tamales and searching for a salad bowl. Pilar sat at the dining room table facing Lori, piles of chopped radishes and green peppers in front of her, along with her plate of pork tamales. Sensing a turn in the fight's momentum, his father yelled, "Pilar, come and watch the fight! Ándale!"

"Oh, it's too violent. I don't like boxing."

After Mayweather was cut in the left eye and Chávez punished him with body blows for a round, Mayweather bled profusely and staggered back to avoid the onslaught. The referee finally stopped the fight in the tenth round. Cuauhtémoc shouted, "It's over! Chávez wins!" and stared giddily at the TV screen, on the edge of the sofa. Marcos picked up his plate and sat down with his mother and his wife at the dining room table while they ate their salads. As soon as Lori and his mamá were finished, Marcos picked up their plates and took them to the sink in the kitchen. His father, still on the sofa, seemed in a trance. His eyes were riveted on the post-fight interview between Larry Merchant and Julio César Chávez. In some ways, Marcos thought, he was, and was not anymore, his father's son.

~

Aliyah recited her first morning prayer. Fatigue spread through her body. Yet the prayer, in part for the ailing health of Imam Khomeini, for her family, and for Mohammed's new job at Tehran University, lifted her toward God and rejuvenated her. There was a dim yellowish light in the small bedroom of the old brownstone, or what reminded her of a New York City brownstone. Delivery trucks roared by on the busy, dusty Tehran street. The city was exceptionally crowded, like Mexico City. Thousands of new refugees from the war added to a weary claustrophobia in the air. She did not hear the children. Aliyah hoped they were preoccupied or asleep.

As she rolled up her embroidered red prayer rug, a gift from Mohammed's mother, Aliyah remembered she had to buy sangak and Barbari breads for tonight's dinner. She could get the bread when she took the kids for a trip to the new park commemorating the martyrs of the revolution. Her father-in-law was a baker, but his shop was not in her neighborhood. Ibraheem began to cry in his crib in the living room as her oldest, four-year-old Zahira, sweetly pacified her baby brother in a singsong voice. Aliyah had bragged to Pilar about how good little Zahira was at diapering Ibraheem. Her mother had only chided her.

"You are taking advantage of Zahirita, and making her do what no child her age should be doing. You are the mother, not Zahirita," she scolded over the international phone line from Ysleta.

In truth, Zahira was only allowed to change Ibraheem occasionally, and half the time Aliyah had to redo the crooked diaper. Yet Zahira was enthusiastic about helping her mother do housework, and Aliyah didn't see anything wrong with encouraging her to be "Mamani's helper." Aliyah wasn't obsessed with cleaning, as her mother Pilar was, and Mohammed didn't care. So why shouldn't Aliyah encourage Zahira, if she was more like her workaholic abuelita, and less like her own mother?

"Zahira, where's Majdy? You were supposed to watch her while I did my prayers."

"Mamani, I was helping Ibraheemi. I think Maji is in the bedroom," the little girl said, looking wide-eyed at Aliyah in the way that always unnerved her.

Aliyah pushed the old wooden door to the bathroom, and it creaked open slowly. Majdy, her three-year-old, was sitting atop the rickety, unpainted toilet seat, her long skirt at her ankles. Gobs of sky-blue shampoo were smeared on her hands, on the bare concrete floor, around the toilet seat, and even across her cheeks. "Majdy! Oh, my goodness, m'ija!" Aliyah said. This is not for playing!" As Aliyah wiped up the mess, she thought about how her mother had called her "m'ija" so often that as a child Aliyah had assumed her real name was "Meeha."

The hardest thing about becoming Muslim five years ago had not been the religion. She loved to pray, she loved to read the Koran, and for the first time in a long time her heart seemed to have a purpose. It wasn't hard marrying Mohammed, who was a good man, a patient and intelligent partner. Having children changed their lives, but Zahira, Majdy, and Ibraheem were God's will. Creating a modest household without the material obsessions of America was a struggle, but the good life was always a struggle. When Mohammed finished his doctorate in political science, and they made their plans to return to Tehran, a place they had visited for a week or two over the years, Aliyah faced her most difficult challenge.

Her Farsi, which she had thought was decent in conversations with Mohammed's family over the years, was in reality a mishmash of mistakes and misunderstandings. Her command of the language was rapidly improving week to week, as she was forced to use her Farsi to buy food, answer the phone, or strike up a conversation with another mother at the park. Yet Aliyah remained a foreigner. It wasn't that she was Mexican, which was how she described herself to anyone who asked. Muslims from every country and ethnicity lived in Tehran. It was certainly better to be from Mexico than from the land of the Great Satan. Her unease resided not in her background or heritage, but in her broken language.

Aliyah changed Ibraheem and put him into a dark blue jumpsuit (a gift from El Paso). Zahira dressed herself in a long tuniclike beige dress, with long sleeves. Aliyah helped Majdy into a T-shirt and brown elastic pants. Quickly Aliyah made five chicken sandwiches, wrapped them in plastic, and dropped them in a canvas bag that she draped behind Ibraheem's stroller. She grabbed a couple of apples, an orange for Majdy, a banana for Ibraheem, and filled three bottles of water from the old faucet in the kitchen sink. The faucet's copper patina reminded her of the faucet in her mother's garden in Ysleta.

Aliyah assembled the bottom section of her black chador, tied it to her body, then slipped her head through the top section. She arranged it so her shoulders were straight and her hair was neatly tucked behind the light yet sturdy black fabric. Whenever Aliyah had worn her chador in El Paso, many assumed she was a Catholic nun and opened doors for her, murmuring a "Dios Nuestro Señor." Aliyah had returned the blessing and smiled politely. Jesus Christ was a prophet in the Koran, and following the word of God was what mattered, wasn't it? As her black chador floated behind her like a dark cloud, Aliyah escorted the children into the sunny concrete patio in front of their brownstone. Women in black chadors were everywhere, on their way to the market with and without children, on their way to work, or out for a stroll. Some women donned a light headscarf instead of a chador. As Aliyah walked toward the park for the martyrs of the Iranian revolution, a breeze meandered through the warm air. She seemed like any other mother on the streets of Tehran. Her face was a luminous moon surrounded by night.

Aliyah and the children walked for an hour and reached the great fountain, her favorite spot at the park. With brightly blue and gold mosaics and Farsi gold lettering extolling the triumphs of the Iranian revolution (which was celebrating its tenth anniversary this year), the massively round fountain was a sanctuary to be closer to God. She watched her children sprint around its edges with delight, pointing at the Farsi letters they could now read. Zahira trailed Majdy like a shadow.

Aliyah admired the newly planted red tulips around the fountain, a giant swaying wheel. Each tulip commemorated one of the thousands of martyrs of the revolution. "Let their blood reach to Heaven, let it pave our commitment to God, let it be a sacrifice worthy of the most Holy," the inscription read. The tulips always inspired Aliyah to soft tears, a rapturous belief that Muslims would win their struggle against the West. When Zahira came up to her and asked her what was wrong, Aliyah replied, "Oh, my little one, I am just happy to be with you. Happy to be enjoying the sun. I am remembering those who died for us."

Aliyah noticed a woman about her own age circle the expanse of the fountain once, and then distractedly approach a crosswalk, only to turn back slowly toward the fountain. She did not wear a black chador, but instead a white hijab around her face. A simple dark brown dress covered her shoes. She carried a large black suitcase in one hand.

"Help you may I?" Aliyah said, smiling politely at the woman.

"Oh, yes. Please. I'm looking for the Ministry of Labor and Social Affairs. I need to . . ." She slumped next to Aliyah on the park bench. The woman's suitcase had a gash across it. Her hands were shaking. The hem of her dress was ripped where she had repeatedly stepped on it. Ibraheem toddled to the suitcase and stared at the woman. Zahira and Majdy were at the other side of the fountain, playing with something in the water.

"I think on this street twenty or thirty seconds—I mean minutes—right where Mosque of the Golden Dome. I am sorry for my Farsi," Aliyah said. The woman solemnly stared at her hands, which seemed strangely older than her face. She smiled wearily at Ibraheem, who hadn't taken his eyes off her.

"How old is your child?"

"Ibraheem, he is, he is, how do you say it? Almost one year."

"I have two children too. A boy and a girl. You are not from Iran?"

"From Mexico. My husband is Iranian," Aliyah said slowly and carefully.

The woman suddenly started to cry.

Aliyah sat closer to the woman and placed a hand lightly on her shoulders. "Maybe I can help you. Are you okay?"

"My children. My husband. I, I don't know what to say. You are very kind."

"Here, please, water for you," Aliyah said soothingly as she handed the woman one of her water bottles from the stroller. Even Ibraheem had guided himself closer to the woman, and placed a tiny hand on her knee. The woman's hands shook wildly, as if the baby's touch shocked her.

"How can I help you?" asked Aliyah.

"I just arrived in Tehran this morning. From Qum. I am so tired. Please forgive me. I don't know what to do."

"I arrived in Tehran almost ninety, no, sorry, nine months ago. My husband a professor is at Tehran University. These are our three children, little Ibraheem, and two girls, Zahira and Majdy," Aliyah said, pointing at the girls who were racing around the far edge of the fountain. "I take care of them. I am at home."

"You are a good mother."

"Thank you. Where is your family?" The woman looked as if she had been slapped.

"I am sorry. I not ask that."

"No, it is okay. Last year my husband became a martyr," the woman said, staring at the hundreds of gently dancing tulips in front of her. "I knew so many war widows in Qum because I was on a local committee to help them, to make their sacrifice for our country easier. I imagined that if I worked hard for the war widows that, somehow, God would spare me. I had heard rumors that the war was about to end, but I tried to push them away from my mind. I did not want to hope. I did not want to feel joy. I did not want to betray my husband and his readiness for martyrdom in God's eyes. But God did not spare him.

"At Shalamjah, O Shalamjah! When a member of the committee for war widows and a volunteer came up to me one day, I thought he would reassign me to another location. I thought they might tell me to go home. Never did I imagine . . . it was time to tell me my husband had died at Shalamjah. They didn't even have to get in their car and use gasoline to tell me the news.

"It was very difficult for the first few months. But we survived, my children, my boy and my girl. The government provided us with some help, I kept working with the war widows committee, and they began to pay me. I only worked part-time, because I wanted to be with my children when they came home from school. They are but a few years older than your oldest. Then my in-laws asserted their right to their grandchildren and took my children away—and the government allowed it. What kind of law is this? What was the point of my sacrifices? Where in the Koran does it say a good mother must lose her children? I told my in-laws I would happily be their slave to be near my little ones. But they said no.

"I have tried for a month to get my children back. I spoke to officials in Qum, the war widows committee, our cleric at the neighborhood mosque. I begged them to help me, but nothing has happened. Where does it say in Islamic law that a family must be ripped apart? I came here on the train last night to talk with the Ministry of Labor and Social Affairs, to see if someone, anyone, would help me. I don't know what to do."

"I will walk you there. Aliyah my name is."

"You are an angel, Aliyah. I am so desperate. I have no money. I have no friends in Tehran."

"I will walk you there, after my children lunch have."

"My name is Fatemeh. Fatemeh from Qum."

"You can stay with us, Fatemeh. I will talk to my husband. He is a good man. And I know he will allow to stay you with us for a few days."

"You are like the angel Gabriel, Aliyah. Thank you."

The Noblest of Blood
SEPTEMBER 1992

The blue-and-white bus lurched forward. Pilar's fifty-seven-year-old legs were cramped from the long plane ride from Germany. Her arms were sore after carrying her suitcase to the Tel Aviv bus terminal. She tucked her black suitcase underneath her legs and rolled the plastic bag of food into a ball on her lap. Cuauhtémoc had lugged his own heavy suitcase and their backpack farther than she had, in search of the bus to Jerusalem at the Tel Aviv airport. At the Jerusalem bus terminal, Cuauhtémoc gave himself his insulin shot in a public restroom that he effusively praised as extraordinarily clean.

Dozens of young Israeli soldiers patrolled the terminal, carrying black machine guns and inspecting luggage, and never for a moment smiling. Cuauhtémoc exclaimed, "I bet you these Israeli soldiers aren't watching television for three hours a day, or putting makeup on all morning. I wish some of the stupid tirilónes from Ysleta could spend a year or two in the Israeli army."

On the bus Cuauhtémoc looked exhausted again. His coarse black hair was matted against his forehead, his thick neck was flushed, and his left hand trembled slightly. Yet his eyes flashed with a boyish excitement at the narrow, cobblestone streets, ancient stone edifices, and the Jewish men in long black robes, thick beards, and curly sideburns. Pilar and Cuauhtémoc were in the Holy Land, breathing the very air that Dios Nuestro Señor had once breathed almost two thousand years ago.

"Oye, Cuauhtémoc, where did the man say we should get off to find a hotel?" Pilar asked.

"I didn't understand all he said. He talked too fast in English, and he had a strange accent. He said Bus No. 18, but that's all I got."

"Well, you better pay attention and help me find a good neighborhood. Didn't he also say about half an hour on the bus?"

"Yes, half an hour."

Ismael couldn't believe his parents traveled to a country without hotel reservations, nothing but the suitcases in their hands. "That's how Mexicans do it," they had said to Ismael. "We just look around and ask people. The locals know what the best places are. We're not gringos, with hotel reservations at la Sheraton or la Marriott. Who's going to pay those exorbitant prices?" Ismael warned his parents about getting lost, about getting into bad neighborhoods by accident. What if they ended up robbed, or stabbed, or worse? "You worry too much, m'ijo," they had said. "Remember that couple from Peru we met in Barcelona? And that viejito chueco at the Biergarten who told us about taking a boat on the Rhine River? If you give people a smile, and you're polite, you'd be surprised how nice strangers are! Also, don't ever tell them you're American. Tell them you're Mexican. They'll treat you much better. We don't wear clothes that announce to the world, 'Hey, here are rich tourists. Come and rob us!' We've never thought ourselves as muy muy. We're from Ysleta."

"Did you notice when we got on this bus?"

"Yes, a little after five o'clock."

Pilar was anxious about finding their hotel before nightfall. Two little girls and their mother, in matching black chadors, sat near the front of the bus. Pilar imagined this was how her grandchildren might look in Iran with Julieta. They had come to El Paso to visit for two weeks this summer, including Mohammed, "El Narizón," as they called him behind his back. The thin, exceptionally tall Mohammed had been quiet, and generally respectful, until the topic turned to politics. Mohammed lectured them on how the Republican and Democratic parties weren't that different, how these politicians were puppets of big business and the military, and how their unqualified support for "the terrorist state of Israel" was a reflection of American political corruption. Why had Cuauhtémoc opened his big mouth and mentioned their trip?

What was the point of arguing with Mohammed and Julieta anyway? Instead, Pilar had taught seven-year-old Zahira how to make flour tortillas from scratch. Julieta tried to order Zahira to help her clean the green beans, but Zahirita said, "Mamani, no! I am helping Abuelita with her tortillas!" This little girl had a mind of her own and was muy lista. Just wait, Pilar had thought, that little spitfire will grow up to resist her mother's and father's brainwashing.

"Excuse me, señora, I heard you talking in Spanish. Are you looking for a place to stay?" a beautiful young woman sitting across from Pilar asked. She was wearing jeans and a tight white blouse and was in her midtwenties. Athletic, even tomboyish, she had curly black hair, deep brown eyes, and very fair skin.

"Oh, sí, señorita."

"Maybe I can help you." The bus slowed suddenly, its wheels squeaking to a halt at a signal light. All of them swayed forward and then backward in unison, as if in sync to a soundless song.

Sofia Gandaría Muñoz told them about Jaffa Street, not far from where they were now. She said it had reasonable hotels, a little plaza, many stores, and was only about twelve blocks from one of the gates to Old Jerusalem. Her own parents had stayed on Jaffa Street when they had visited her from Cordoba, Spain.

Pilar asked her about the Via Dolorosa, and which entrances to Old Jerusalem would be best suited for it. Cuauhtémoc asked her about Orthodox Jews and Muslims, and how Sofia could tell them apart. The young woman smiled politely and pointed out the pedestrians on the sidewalk as the bus rumbled by, noting the different garb and what significance it had.

"We have a daughter who converted to the Muslim faith," Pilar said, "and she wears a chador. But we are Catholic like most Mexicans and Spaniards."

"That's true. But even Spain has a long Muslim and Jewish history. I am a Spanish Jew, for example."

"Really?" Cuauhtémoc exclaimed, his green eyes flashing. "I knew about 'Cuidado, hay Moros en la costa.' And we have visited the giant mosque in Cordoba. But are there a lot of Jews too?"

"Well, not anymore. They were called Sephardim, for Sepharda, the old Hebrew name for Spain."

"Our son, Ismael, is marrying a Jewish woman from Boston later this month. So soon," Pilar said, her eyes bright with happiness, "we will have a Jewish daughter too."

"How wonderful!" the young dark-haired woman said. "Your familia is recreating the wonders of Al-Andalus, Muslims and Christians and Jews together. Here we are. This is our stop."

~

"Look, Cuauhtémoc, there's the wall of the old city, just like the girl on the bus said. Jaffa Gate. Those stones must be thousands of years old!"

"Did she say 'Jafra,' or 'Chaffa'?"

"Cómo crees? She didn't say 'chafa.' The man from the hotel said go through the stone entrance called Jaffa Gate and follow the road next to the Tower of David, and make a left for the Via Dolorosa," Pilar said. "We're the only 'chafas' around here."

"Speak for yourself, señorita. I come from only the noblest of blood."

"Ay Cuauhtémoc, it's so dark in here, and yet in my heart, I am so happy. I can't believe we're here."

"I know what you mean. We're here. It's real. Finally we're on the streets Dios Nuestro Señor walked. Oye, let's walk fast, el viejo over there kept tugging at my shirt, trying to get us into his store. Híjola, they're aggressive. It's like El Mercado in Mexico City. Maybe we shouldn't ask directions anymore."

"Al-Silsilah Street? I think that's what it says over there."

"Así se lée? What kind of a name is that?"

"Probably Árabe. Maybe that old man is just sending us to Julieta's friends."

"Look, oranges, tomatoes, T-shirts, pendants. It's surprising how they let this happen here on sacred ground."

"But not every inch of it is sacred, Cuauhtémoc. It's just a city, like any other. I bet you they won't allow that at the Church of the Holy Sepulcher."

"Ese chavalito looks like a little Mexican boy. A street rat, just like I once was."

"Quizás eres Árabe, with that nariz of yours. You ever think of that?"

"Ask that Jewish viejito with the table where we're supposed to turn for the Church of the Holy Sepulcher. Ándale. Me don't speak-ity English anymore," Cuauhtémoc said.

"Ay no."

"I'm not going to ask another Árabe after that first barbón. At least the Jews haven't tried to trick us into their stores. They look at us like wolves."

"He said turn left at the next street, follow it, and we'll be in front of the Church of the Holy Sepulcher."

"You see that little box strapped onto that child's head?"

"What was that? Why are they carrying a table with them in the middle of the street? El viejito also said when we come back, if we go straight ahead, we can get to the Wailing Wall." Pilar had always wanted to leave a special prayer within the only wall left of the Jewish temple.

"Tomorrow I want to walk la Via Dolorosa. The way Dios Nuestro Señor walked on His last day on earth. We're just stumbling around today, asking random Arabs and Jews which way Jesus Christ walked. We're doing everything backwards."

"Paciencia, paciencia."

"Oh, my God, my knees are weak. I am so excited we're actually here. I wonder when it was built. Look at these massive walls. Mira, that monjita's walking and praying, not even noticing who's around her."

Pilar did not say anything as they entered the shadows of the Church of the Holy Sepulcher. She could smell the incense and burning candles in the dense air. She could hear chanting and praying in different languages. Cuauhtémoc seemed ecstatic. As their eyes adjusted to the darkness, they began to take it all in: the ornate altars, the mosaics on the floor, the flickering light of candles. Pilgrims on their knees prayed, and many women donned multicolored scarves. Some men undulated with their eyes closed. Pilgrims walked to different chapels, alcoves, and other recesses within the labyrinthine church. Pilar reached a dark reddish-brown platform on the floor, with eight-foot-high brass candles at each corner and eight white candle lamps etched with tiny red crosses dangling above. Three women splayed their hands over the Stone of Unction, quietly praying, one sobbing.

Pilar knelt and began to pray. For a second, she imagined a white-robed Mary next to her, also lamenting and praying, also a woman on her knees. How could Mary have endured the unendurable?

"This is where She prepared His body before burial," Pilar whispered quietly to Cuauhtémoc. He had finished uttering his own silent prayer and stood up.

"But we're starting this backwards," he said tight-lipped, his hands clasped studiously in front of him. "We should follow the Via Dolorosa the right way. Where He first meets His mother as He carries the Cross. Where Simon helps Him carry His burden. Where Veronica wipes His face."

"Tomorrow, when we find out where the first station of the Via Crucis is. We're here now. We need to find what's here first. Let's go over there. It's Golgotha, those dark chapels."

"Here, or over there?"

"Look at the mosaic, Cuauhtémoc. Dios Nuestro Señor is on His back and they're driving nails through His palms. The Virgin Mary is on Her knees. This is the Altar of the Nails of the Cross."

"But why is there a shrine to Mary over there? I don't understand."

"It's Our Lady of Sorrows."

"I don't like that we're doing this backwards. First we see where His body is anointed after He's dead, and then we're going to where He was crucified. It doesn't make any sense. That's not the story, Pilar."

"We're coming back every day for two weeks. We'll get it right once we know where everything is."

"You know what strikes me?"

"What?"

"That it was real. That these are historical sites. That on this ground is where He walked, where He stumbled, where He died."

"But it's not a museum, Cuauhtémoc. People believe. I believe."

"I have always believed too, por supuesto. But now I see what I have always believed in. You know what I mean, don't you?"

In silence, they walked out to the plaza of the Church of the Holy Sepulcher. Cuauhtémoc studied their map. The Jerusalem sun was bright, and a dry breeze wafted through the plaza, as more pilgrims, nuns, monks, priests, and tourists milled around the church entrance.

As three children and a mother in a chador entered the shadows of the church, Pilar was overcome by an incredible sadness. Why had her children abandoned the church? Why had they become like grains of sand scattered throughout the desert? Had she and Cuauhtémoc given Julia, Francisco, Marcos, and Ismael too many freedoms and opportunities in El Paso? Why had she not succeeded in transmitting her culture, her faith to them? What had she done wrong? What had happened to their family?

~

September 27, 1992. Lilah had wanted to be married after graduating from Harvard's John F. Kennedy School of Government, but not immediately afterward, so that she at least had a summer to move wherever she found a job. Jenny Kantor had imagined a spectacular late September wedding for her daughter to take advantage of the fall foliage of New England. Mrs. Kantor had also asked important family members from Baltimore to Seattle to save the date.

Lilah and Ismael had also found an old Reform rabbi to officiate at their mixed wedding. Ismael had convinced Father John Ludek (who had known Aliyah in San Antonio, during her radical Catholic days) to assist Rabbi Zuckerman with the ceremony. They had chosen the Ketubbah from West Side Judaica on Manhattan's Upper West Side. After Lilah's graduation and Ismael's acceptance into Columbia University's master's program in philosophy, they had moved in together. Two nights ago, on Friday, Lilah and Ismael had hosted a Tex-Mex barbeque in the two-acre backyard of the Kantors' house in Wellesley, catered by El Burrito Loco, a funky, innovative Cal-Mex restaurant in Somerville. Ismael's brother, Francisco, was the best man, and Lilah's younger sister, Deborah, the maid of honor. Even Mrs. Vega, Ismael's third-grade teacher from Ysleta, had flown to Boston to attend the festivities. That señora Vega was always ready for a dance party.

Ismael felt a knot in his stomach as he stepped out of the shower on his wedding day. He could already hear the commotion downstairs. On the first floor, Mrs. Kantor argued with Deborah about making sure the photographer was on time. Ismael had to fetch his parents at the Holiday Inn in Wellesley, only ten minutes away. The family photo would be shot before the ceremony at noon. The wedding would be at the quaint New England chapel of the Griswold Academy, Lilah's old high school. Dr. Kantor and Becky's husband, Danny, also a doctor, had spent last night opening the windows of the old chapel, because the wooden pews had been newly varnished and weren't quite dry.

He needed to shave meticulously, yet avoid slashing the small mole above his lip. Ismael carried extra copies of the poetry Lilah's sisters would read at the ceremony. The honeymoon tickets to Hawaii were already in his suitcase for tonight's stay at the Boston Marriott, as well as a change of clothing, his good oxford wingtips, one thousand dollars in American Express travelers cheques (Lilah's money), their new camera, and Lilah's change of clothes.

What if he failed to smash the glass at the end of the ceremony with one stomp of his foot? Would these dark morning clouds unleash more rain today? Would old Rabbi Zuckerman lose his way driving from Lexington to Wellesley? Ismael's stomach churned. A spurt of acid surged up his throat and receded as his mouth gaped above the bathroom sink.

Ismael worried most about his parents. Would they be disrespected by the Kantors' rich friends, or Lilah's aunts or uncles? At the Friday barbeque, Ismael had been pleasantly surprised. Lilah's sister Deborah and Aunt Lilly had made it a point to escort his parents everywhere and introduce them to dozens of friends. Aunt Lilly—redheaded, massive like a wrestler, with piercing green eyes—guffawed at their table. She traded recipes with his mother and listened carefully to Cuauhtémoc's and Pilar's stories of their recent trip to Israel and Egypt. "Aunt Lilly es muy simpática," his parents would later tell him.

Aunt Lilly had once confided to him how her sister Jenny (that is, Mrs. Kantor) "never smelled the shit coming from her own children." Lilly was tough, down-to-earth, and divorced, a single mother who had survived to become an independent professional. Lilah's mother, however, rested happily within the confines of her husband's money and prestige. Most of the people at the wedding would be like Mrs. Kantor and her friends. How would Ismael's mother, who had once wrenched the neck of a chicken with her bare hands, fit in with this crowd?

Ismael wasn't ashamed of his father and mother. He was proud of what they had accomplished. They had come to the United States with less than nothing, built their home with their own hands, and saved enough money to put each of their children through college. Now they had traveled the world, unlike many of the well-to-do snobs of New England. Ismael knew his parents were one of a kind. He just worried that other people wouldn't take the time to appreciate what he understood.

But his family's behavior had angered Ismael in other ways. Pancho had pointedly refused to give a best man's speech even though Ismael had begged him to do it. Ismael had even offered to write it for his ridiculously shy brother. But Pancho was adamant and Ismael was mortified. Pancho declared he was happy to be his brother's best man, but did not want to get up at the reception in front of hundreds of people. What the hell was wrong with Pancho? Why couldn't he for once conquer his fear of public speaking? The man was thirty-three years old!

Two days ago, he, Pancho, Dr. Kantor, and Danny had tried on their tuxedos at Mr. Tux. His brother had struggled to stretch enough of his white dress shirt over his huge stomach and into his too-tight pants. Pancho just smiled, resigned to endure the ignominy like the good obedient Catholic boy he was. Ismael immediately got the attention of a salesman and demanded larger pants, a roomier shirt, and a proper vest. Ismael had learned from years of watching Mrs. Kantor demand the best for her children without justification or apology. Why couldn't Pancho do this for himself? It was called chutzpah.

But at least Pancho was trying. Marcos had decided to skip the wedding entirely. His annual two-week training with the Army Reserve was in Africa's Ivory Coast, and Marcos wouldn't be finished with his army exercises until the Monday after the wedding. One month earlier, Ismael had chatted with Marcos's wife, Lori, while she and their two-year-old boy, Noah, were visiting his parents in Ysleta. She had graciously congratulated Ismael on his wedding and said it would be hard to take Noah to Boston by herself. Couldn't Marcos have changed the dates of his two-week Army Reserve training months ago? If not, why couldn't Lori attend the wedding with Noah? Had Marcos instructed her not to go? Why hadn't Marcos, as a courtesy, called Ismael and Lilah before leaving for the Ivory Coast to offer his regrets?

It had not bothered Ismael one iota that Julia was not attending and had not offered an explanation for her absence. Ismael never expected much from her. She didn't have any money for travel and her hands were full with her large family.

Ismael knocked on the door of his parents' suite at the Holiday Inn. Pancho answered the door. "Are you guys almost ready? We need to be at the Kantors in about twenty minutes for the pictures."

"You know how to do this? I can't seem to get it right." Pancho handed him a black-and-white striped silk tie. "Do the little collars go underneath, or over, the tie?"

"Let me do it for you," Ismael said, stepping inside and in front of the mirror behind the door. He draped the tie over one hand while he struggled to fasten the shirt button around his brother's thick neck. "Y Mamá y Papá?"

"We're ready," his father said from somewhere inside the hotel room, "I'm just finishing combing my hair." His father stepped into view, wearing an expertly tailored dark blue suit and tie and looking like a Wall Street mogul. "What do you think?"

"That's a terrific suit. Where did you get it?"

"In El Paso. I know how to look good when I have to. But you! What do you call that long coat? Es medio estilo Rockefeller. Mira, Pilar, tu hijo! Qué guapo!"

"It's called a morning suit."

"I remember it from movies like Pedro Infante's *Ahora Soy Rico*. But wait till you see your mother. Are you nervous? I was so nervous on our wedding day thirty-five years ago, I almost fainted at the altar."

"I'm okay," Ismael said, now worried about fainting. He wasn't nervous about marrying Lilah, whom he loved and who he knew loved him. But he was nervous about himself. Lilah had a job and was done with school. He was just starting a graduate program in philosophy. She would be the breadwinner. Was that a position a newly married man was supposed to be in? What kind of job could he get as a philosophy graduate student? Lilah encouraged him to follow his dreams and wanted him to keep writing. Dr. and Mrs. Kantor had not said anything, except to ask politely what he would be doing in New York. "There comes a point where you have to think about a career, don't you think? Lilah, you remember Rob, that nice Jewish boy you liked in high school? He's already a biochemistry professor at NYU." Ismael never told his parents about these dinner-table conversations in Wellesley. His own parents urged him to do his best and get a job as soon as possible, perhaps as a teacher.

"Y mi mamá?"

Ismael's mother walked cautiously into the hotel living room. She was wearing a rosé silk jacket with a matching skirt and an embroidered rosé silk top, her jet-black hair in a Lady-Di do, a long strand of pearls dangling around her neck, and a matching rosé silk flower in her hair. Pilar looked like those dark-haired, ivory-white-skin Hollywood beauties at a movie premiere, à la Jane Russell, but better.

"I told you she looked good," his father said, beaming.

"Do you like it, m'ijo? I got it especially for your wedding. I bought the earrings in Israel."

"It's gorgeous. You look wonderful, Mamá."

"Did you know your mother used to be a model for a department store in Juárez?"

"Ay, Cuauhtémoc, that was forty years ago. I'm just una panzona today."

"On the contrary, Pilar. The only woman who will look better than you today will be our new daughter Lilah, as it should be. But you will always be my bride." Cuauhtémoc kissed Ismael's mother lightly on the lips. For once Ismael did not look away in embarrassment.

~

As Ismael marched in what seemed like slow motion down the aisle with his mother, he did not notice the hundreds of eyes staring at their every move. By this point things were beyond his control, and in his mind he released his worries into the thick chocolate-colored rafters of the old New England chapel. He watched his father march down the aisle in a studied formality, like a sergeant at arms in parliament. Mrs.

Kantor had begrudgingly complimented his mother about her beautiful outfit, having recognized she had been outdone by this Mexican lady from Texas. Deborah had sprinted down the stairs to the living room and shouted "Wow!" before proceeding to interview his mother about every detail of her ensemble. Ismael kissed his mother on the cheek, hugged and shook hands with his father Cuauhtémoc in front of the altar, and swelled with pride. In large ornate letters carved behind them on a gigantic slab of ancient wood, it read: "Love never faileth: but whether there be prophecies, they shall fail; whether there be tongues, they shall cease; whether there be knowledge, it shall vanish away. For we know in part, and we prophesy in part. But when that which is perfect is come, then that which is in part shall be done away. Corinthians 13."

More than a hundred people were crowded in the chapel, friends from college, old roommates, Lilah's aunts, uncles, and cousins, his Aunt Rose from California, Mrs. Vega, and dozens of the Kantors' friends from Wellesley, Cambridge, Lexington, and Newton.

Lilah gingerly walked down the aisle with her parents and reached the steps to the altar. Ismael stepped down to meet them. He heard her ivory silk dress rustle gently as they walked up toward Rabbi Zuckerman. Lilah's enormous blue eyes shined at him. Ismael knew she, like him, wanted the ceremony to be perfect, and wanted it to be over. Lilah looked more beautiful than ever. Her smooth white shoulders were exposed by the silk straps of her dress. The veil around her face was like a misty, sparkly glow. This blue-eyed brunette, with whom he had been smitten immediately after spotting her at Harvard, was a good-hearted person who was at ease with herself. Lilah was more comfortable in small-town Ysleta, on the porch under the mulberry trees with a cup of coffee in hand, than he had ever been.

Rabbi Zuckerman seemed momentarily reinvigorated by the ceremony. In Newton, at their first and only meeting with the rabbi, Zuckerman would get distracted and start rambling about Israel, or his adventures in South America, or even his children and grandchildren. Lilah had found the rabbi through a friend of a friend in Massachusetts in order to make the marriage "Jewish" for herself and, most importantly, for her family. There was a sense that they had picked a rabbi somewhat on the fringe, one who would regularly perform "interfaith marriages" when others wouldn't. When Zuckerman agreed to include Father Ludek in the ceremony, Ismael and Lilah were thrilled, but Lilah's parents stared at each other as if to say, "What the hell is going on with Zuckerman?" Ismael wondered if Zuckerman's marriages were even legitimate and was secretly pleased that earlier this week they had been married legally at the town hall in Wellesley.

Yet Zuckerman seemed in decent form as he talked about the chuppah and how it symbolized the new home Lilah and Ismael were now creating. His bald head was covered by his yarmulke. His white prayer shawl flapped behind him like weak wings. Becky and Deborah read love poems, which Lilah had selected from *A Book of Love Poetry*. Father John Ludek stepped forward. Ludek was a young priest with a booming voice. Every pair of eyes was suddenly mesmerized by this tall, handsome, blond-haired dynamo. Ismael had asked Ludek to be part of the wedding because he was the only priest Ismael could tolerate. Julia had brought Ludek to dinner just before she left for San Antonio to join the Sandinistas, or whatever the hell she was doing in Central America. Ludek had worn jeans and a T-shirt and chatted about sports. More importantly, Ismael's parents knew Father John and had treated him like royalty every time he came to dinner in Ysleta. His mother in particular relished saying grace with a priest at the dinner table.

Ismael was just as surprised as everybody else when Father Ludek began to address the congregants in Spanish and English. For a moment, Ismael imagined all the unpredictable collisions at the altar: Spanish and English, Ysleta and Wellesley, the Martínezes and the Kantors, the priest and the rabbi. Under the flowers of the chuppah, Lilah beamed at him, and that was all that mattered to Ismael.

"As we join these two cultures, two languages, and two religions in this holy union, in the persons of Lilah and Mayello, their love will show us the way. Their love will give substance to how we can love God and His works in this new world. Their love will be an example of how we can create a holy community to practice the word of God. May their union be blessed, for now until eternity." Father John stepped back to allow the rabbi to continue the service. Ismael glanced at the crowd. For a moment they seemed to want to applaud the priest, yet they didn't. The rabbi stepped forward with a quizzical look in his eye.

"Let us turn now to the conclusion of our ceremony for Lilah and Manuelo," said Zuckerman.

Lilah almost burst out laughing. Ismael turned red, but just grinned and turned to the crowd and shrugged. When Rabbi Zuckerman called him "Manuelo" again, half the congregation yelled in unison, "His name is ISMAEL! ISMAEL!" Rabbi Zuckerman looked stunned, staggered back a step, and apologized. Lilah rolled her eyes and grinned. Mrs. Kantor, in the front row, looked as if she wanted to grab a stanchion and stab Zuckerman through the heart.

~

"Oh, it was nothing," Ismael said, smiling to guest after guest at the receiving line at the Wellesley Country Club. "It's not his fault. Father John used my childhood nickname, Mayello, and the rabbi must have heard 'Manuelo.' It was an understandable mistake." Father John, at his parents' table, was surrounded by well-wishers. Aunt Lilly came up to Lilah and Ismael and exclaimed, "Where the heck did you get that Father Ludek? He was great!"

Lilah had whispered to Ismael that he had defused the situation by explaining what had happened to everybody, by defending the rabbi, and by not making a big deal about it. They all took their cue from him, and she was proud of him. She also thought Father Ludek had been extraordinary.

But an hour before, Mrs. Kantor had cornered Ismael when no one else had been nearby. His mother-in-law wore a dark purple dress dotted with wildflowers, a dress that matched the dark rouge of her cheeks and sent a wild flash of light whenever a fold in the fabric caught the sun just right. "That moron," Mrs. Kantor had hissed at Ismael. "He almost ruined the entire wedding! You planned this, didn't you? With that old idiot next to your friend, the young priest. You planned it so the Jews would look like idiots."

Ismael had stared incredulously at Mrs. Kantor. "What are you talking about?" he had muttered and walked away.

As Lilah and Ismael greeted more guests at the reception line, he noticed that his parents were smiling at the table with Father Ludek. Aunt Lilly chatted with John, and Deborah and a few of her girlfriends were also there. Lilah's great Aunt Miriam also sat at the table, beaming at Father Ludek and waiting patiently for her turn to talk to him. Aunt Miriam, in her midnineties, was one of those figures in the Kantor family who commanded everybody's respect. Ismael had heard a story from Lilah that her Aunt Miriam had been (romantically?) involved with John Reed and other Communists in the early part of the century. That must have been a helluva time to be young.

Two Brothers

FEBRUARY 1997

Carmen, their Guatemalan babysitter, had just left. Little David was asleep in the crib that would soon be too big for him, and Ismael had one hour, perhaps two. The taxis and buses on Broadway slowly made their way through the snow-clogged intersection next to Fairway Market. Under the smudgy living room window of their pre-war apartment, the radiator gurgled. Last month, Lilah had detected a sharp odor in their bedroom, which faced a shadowy courtyard of wrought-iron staircases. Ismael had yanked up the metal cover of the radiator next to their bed and discovered a dried-up mouse on its back, its nose in the air. Now Ismael sniffed the air and smelled nothing but David's A+D ointment.

It was a shame they would never get to use the fireplace, Lilah's favorite feature in their first apartment together as a married couple. Lilah loved the Astor, their home for the last five years, and where they had brought their newborn son from New York Hospital fifteen months ago. In their crowded one-bedroom on the fourth floor, jam-packed with used furniture from their college and graduate school days, Lilah and Ismael did not have many luxuries. But Lilah loved the cream-colored fireplace mantel: a slab of white marble with black streaks, and etched in it a pair of laurel leaves in an oval shape about the size of a large orange. She also loved other architectural quirks at the Astor: the high ceilings, the marble trim in the lobby, the brass mailboxes. In two months, however, they would close on a two-bedroom co-op in a ten-year-old building eleven blocks north. Their new building had a pool, a health club, and a gigantic playroom.

Lilah's confidence in Carmen allowed her to return to the Federal Reserve after only three months of maternity leave, and to push herself at work so that she won a promotion to senior analyst two years before. Without that promotion, they would never have saved enough for the down payment on their new co-op. The classes Ismael taught at Columbia University, as a lecturer, did not even cover Carmen's salary. That the nanny made more than Ismael haunted him for a while.

One night, when he had ranted to Lilah about feeling like a failure, she encouraged him to keep writing and had reminded him of his recent publication successes. What really mattered, she said, was that they were a family, happy and in love. That evening Ismael had kissed Lilah a bit more deliberately, prompting a delicious night for both of them. In their darkened bedroom, he pleased her to thank her for being so kind and for loving him despite what her family and he himself imagined a man and a husband should be. Lilah had curled up and fallen asleep in his arms, and he stopped hating himself.

The nanny also made it possible for Ismael to write. Yet while he was grateful, he was always relieved when she left for the day. Carmen was playful and affectionate with David. She took him to the park, playdates, the second-floor children's section at the Barnes and Noble on 83rd Street, the American Museum of Natural History, and the Children's Museum of Manhattan. She spoke only Spanish to David, the reason why they had hired her in the first place. Lilah and Ismael wanted David to know the language of his abuelitos. Ismael's mother had even initiated impromptu phone conversations with their nanny in Spanish. Over Christmas in Ysleta, Pilar had told him how lucky they were to find such a caring woman they could trust with their child. Even his mother didn't have a problem with their raising their son with the help of a nanny.

But Carmen was not that smart. As David was strapped into his blue-and-white high chair, Carmen would convince the child to eat what he didn't like, sweetly at first, but soon enough with tricks to force him to swallow his peas, broccoli, or eggs. If David did not want to go to the park, Carmen told David they were doing something else, just to get him into the stroller, and then take him anyway. Ismael had had conversations with Carmen about really listening to David's wishes, about not using trickery to get her way, about having the patience to deal with a very bright kid who knew exactly what he did, and did not, want. The nanny would nod her head politely and gently remind him that she had decades of experience with children.

It was true that even he and Lilah sometimes resorted to underhanded tactics to deal with their gregarious, energetic, and stubborn little boy. But as David got older and needed someone to interact with him at a more complex, intelligent level, Carmen Pacheco would not be up to the task. She was good for hugging their toddler, making David laugh, and making sure he was safe inside their apartment, in the park, or in the cavernous halls of a museum. Yet when David asked an offbeat question, or waved a book in the air, or stopped in his tracks to study a peculiar stick on the ground, more often than not the nanny squelched the child's curiosity rather than nurtured it.

When David asked her why he shouldn't touch the radiator, she said, "Está caliente, and you shouldn't go near it, okay? Let's go visit Zachy today." For a second, David waited for an answer, then ran to the stroller in the hallway. Seeing David's expectant face ignored, Ismael felt a stab to his heart. Ismael immediately knelt in front of David and explained how hot water ran through pipes throughout the building. Ismael walked him back to the radiator, yanked open the metal cover, and showed David the accordionlike pipes, the black handle to increase or decrease the heat, and the stainless steel steam-release valve, which in action unleashed a low whistle. Ismael pointed to the snow outside and explained how the heat came from the radiator only during the winter, and when the weather got warmer the radiator would not be hot anymore. Instead of wandering aimlessly around the room, David's dark brown eyes focused on what his father was saying. The little boy followed the outline of the pipes, while his fingers carefully gripped the black handle. Ismael could tell his son was figuring it out. You needed to take even a toddler's questions seriously.

Carmen, whom others at the park had repeatedly mistaken for David's grandmother, did not read the newspaper, except for scandalous celebrity gossip from *El Diario*. After Lilah had showed Carmen where everybody's clothing belonged for the third time, Ismael still found Lilah's T-shirts in his bureau, or all his athletic socks in Lilah's drawers. Carmen wasn't ignorant. She just wouldn't adapt to new situations. She lacked curiosity.

Ismael had finished writing his midterm for Philosophy in Literature early, and no undergraduate had signed up for Tuesday morning conferences. So he surprised Carmen by asking whether he could join them for their trip to the American Museum of Natural History. At the foot of the tyrannosaurus skeleton on the fourth floor, Carmen pointed out to David the ominous head and the rows of teeth encased in a glass box, each tooth the size of a carving knife. "Mira, que dientes tiene el dinosaurio. Qué grandote. Mira, tiene hambre." Objects were to be stared at, not explained. Wonder was never to be transformed into comprehension. When David asked, "Why dinosaur look like big duck?" she looked confused. To her credit, she tried to read the description on the platypus skeleton, but then she strolled to the next exhibit, excitedly waving at David to join her. Before they left the museum, Ismael brought Carmen to the Discovery Room on the first floor next to the American Indian canoe and showed her where to sign up ahead of time to gain entry. They spent the last hour digging up replica dinosaur bones in a grainy, tan-colored resin that was reset every couple of hours for the next group of children. David worked furiously at the resin, with a brush and a soft spatula, and beamed with pride after he had uncovered all the bones. His eyes said, "Look at what I have done. Look at what my own two hands have uncovered."

Another problem was that except for a few key phrases Carmen could not speak or read English. How she had lived in New York City for over thirty years and not learned English was something Ismael could not understand. Even his parents—who lived a few hundred yards from the Mexican-American border where everybody spoke Spanish—knew more English than Carmen. Ismael would have been happy had she tried to answer David's questions in Spanish. But Carmen was not interested in explanations, in English or Spanish. Ismael suspected she did not want to seem incompetent and perhaps knew all her children would eventually not need her anymore. Their English skills, even as toddlers, would quickly surpass hers. Sometimes, this short, plump woman washing their dishes, or cheerily changing David's diapers, or lugging a load of laundry from the machines in the hallway, reminded Ismael of his mother's older friends, like doña Cuca. "Why do you think you stay friends with people from el rancho your entire life? They might be simple, they might not be interested in what those people from Harvard are interested in, they may not be as smart as you are, but they do not betray you. Who they are and what they are are right there in front of you. You leave that pobrecita Carmen alone, and let her do her job. She is a very good woman, and you are lucky to have her. Just look at what a happy little boy David is," Pilar had admonished him.

Ismael tiptoed into the dark bedroom, past David's crib, and took out his yellow legal pad and a Pentel mechanical pencil. He sat in front of an old postal desk with mail slots at one end, which Lilah had bought at a warehouse in New Haven for fifty-six dollars. Ismael wrote a few notes for another story he had in mind, about three young boys playing a dangerous game in an irrigation canal. Suddenly David exhaled deeply in his sleep. Ismael put his pencil down, rubbed his eyes, and glanced at his philosophy and ESL course books piled on the desk. How had he ever gotten himself in this situation? He couldn't write, or at least not for very long, before he had to tend to David, pay the bills, or buy groceries. He couldn't write before Lilah would walk in from work and ask what movie they'd be seeing on TV. Only after midnight, after Lilah and David were asleep, when the phone stopped ringing, when Carmen was miles away in Queens and not in their apartment asking him for laundry money, only then could he write.

Sometimes Ismael couldn't write for too long a stretch before his own, perhaps misplaced, sense of responsibility forced him to focus on grading papers, compiling the tests he'd hand out this semester, or rereading the books listed on the syllabus. On his desk were specific and definable tasks with deadlines. In his mind, however, were elusive, fragile stories, like orchids that demanded his attention and care. Ismael yearned to write these stories. Nothing thrilled him more than finishing one story in the dead of night, and knowing it was good. His head would be hot for hours, immersed in a nether world. But he had no time anymore. These dirty white walls at the Astor—"off white," the Polish super claimed—seemed to close in on him. How had he gotten himself into this trap?

Ismael blamed Lilah. Unlike his other girlfriends, who had moved on because of his lackadaisical attitude toward women, she had pursued him. She had been eager to get married, had promised he would never lose his space and his time to write. When Lilah had become pregnant with David, she had said they would hire a nanny, and they did. It had been an imprisonment of kindness.

But she had also healed him. She had taught him that he did belong at Harvard and that a woman he could have delicious sex with could also be his friend. When his old temper flared and he shook with a murderous, silent rage, she did not leave him. Instead she forced him to face and overcome his anger. She defended him against her parents in Massachusetts. ("When do you think Ismael will get a 'real' job?") She gave him a family. In the delivery room at David's birth, cutting the umbilical cord had been one of the proudest moments of his life. His father had never done that, had never been as much a part of Ismael's life as he was now a part of David's.

Ismael had wanted these things, just as much as Lilah. He couldn't deny that. He had wanted to go to Harvard, he had wanted to go to Yale, he had wanted to live in New York City, and he had wanted children, too. Whenever he told Lilah he had to go into their bedroom, close the door, and work on a story, she never stopped him. Lilah had even pushed him a few times to go to Columbia after she came home from work so he could spend the evening writing at Butler Library. She would give the baby his bath, read to him, and put him in his crib, even though she was exhausted.

No, it wasn't Lilah's fault at all. Ismael had gotten himself into his predicament. Ismael *was* the predicament.

He lacked talent. A great writer would have been able to work around babies, nannies, wives, loud city noises, and insomnia. A great writer would have dominated a restless, pumping right leg that seemed to have a mind of its own as soon as he sat at his desk to write. What was wrong with him? His own body was his enemy. Lurking in his bones was a deep urge to do, rather than imagine.

Other writers he chatted with at Columbia's many literary readings seemed blissfully cut off from the world. He envied these self-absorbed types, their production, and complete focus on their work, on their craft. Ismael could act like that, Ismael had acted like that, yet part of him would soon enough abandon writing to rejoin the world wholeheartedly, even desperately. Why did he even keep trying to write? How could he rise above his strange, contradictory existence?

Yet in Ismael's quietest moments, Kafka's stories mesmerized him. Ismael would lose himself in Dostoyevsky's or Tolstoy's sentences, their scenes, the gigantic dramas of their novels. Their questions resonated in him for years. Ismael's love of stories was both a strength and a weakness that propelled him to write, to hate himself whenever he had written nothing for weeks, to admit he was a decent husband, perhaps a good father, but not much of a writer. This knowledge was a torture relieved only by working. He simply had to keep working to capture who he truly wanted to be.

"Ayiii! Ka-men, Ka, Ka. Ka-men!"

"Oh, my little one, you're up. Carmen's gone. Dada's here."

"Dada. Up," David insisted, standing unsteadily on the crib

mattress. The toddler held his arms high so he could be hoisted onto the floor. In a few days, David would probably learn to climb over the white rail regularly. He had already done it twice in two weeks in the middle of the night.

"I think I smell poop. Let's check."

"Poop!"

Ismael carefully laid the child down and handed him a cloth book. With one hand on David's tummy, Ismael grabbed a cushiony diaper from the ripped plastic bag at the foot of the "changing table," Lilah's old white bureau from Wellesley upon which Ismael had attached a small curved changing bed with a blue terry-cloth cover. Ismael quickly cleaned David with a wet wipe and rubbed a dab of A+D ointment on the child's bottom. (The process put him in mind of hoisting a piglet by its hind legs.) Snugly fitting the diaper onto David's waist with the white adhesive tapes, Ismael pulled up the toddler's elastic pants. He knew he had changed twice as many diapers as Lilah. He was better at it. Hers were often crooked or saggy. Sometimes Ismael would redo them when she wasn't looking.

Ismael set David down on the floor and surveyed their living room to make sure Carmen had left nothing potentially dangerous within arm's reach of David. The iron and its extension cord. A glass half full with water. A bobby pin, just the right size for David to pop into his mouth and choke on. When Ismael was satisfied the room was clear, he dragged out David's toys, which were stored in white plastic laundry baskets underneath the crib. David rummaged through the heap of plastic balls, colorful doughnuts meant to be stacked from bigger to smaller on a yellow pedestal, and a pile of books. Ismael shoved his notes into the uppermost slot in the postal desk in the bedroom, out of David's reach. He stepped around the corner into their closetlike kitchen, big enough for only one adult at a time. On the stove were boiled peas and two chicken legs Carmen had prepared for David's dinner. Ismael would have to separate the meat from the bone and skin, which David did not like, but that would only take a few minutes.

"Dada! Dada!"

"What's up, my little one?" asked Ismael, stepping out of the kitchen for a second.

"Dada, read a book!" David's chubby little hands gripped a huge red picture book featuring apple cars, foxes handy with a wrench, and a pig-man who kept losing his hat.

"One second, I'll be right there."

"Dada, read book!"

"Okay, okay. But after this, we're going to get the mail and get dinner ready." Ismael sat down on their dark blue sofa, while David climbed up beside him and leaned against his father's shoulders. David's little body felt warm against his. The wind whipped across Broadway, and the slushy ice had frozen again. Lilah had not called. She usually did after she left work, a habit that had often annoyed Ismael, particularly when he was in the middle of washing the dishes or throwing the trash out, or when David was asleep. Yet whenever she did forget to call, Ismael worried that something awful had happened. Last week, a psychotic homeless man had shoved a middle-aged mother onto the subway tracks near Herald Square. The poor woman had been crushed by the steel wheels of an uptown No. 1 train.

David sucked his thumb as the radiator hissed and whistled.

"Farmer Pig is growing corn, for making grain and bread. He needs to pick it up from the field with the green machine and take it down the street," said Ismael, pointing at a pig on a tractor reaping the corn. Next to the tractor was a mound of grain and what appeared to be a red flour mill slowly grinding the grain, which was manned by another pig worker. "They also make tortillas out of corn."

"Ka-men make me quesadillas."

"Yes, she makes quesadillas, with corn tortillas and cheese. Queso. Mmmm. That sounds delicious."

"Mr. Frumble lose his hat."

"Yes, here he is again. 'Where's my hat?' he says. Maybe we should give Mr. Frumble a quesadilla so he feels better because he lost his hat."

"Mr. Frumble fat."

"Well, maybe you are right. Maybe Mr. Frumble ate too many quesadillas last night. Look, Lowly Worm's reading a book behind the barn. Huckle Cat is looking for him. 'Where's my best friend, Lowly Worm?' he says. You see that?"

"'Here, Huckle!' Lowly like to read. He hide from Huckle."

"David likes books. Dada also likes books. Maybe Lowly could read a book to Huckle, just like Dada is reading a book with David."

"Sergeant Murphy! The Corn Car getting ticket!"

"Va-room! Va-room! The Corn Car's too fast, and Sergeant Murphy's giving it a ticket. 'Don't drive too fast,' says Sergeant Murphy. 'Be careful.' Oh no. There's Lowly Worm again, reading a book while he's driving!"

"Careful Lowly Worm! No read book!" David's tiny legs, which did not reach over the edge of the blue sofa, flailed with excitement.

"That worm's going to crash into that ambulance. You hear that? Outside? An ambulance." Ismael raised an index finger in the air. David stopped staring at the book and listened to the ever-louder wail of the ambulance siren on Broadway or Amsterdam.

"The ambulance, the fox," David said slowly, turning to his father, his eyes wide with the fascinating possibility of reality mirroring the book.

"Well, that might be another ambulance. A New York ambulance. This is the Busytown ambulance, in the book. It's probably faster than the New York ambulance."

The little boy thought for a few seconds, not quite willing to give up his fantasy, then turned to the book again. "Busytown 'bulance. Faster. Look at Huckle. He n-gree."

"He does not look angry. Why do you think Huckle's angry?"

"Lowly not listening. Lowly reading a book."

"Well, maybe you're right. Maybe Lowly should read with Huckle. Then maybe Huckle won't be angry. Huckle wants to be with Lowly."

"Huckle want-bee with Lowly."

"Look on this page. Lowly has a library in his house. A room full of books. Huckle's happy on the chair, reading a book. Lowly has marshmallows and a pipe with bubbles. Lowly loves to read."

"Huckle not n-gree in house."

It took them a few more minutes to get to the end of the Busytown book. Whenever Ismael had tried to stop reading a story before the end, David would protest, even cry. Leaving a story unfinished was as bad as waking him up prematurely from a nap. They went downstairs to pick up the mail in the Astor's lobby. David loved to push the L-button and stomp down the echoey halls of the old marble and ceramic lobby. It was usually empty. Only the uniformed doorman sat at the far end in front of the 75th Street entrance, across from Citarella, the fish market. A sticker had been placed on their brass mailbox, and so Ismael and David walked down the hallway, hand in hand, to pick up the package from the doorman. As soon as Ismael read the return address, his heart skipped a beat.

David ran into their one-bedroom apartment as soon as Ismael opened the door, disappeared around the corner to the living room, and rummaged through his toys again. Ismael flicked the kitchen light on, poked his head out to make sure David wasn't standing on the couch, or yanking the leaves off "Moe," the Spathiphyllum he had had since his Harvard days. Ismael ripped open the package and took out a large paperback book, *New World: Young Latino Writers*.

"Mira, David. Come here," Ismael said, suddenly hoarse. He dropped the book onto the couch. David pushed himself off the floor, stood in front of his father, and put one hand on Ismael's knee. "Mira, Dada's first book. I mean, I wrote one of the stories in this book."

The little boy gripped the book, turned it over a few times, and opened it, only to find a sea of gray words, but no pictures. David dropped the anthology back into his father's hand, holding it by one page as if the book emitted a malodor. He demanded, "Dada, read this book," and shoved the bright yellow Busytown book *How Things Work* onto his father's chest. The little boy climbed onto the couch and sucked his thumb as he waited for his father to read the story.

~

Marcos glanced at the classic 1960s-vintage red Ford Mustang in his rearview mirror as it sped out of the Army Reserve training center at Fort Bliss. His calves ached, his thighs burned, and his shoulders creaked like rusty hinges whenever he raised his arms to the steering wheel. He was wearing dark green army pants with cuffs and a short-sleeve khaki shirt with his rank of first lieutenant, a single silver bar. His weekend of training had ended early as expected, at 3:00 p.m.

As the engine to his silver Camry turned over, Marcos got excited thinking of Jenna. She would meet him in about an hour at the Marriott Residential Suites on North Mesa after checking on her five-year-old daughter who was staying with her grandmother this weekend. Jenna, a warrant officer also in the Army Reserve at Fort Bliss, had already handed Marcos their electronic room key and whispered to him their room number. With the clear manicured nail of her index finger, she had gently stroked the inside of his wrist as her hand passed him the key. In the hallway outside their empty classrooms, a shiver raced down his spine and to his loins. Marcos realized what had happened. Jenna marched down the hallway without turning around, not missing a step, smiling to herself for being so clever. She had taken care of every detail. That take-charge, no-nonsense attitude thrilled Marcos. Jenna Jimenez wanted him and nothing else whenever it was convenient for both of them. She had her life as a mortgage banker for the El Paso Savings Bank. She had sole custody of her daughter from a previous marriage. She owned her own home, on Resler Drive on El Paso's west side. And she never made Marcos feel guilty about anything.

In the parking lot at the Marriott, Marcos called his house on the east side, and Lori answered the phone. He could hear the television set in the background, the theme song from a cartoon he did not recognize. "How's everybody over there?"

"Oh, we're just fine. You almost done?"

"Yeah, we're on a break for a few minutes. I'll be here a little late, 'cause the new commissioned officers have to watch a training film on the Middle East and desert combat. They're apparently thinking of expanding Fort Bliss, but the plan's still in the early phases."

"Your mom called and said we should be in Ysleta for dinner about seven or eight."

"I'll meet you there. Is that okay?"

"Of course. You do what you have to do. Did you get your first lieutenant bar already?"

"Oh, yes, they gave it to me today. I'll show it to you tonight. The kids haven't been watching television all day, have they?"

"No, no, no. I took Noah and Sarah to the Chuck E. Cheese near Kmart on McRae, and they ran around for almost two hours after lunch. Sarah got stuck in one of those climbing tubes. Well, she didn't get stuck, but I think she was afraid, or confused. Don't know exactly what happened. Anyway, I sent Noah to get her, but he came back and said she couldn't, or wouldn't, come out. So I had to climb in there and get her myself. It was an adventure, let me tell you. Those tubes are not made for adults."

"Is she okay?"

"Oh, she's fine."

"I have to go. I'll meet you in Ysleta at about seven thirty, okay?" Marcos's eyes followed a red Mustang, but a newer model, not the right one, as it pulled into the McDonald's parking lot across the street.

"Great. I'll let your mom know. Wear your uniform, will ya? Your parents will be very proud."

"Love you."

"Love you, too."

~

As Marcos climbed out of the shower, Jenna said, "Hey, Marcos!" from the bedroom. She was under the copper-colored covers, a big smile on her face. A pair of jeans and white Western blouse with tiny black enamel buttons were neatly laid out on the couch next to the bed. "I have a surprise for you," she said coyly, in her West Texas drawl. Marcos climbed into the bed and slipped under the covers. His heart pounded inside his chest. Jenna pushed him back and flung the bedcovers to one side.

She had donned a new red-laced teddy. Her breasts pushed at the seams of the garment. Her smooth, tanned skin glowed like the skin of an athlete, with energy, tone, and muscle. Her legs were long and perfectly shaped. Jenna had the silky brown skin of a Latina, with enormous hazel eyes, eyebrows perfectly plucked, and delicate, seductive eyelashes that had taken hours to perfect. Her shiny brunette hair flowed over her shoulders and brushed against her breasts. Marcos stared at Jenna for a few moments as if he couldn't believe his eyes, or his luck. Jenna Jimenez, who rarely referred to herself as a "Mexican American" and never a "Chicana," who looked more like a Victoria's Secret model than a banker, did not spend every waking day agonizing about her parents or praying to her saints or cooking flautas or enchiladas. "Let me give you my surprise," he whispered, a hair's breath away from exploding indecorously on the sheets. Adrenaline surged through him. He held it back, to release it slowly for hours and fulfill this exquisite beauty. Marcos cherished Jenna as a sort of talisman of what he could still have, as well as what he had lost forever.

~

As he drove back to Ysleta, Marcos kept the Camry's windows open to make sure his hair would be dry by the time he arrived at his parents' house. He had taken three showers today: at home in the morning before reporting to the Army Reserve; at the Marriott before Jenna arrived; and again at the Marriott a few minutes after Jenna had left. Even so, he thought he could still smell a trace of Jenna's intoxicating scent. He was utterly spent. That had been one of the most luscious afternoons they had spent together. At one point, Jenna had tightened her grip on his hair and gasped for the first time that she loved him. She promised she didn't want him to abandon Lori and his children. She just wanted to see him more than once every three or four weeks. "I just need to be with you as often as possible," Jenna had pleaded, gripping his shoulders.

The silver Camry streaked over the gigantic hump of the Yarbrough overpass as if he were flying across the desert landscape. He deserved this, Marcos thought, his heart beating faster. He deserved it for working twelve-hour days in the thankless job as a high school assistant principal. He deserved it for being born poor, for leaving this nowhere town and coming back. He deserved it for dealing with self-important gringo idiots and self-styled Chicano saviors in the school districts, especially on the school board, who seemed more interested in contractor kickbacks and promoting kiss-asses than in educating children. He deserved it for marrying a woman who had stopped exercising, who had become soft around the edges of her body and her mind, who seemed to spend every waking moment obsessing about doilies or sales on pictures frames at Michael's. Lori loved to depend on him. She loved to be the stay-at-home mom. She loved to be the sweet, steely queen of the house. But Marcos deserved better. He deserved to squeeze every drop of precious blood from this awful desert.

Marcos stopped his car on San Simon Street, around the corner from his parents' house. He noticed Lori's Subaru was already there. Diagonally across the street, on one of the vacant lots where he used to play baseball with his childhood friends, a new white-brick house was under construction, along with an elaborate curvy brick and wrought-iron fence. His parents' rough-hewn fence of stone and rusted black-metal bars seemed humble by comparison. The three giant mulberry trees in the front yard had been pruned to short stumpy branches. His father had also entombed their front yard with thick, hexagonal rosé bricks, to extend the driveway to hold two spots for their cars. Already a grease spot had smudged four of the hexagonal bricks black.

"Señora Big," Marcos said, patting his mother on the head as she diced one final jalapeño for the salsa. The dining room table was already set. The stove was splattered with specs of corn oil, from the flautas or enchiladas. Two large plates were covered next to a black skillet on the front burner. "Where's Lori and los niños?"

"M'ijo, we've been waiting for you. Where have you been?" Pilar searched his eyes for a moment and kissed his forehead.

"It was a late night at the Army Reserve."

"You look so guapo in your uniform! Let me see, is this it? This bar?"

"Yes, that's it. I'm the youngest first lieutenant in my group, Mamá."

"Lori told us. She's in the back watching the kids play with the dog. We are so proud of you. Go show your father," she said, wrinkling her sixty-two-year-old brown eyes. In a whisper, Pilar continued, "He hasn't been feeling very well. His back." Cuauhtémoc had fallen off a ladder while fixing a leak on the roof above señora Grijalva's apartment. He had fallen only a few steps, but he had injured his back. "He's been able to walk only from the bedroom to the TV set and back. He's in a lot of pain."

"Why doesn't he go to the doctor? And where was Pancho? Papá can't be climbing on the roof anymore. He's lucky he didn't fall off and kill himself."

"You leave my pobrecito Pancho alone. He has been helping your papá for decades, more than you, or Ismael, or Julia. Pancho's busy with his job and his girlfriend. He wasn't going to be your father's slave forever. Why don't *you* help your papá?"

"I have even less time than Pancho does, you know that Mamá. I'm an assistant principal, I'm in the Army Reserve, I have Lori and the kids and the house to take care of."

"Well, your father likes working on his departamentos. It keeps him busy. He's just a little decaído, you know. He spends all his time watching TV. Go talk to him."

"Y Pancho?"

"He should be here any minute now. I'm not sure if he's bringing Isela with him or not."

In a few minutes, three-year-old Sarah and seven-year-old Noah were at one end of the dining room table. Lori and Pilar brought Sarah spoonfuls of green peas, mashed potatoes, and diced chicken breast and gave Noah one flauta. He gnawed on it for a few minutes before he seemed to swallow it whole and begged for another. Marcos served himself a plate with flautas and yesterday's enchiladas, which he preferred refrigerator cold. He squeezed next to his father at the head of the table. Cuauhtémoc winced with pain as he twisted uncomfortably in his chair, yet smiled gamely at Noah and Sarah with webs of new wrinkles around his sunburnt face. He ordered Pilar to bring another flauta to Noah, who had suddenly discovered the sour cream in front of him.

"How's your back, Papá?" Marcos asked, his green eyes glistening at his father for what seemed a brief second.

"I'll be fine. I just have to rest. Pilar, why don't you just bring the plate full of flautas for this niño? Look at him go!"

"Here comes big Uncle Pancho; I see his red truck!" Noah squealed, pointing at the picture window.

"Honey, don't say 'big.' It's not polite. Your Uncle Pancho is extremely strong. Say 'strong' instead," Lori said in her high-pitched southwestern twang, handing Noah another flauta and winking at Marcos.

"He's big and strong."

"Noah."

"Lori, please sit down. It's okay," Pilar said, running her hand through Noah's blond hair, which she had always admired. "Panchito knows he's big. I don't see Isela with him."

"Hey, how's everybody?" Pancho said in a cheery, gravelly voice as he walked through the screen door. Instead of slinking away to the kitchen or the bathroom, Pancho lingered at the table and jostled Noah's hair. Pancho seemed to have gained weight. His belly hung over and hid his belt, yet his small dark brown eyes gleamed. Two months ago at Christmas, as the entire Martínez family was ripping open their presents in the living room, Noah had blurted out, "Uncle Pancho reminds me of a Mexican Santa Claus." Without missing a beat, Pancho had belted out, "Ho, Ho, Ho!" Maybe his perennially shy brother was changing, Marcos thought. Maybe he was feeling better about himself and having a new job as a government teacher at Riverside High School.

"Y Isela? Is she coming? Everything okay?" Pilar kissed his forehead, even though Panchito towered over his mother. "Sit down here, next to Lori."

"She'll be here soon. We were just at her parents' house; she was helping her mother with some dresses she bought. She said it might take an hour. So she's meeting me here."

"Qué bueno, m'ijo."

"We already ate a little bit at her mother's, Mamá," Pancho said, washing his hands at the kitchen sink.

"Here, just a taste. I know her mother's frijoles are not better than mine."

Pancho sat down with a plate of flautas and frijoles and his mother's special soupy concoction of corn mixed with zucchini and melted Muenster cheese, which she called "calabaza con queso." Before Pancho picked up his fork, he said a quick, quiet prayer to himself, his eyes closed, and crossed himself. Noah stared at his favorite uncle, puzzled by the ritual. Pancho opened his eyes, grinned, and blurted out, "Papá, Mamá, I have an announcement. Isela and I have decided to get married."

"Bendito sea Dios!" Pilar screamed, accidentally dropping a plate of flautas on the linoleum floor with what sounded like a rifle shot.

"Oh my God! Congratulations!" Lori shouted, and hugged Pancho before he could even struggle out of his chair. "That's wonderful!"

"Congratulations." Marcos hugged his brother. Cuauhtémoc tried to stand up, but winced with pain. Marcos held one hand on his father's shaky arm to support him.

"M'ijo, what great news! When are you getting married?"

"Bendito sea Dios," Pilar repeated, as she held Pancho's face in her two hands. She looked at her son for a second, then kissed both of his cheeks. All three-hundred-plus pounds of Panchito seemed to melt.

"Your Uncle Pancho's getting married!" Lori squealed delightfully to Noah and Sarah. The children seemed thunderstruck at the adults and their commotion.

"Can we go to the wedding?"

"Of course you can, No-ee," Pancho said sweetly, sitting down. "Maybe you can carry the rings in the church, and your little sister can sprinkle flowers across the aisle."

"The ring bearer and the flower girl! This is so exciting, kids! These are very important and fun jobs at a wedding! You get to dress up!" Lori said.

"My sister will like that. She's good at throwing things!"

"I'm going to church tomorrow morning and say a prayer for both of you," said Pilar.

"We're going to ask Father Lucero to marry us. He knows us so well from running the food and clothing drive at Mount Carmel on Sundays."

Isela was the perfect mate for Pancho: she was also a teacher from the Lower Valley, she was overweight, and she valued Pancho for his kind and helpful nature. After they ate and took the dishes to the kitchen sink, Pancho said, "Ese, Marcos, like your uniform."

"Thanks, but you're getting married! That's great, carnal." The two brothers were unlike in so many ways: one adventurous, the other shy; one athletic, the other overweight. But Marcos and Francisco both loved sports, they loved being their own bosses, and they loved the town of Ysleta and the city of El Paso. They joked bitterly about digging ditches and slaving away in los departamentos for their father. In the living room, as they watched the Dallas Cowboys, they often derided the imbecile politicians who ran El Paso. The two brothers had also been the ones left behind. "Can't wait to congratulate Isela. She coming soon?"

"She'll be here. Ese, wanted to ask you something important."

"What?" For a second, Marcos imagined his older brother had seen him pulling out of the Marriott Residential Suites parking lot.

"Will you be my best man at the wedding?"

"Of course. I'd be proud to."

"I already talked to Isela about it and she thought it was a great idea. Lori can be a bridesmaid or whatever they call a bridesmaid who's married. A bride's matron? Anyway, Isela's sister will be her maid of honor."

"Lori will be thrilled. She likes the whole idea of a big pachanga wedding. Dressing up the kids. And now she'll get to dress up too. Wait 'til I tell her."

"Oye, you think Mayello will feel left out?"

"You not inviting him to the wedding?"

"No, I mean that he's not the best man."

"Nah, he'll be fine. Para que se fue! It's his own fault. Nah, don't feel bad about it, Pancho."

"That's true. He left, el güey, to the New York Giants. Heard anything from Mamá about him? I'll call him tonight and tell him the news."

"He takes care of David while Lilah's at work."

"Órale."

"He's teaching a course or two at Columbia. They also have a nanny, I think."

"So el pinche Mayello's changing diapers. With that Harvard education."

"A househusband, el cabrón. You believe that? What's the point of writing anyway? He's been doing that for years. He sent me a book he's in. An anthology."

"Know, I got that one too."

"But how much money can he make doing that? Está mantenido, el güey." Marcos and Francisco snickered. The door slammed shut, and Isela walked into the kitchen. Pilar hugged her, and everybody stood up and surrounded the new bride-to-be.

The New Jerusalem
NOVEMBER 2001

Ismael left five-year-old David at the Margaret Wise School for
Children at 8:45 a.m., after staying for a few minutes to make sure
he had placed David's tiny backpack with his lunch in his cubby.
Immediately David started building a block city with his friend Diego
on the white linoleum floor. Ismael kissed David on the cheek and
said good-bye. Instead of returning to their co-op on 86th Street, or
crossing the street to Columbia University to find a quiet, secluded spot
deep inside the Butler Library stacks, Ismael was headed *there* for the
first time. His book, *San Lorenzo Street,* a collection of fictional stories
about growing up in Ysleta, had been published a little over a year ago,
to excellent reviews and even a modest success in sales. It had already
been reprinted once, and his university publisher seemed pleased and
printed the new edition with an extra page of review blurbs. But *there,*
this heap of metal and glass and bodies, had pushed aside any kvelling
about his first book, or the thrill of seeing it occasionally in a bookstore,
or the need to write more.

As Ismael rode the downtown No. 1 to as close as he could get
to the World Trade Center, he remembered that Tuesday. Ismael had
dropped off David at the Wise School—the second day of school—and
walked home. Jean-Paul, their French-speaking doorman from the
Antilles, said somewhat excitedly that a plane had crashed into the
Twin Towers. Once inside their west-facing two-bedroom co-op on the
fifteenth floor, he turned on CNN. The sleek silver skyscraper smoked
and burned on TV. While listening to the breathless chatter of the
commentators, he washed the dishes, threw out the trash, and prepared

a toasted bagel with butter before he left for Columbia. The talking
heads seemed gleeful to have another catastrophe to report. A live shot
of the evacuation at street level showed nervous emergency workers
sprinting toward the chaos. The grooved aluminumlike façade of the
skyscraper was agape with a wound of black smoke and red fire pouring
out into the blue sky. There were reports that a "small plane" had been
flying near the Hudson River. Perhaps in distress.

Ismael finished munching on his sesame bagel, aware he was
wasting time. As he stood up to turn off the TV, he froze in mid-chew
as a new flash zoomed behind the Twin Towers. A second later a giant
fusillade of smoke and fire exploded from the second building.

"It's not an accident," Ismael whispered to himself. His stomach
dropped a foot inside of him.

Ismael looked at their panoramic view of the Hudson River and
New Jersey and suddenly felt ominously vulnerable fifteen floors above
Broadway. "We're being attacked."

Ismael spent black Tuesday staring dumbfounded at the TV
images of the charred walls of the Pentagon and the brown haylike
field in Pennsylvania where a small smear of black was all that was left
of another hijacked passenger jet. He must have seen three replays of
the sickening slow-motion collapse of both towers. In the video, the
gigantic antennae eerily pointed and tumbled at him.

The next day, he walked. Ismael walked to feel the air, to see other
people's faces. Overnight Manhattan had become a near ghost town.
Could a poison gas attack be next? Were the subways the next target?
Should they stay in New York City? Lilah was six months' pregnant;
David was five years old. Should they go stay with Lilah's parents in
Wellesley? Or to the countryside? Or to a motel for a few weeks? Ismael
walked to get away from himself and to find answers.

He walked from 86th Street down Broadway, all the way to
Times Square. Over forty blocks. He walked by the New York Public
Library, where he had edited his book, and to Grand Central Station.
Strangely, newsstand after newsstand had stacks of bundled, unbought

newspapers. When Ismael reached the train station, he turned around and walked home. At the glittery spectacle of shops on Fifth Avenue, an older, well-dressed couple cried in front of Fortunoff's. A small suitcase was between them. Central Park at 59th Street was bereft of the usual pandemonium of traffic, horse-drawn carriages, and weary old horses. An old woman slipped about half a block in front of him. Two construction workers helped her up and even volunteered to help her across the street. This Boy Scout friendliness seemed so out of place in New York, as if the terrorist attacks had reminded everybody, for better or worse, they were on this godforsaken island together. At Strawberry Fields, John Lennon's memorial, dozens of New Yorkers sat together in front of candles on the shadowy asphalt and sang songs of peace.

His birth in Ysleta automatically made Ismael an American citizen. But 9/11 had transformed Ismael into a New Yorker. He would never forget the details of that day.

Ismael exited the No. 1 downtown train at Franklin Street and headed south. In the distance, smoke meandered slowly toward the heavens. What kind of fire burned for five weeks? One fire truck roared on West Broadway, sirens and lights off. Another turned and rumbled down a side street, toward the Hudson River. At a corner, two National Guard soldiers, rifles in hand, drank Starbucks coffee. On this block, a Gristedes supermarket and a Duane Reade drugstore had their gates closed. Many other businesses were also shuttered, with two-by-fours and plywood covering their windows. Police cars and ambulances were parked in the middle of streets that had once been teeming with taxicabs, city buses, and bicyclists.

Ismael edged closer to a street that was not a street anymore but a promenade filled with tourists with cameras, curious onlookers, and even a few mothers with baby strollers. One block away, he noticed the road had been blocked off with a ten-foot-high makeshift chain-link fence. On the horizon, just above the heads of the crowd, were three stories of metal, glass, and unrecognizable debris. From a distance, tiny fire trucks surrounded the gigantic mound. Television images failed to capture the scene of what was left of the Twin Towers.

As he had angled for a better view, Ismael had detected the pungent, acrid scent of barbeque in the air. It had made him hungry. But now, with a clear view of the Twin Towers, he understood what it was: the remains of the dead cooked inside the smoldering mountain of rubble. A spurt of acid lurched up his throat and almost gushed out of his mouth. But he forced it back into his stomach. There were no answers here, and he walked home.

~

As he sat down to grade thirteen five-page narratives on a third-person-voice exercise he had devised for his Columbia students, the phone rang on Lilah's old postal desk. For a second, he thought of ignoring it and letting the machine pick it up, but he grabbed the receiver.

"Hello," Ismael said, half-annoyed.

He heard nothing but static.

"Hello," Ismael repeated.

"Mayello, it's me," Ismael heard faintly. "Your sister, Aliyah. I'm calling from Iran and I wanted to know how you and Lilah are."

"Hey, hello. From Iran? Isn't that expensive?"

"I'm using the Internet. There's a delay. But it's cheap this way. How are you, and Lilah and David? Mom told me Lilah's expecting again. That's wonderful."

"Fine, we're fine. I'm working, teaching. Writing when I can."

"Oh, that's good. We're fine over here, too."

"That's good," Ismael said curtly, staring at the papers he had to grade by tomorrow. His sister had not called him in years. Ismael usually heard news from Iran from his mother or father, who received intermittent calls from Julia whenever she was back in the United States, or whenever she was planning another visit to El Paso. When his first book was published, Ismael had e-mailed his sister a few of the early reviews and had received a few short congratulatory emails

from her. Ismael imagined the profanity and occasional sex scenes in
his stories would not be embraced by the literary mullahs in Iran, nor
by his sister, who was translating Imam Khomeini's works into Spanish
and English.

"I would have phoned earlier, but the Internet was out for a while.
Then I couldn't get through. We saw the news. You, Lilah, David okay?
Not next to the Twin Towers?"

"Well, if we had been dead you would have probably heard by
now. No, the Upper West Side is about three or four miles from Lower
Manhattan where the Twin Towers were. We could see the smoke from
our window. We weren't close, but it's been devastating to New York
City. You must be happy."

"Ay, Ismael. How can you say that? I'm not happy about this at all.
Thousands of people died."

"Isn't that what you wanted? To attack 'America the Great Satan'?"

"I didn't want this at all," his sister said carefully, over what seemed
an occasional electronic gust of wind on the phone lines. Ismael
imagined his sister's brown eyes across the Formica kitchen table in
Ysleta, glaring at him in anger, yet her tone calm and deadly.

"How many times have I heard you argue America oppresses the
world, that we slaughter the Palestinians through our Israeli agents, that
we propagate a materialistic, hedonistic, godless culture to the world?
Your Muslim religion is a religion of killers. Did you know women
jumped off the Twin Towers with their babies, women who were
trapped dozens of floors above the fires? Did you know tourists jumped
to their deaths? Did you know that?"

"Ay, Ismael, the people who did this weren't Muslims. They're
fanatics."

"Yeah, and you have egged them on. You and your friends. This is
what your rhetoric supports. You want to wash your hands of it now,
when blood is splattered on the sidewalks, but you have supported
this. Of the nineteen terrorists on those planes, fifteen were from Saudi
Arabia. All of them called themselves Muslims. How can you explain

that? After the planes hit, they were dancing in the streets of your great Palestine, in Mecca and Medina, in fuckin' Tehran."

"Ismael, maybe some people, some ignorant people, were happy about what happened. Maybe the United States is now getting a taste of what it has done to the Third World for years. Did you know America funded Saddam Hussein, who slaughtered hundreds of thousands of Iranians, who gassed them? Did you know Israel has dropped bombs on apartment buildings with women and children? The people who call themselves 'Muslims' who did this are no different than the worst of what America has to offer. The Muslim religion is a peaceful religion. You don't know what you're talking about."

"I'm sure it's peaceful, when it's convenient for it to be peaceful. When the United States is thinking about dropping nuclear bombs on Tehran, on Saudi Arabia, on Afghanistan. Suddenly, yeah, the Muslims are peaceful. You are such a liar. I've heard you with my own ears express your hatred of this country. I've heard you say 'America sows murder in the world. America is the Great Oppressor.' You and Mohammed have said these things in Ysleta. Where did you think that hatred would lead? When Saudi Arabia trains children in its Muslim schools to think of Americans as 'infidels' who deserve to have their throats cut, what did you think would happen? You can run away from your rhetoric now, when it's convenient. Conceal the pride you have in that idiot Bin Laden and what he has accomplished. Conceal your glee. But I know it's there."

"How can you say those things? We are not proud of killing innocents. If a Christian religious fanatic blows up people with a bomb, does that mean every Christian is responsible for that act? Does it mean the Christian religion somehow supported it, encouraged it, or made it a policy of the religion to kill innocents?"

"Well, didn't Muslim religious leaders declare 'jihad' on the United States? What Muslim leader has stood up to condemn Bin Laden? Just name one!" Ismael stood in front of Lilah's desk shouting into the phone. His face was contorted with a black and bitter anger. He wiped the saliva off his lips.

"It's terrible what happened. Real Muslims don't support this. I think you're naïve to think the United States didn't bring this on itself. With its support of Israel. With its support of dictator after dictator, from Pinochet to Hussein to King Fahd. I just called to see how you were, to make sure you're all right. I didn't call to get into an argument with you."

"You called to free yourself of your guilt. You know, Lilah knew people who were in the Twin Towers. Thousands of families have been destroyed. That moron Bin Laden and his henchman even killed Muslims who worked in the World Trade Center. And you didn't answer the question. Name one Muslim leader who has stood up to denounce this. Publicly. The king of Saudi Arabia? The president of Iran? Where are they?"

"Plenty of people have condemned this."

"Well, you don't hear about it. You don't see it on television."

"You think whatever appears on CNN or Fox News is the truth? You think if it doesn't appear on cable, then it must not have happened? You need to see the world from other people's eyes, Ismael."

"Have you condemned this? Have you stood up in your mosque and denounced this? Of course you haven't. They'd stone you if you did. I can't respect who you are or what you have become unless you stand up and denounce this! And that is the problem. There is no serious internal criticism within the Muslim community. Why? Because if you criticize other Muslims, if you support a free democracy, a free discussion of ideas, something other than old religious mullahs deciding what's right and wrong, you get shot, you get killed. Isn't that the truth? It's about toeing the line, it's about obedience, it's about a religious dictatorship of old men. Stand up and denounce this if you have the guts."

"I will. Why are you so angry with me? I told you I don't support what these terrorists did. They are not following the Word of the Koran. I called to see how you are and you attack me."

"Why shouldn't I be angry? Look at what happened in New York. If they kill more people, if some moron drops an anthrax bomb and harms David, I will go after you! You hear me! I'll go after you and your family! I don't care. You are a traitor. You left our family for what? For following old idiots in bedsheets who treat women like slaves. What's the difference between following the priests of the Catholic Church and following the mullahs? What's the difference? You traded one cage for another!"

"Ismael, calm down. Stop making threats. I think you're just angry. And I understand. Women in Iran are not treated like slaves. That's just a distortion of your media. Are you even religious anymore? You don't follow God and so whoever follows God must be a crazy fanatic. Is that what you think? Our own mother is a devout Catholic. You think she's oppressed? Do you think she thinks of herself as oppressed?"

"Why are you bringing Mom into this? She thinks you're a traitor too. Just ask her. Maybe she won't tell it to your face. You know, Lilah's Jewish. What do you think they'd do to Lilah in Iran? In Saudi Arabia? To David? They'd slaughter them. That's exactly what they'd do."

"Jews have lived in Iran for hundreds of years. Peacefully. They can practice their religion. There's a difference between the Jewish people and the state of Israel. The Iranian government protects the Jewish community in Iran."

"I'm sure they do. That's why they're dying to go there."

"Ismael, why do you insist on making this a personal fight between you and me? I didn't bomb the Twin Towers. I don't support what they did. I think it's terrible."

"Why shouldn't it be personal? I live here! My family lives here. You have been talking and pushing your shit on us for years! Now you've ended up on the wrong side! You talk your radical hatred and then you turn around and say you're not responsible for what happened. You're a hypocrite. These nineteen idiots and Bin Laden did what they did because they knew they'd be supported by you and your friends."

"Ismael, I don't support this, I told you. But what choice do poor Palestinians have when they're facing Israeli tanks? What choice do the powerless have against the might of America? Think about it from the perspective of someone who has suffered under the policies of the United States and Europe."

"That's bullshit. Bin Laden doesn't give a damn about the Palestinians. As soon as the Palestinians contradict him, he will have them beheaded. It's about a culture that doesn't know how to interact with other cultures. Discourse is violence for someone who's a dictator, who claims to have an inside track to God. Claim you can talk to God and the next thing you'll be saying is that you should be obeyed without questions. You made a mistake. You accepted a culture of death. A culture that will enslave your own children!"

"I can't talk to you when you're like this. Just say hello to Lilah and David and la familia in Ysleta. Tell them I love them, that I'm thinking of them. I hope you find peace within yourself."

"Fine," Ismael said sharply and hung up. After a few seconds, he imagined his sister standing up at a mosque in Tehran the next afternoon, denouncing the terrorists of 9/11. Ismael imagined a bearded man or two would discreetly follow her back home. At the opportune moment, this man would slit her throat and stab to death Zahira, Majdy, and Ibraheem. Ismael shut his eyes tightly and lifted his head toward the heavens.

~

Aliyah was stricken by an incessant wheezing cough and lay on her flat beige cushion on the floor at night, trying to sleep, wondering whether germs could be transmitted through international telephone lines. In smoggy Tehran in early November, the air became cooler, helping her breathe whenever she walked thirteen-year-old Ibraheem to school. Aliyah realized she didn't need to do this anymore. Her youngest was old enough to go to school by himself. Majdy and even Zahira had volunteered to drop him off when they saw their forty-three-year-old mother holding her chest at breakfast, her face cold and white like snow. But Aliyah would walk the lanky Ibraheem to school until the day her son turned her away.

Aliyah did not tell Mohammed about Ismael's outburst. Instead, when Mohammed returned from teaching his class on the United Nations and its global role, she said Ismael and his family were fine. They spread the flowered plastic cover on the floor of their dining room to get ready for dinner and brought out the giant bowl heaped with saffron rice, another bowl with yogurt and thin slices of cucumber, and a plate of lamb kebab with peppers. Mohammed mentioned that hundreds of students at Tehran University were attending a vigil for the victims of 9/11 that night. The university president expressed his sympathy for America in a letter to the faculty that had been distributed the day before. For weeks, the Tehran newspapers had detailed the chaos and devastation in New York City. Editorial after editorial mentioned Iran's own catastrophic experience with terrorism, warning that Israel should not take advantage of the charged atmosphere by attacking the Palestinians, or by launching "preemptive strikes" against its neighbors.

What struck Aliyah was how much sympathy for the United States poured out from her adopted country. From its politicians, newspapers, and religious leaders. Even from her friends.

For the first time in a long time, the image of the United States had been humanized in Iran. Iranians understood and even venerated pain, blood, and sacrifice. Iranians had been the victims in protracted wars, most recently against Iraq. They had been victims of the Shah's brutal methods for decades. Now the mighty United States, that invincible, faraway foe and the main supporter of Iraq and Israel, was bleeding. Many on the streets expressed a newfound sympathy for America. That the 9/11 attacks had slaughtered thousands of innocent civilians was also inexcusable to many Iranians.

Iranians, like Mexicans, overindulged in the kinship of blood sacrifice, in reverence for enduring the pain of injustice, and even in a view of death as glorious. But unlike most Mexicans, Iranians projected a great pride in their culture and heritage, a sometimes strange insularity that reminded her of the French. This was why Aliyah would always be a foreigner in Tehran, though a welcomed one, for Iranians (unlike the French) had a deep cultural predisposition toward hospitality. The recent events provoked this Iranian insularity in a way. Acting like the United States, as some Sunni Muslims had done on 9/11, was not being truly Muslim, but just a bad Muslim copy of what was wrong with the world in the first place.

The phone rang. Aliyah glanced at her black stove clock; it was not yet noon. "Allo."

"Salaam alei kum. Peace be with you."

"Alei kum salaam," Aliyah said, her voice labored and wheezy.

"Aliyah, it is Azar Shirazi, from the Women's Federation. How are you this fine day? It's suddenly getting cold out there, is it not?"

"Oh, Azar, how could I forget you? I've been meaning to call you. I do plan on signing up to teach a class in January, but I have been so busy."

"My dear Aliyah, I am not calling about your classes. I do hope you will teach English or Spanish again, if you have the time. You sound sick, my dear one."

"Yes, I don't know what it is," Aliyah said. Why would one of the organizers of the Women's Federation in her neighborhood in east Tehran be calling her? Could Azar possibly have a son or nephew too? Was it another one of those calls? Aliyah's stomach tightened. "I'm not sure it's a cold. It might be an allergic reaction to something. But I feel better than yesterday."

"Aliyah," Azar's voice said sweetly, "the reason I am calling is to inquire about your daughter, Zahira."

Aliyah closed her eyes. She had imagined these calls would stop after word got around. At one point last month, Aliyah had dreaded answering the phone and stopped picking it up for a few days to avoid these conversations.

"Your daughter is such an intelligent, dutiful, and religious child. Any mother would be proud to have her as a daughter. You may not know this, but I have a son who is twenty-five and already in dental school. He lives in north Tehran. Have you and your husband thought about when it would be appropriate for Zahira to marry?"

"Thank you for your kind words, Azar. They are very much appreciated. Mohammed and I have discussed this. We believe Zahira is still too young, at sixteen years of age, to consider marriage. We know some girls marry at that age, but we will wait at least until she is eighteen."

"My husband and I would love to come over and talk to you about Jahan. Perhaps you could meet him."

"Well, right now we have decided to wait. When Zahira is eighteen, we will certainly welcome visits to our home about Zahira, from parents and eventually from whoever believes Zahira might make a good wife."

"Oh, so you have had a lot of inquiries already? I am not surprised. Zahira is a beautiful, intelligent girl from the right kind of family."

"Well, thank you. She is first in her class, did you know that? A gifted writer. Your Jahan, I don't think I've ever met him. But he sounds like a good person, focused on his work."

"Aliyah, he is. And I'm sure you will meet him one of these days. I will tell him about your decision, and I am sure he will want us to call again, when you feel Zahira is ready."

"Thank you, Azar. Thank you for being so understanding. It is sometimes difficult to say 'no' to people, and I am not accustomed to doing it. I always hope our decision does not destroy friendships. I would never want that to happen."

"Oh, Aliyah! Of course not. Perhaps because you are not from Iran, originally, that is why you worry. But it is the right of every father and mother to do what's best for their child. So we will wait. Everybody will wait."

"Thank you again, Azar. Salaam alei kum."

"Salaam alei kum," Azar's voice said softly. Aliyah waited patiently until she heard the soft click of the phone at the other end before hanging up herself.

As she finished washing the morning dishes, Aliyah thought about Zahira, who had no clue, as far as her mother knew, that she was the object of such attention. Mohammed and Aliyah had decided not to even mention the interest, not until Zahira brought it up. Zahira was a good girl, always busy with her friends and her school projects, and she had not yet expressed an interest in boys. It was not like in the United States, where a mother might put her head in the sand and wish her sixteen-year-old daughter would not be thinking about sex, or having sex, when in fact she might be. Promiscuous influences did not exist in Tehran, in the media or in school. A young woman having a relationship outside her parents' purview, or getting pregnant—these situations were rare. Aliyah hoped her children would never know how she had grown up as a teenager in Ysleta. Her children were in many ways more innocent than she had been at their age.

In any case, Mohammed and Aliyah would not be making the marriage decision for Zahira. They would first talk to interested parents in a few years. Perhaps after a few dinners, they would invite the boys to meet them, without Zahira and the boys' parents. Once Mohammed and Aliyah had a sense of which boys might be most suitable for Zahira, their daughter would meet the suitors, at their home first. Zahira would see which boy she would be happy with, after getting to know the suitors by herself. Mohammed had promised Aliyah that he would, point blank, ask every boy if he'd let Zahira be the mayor of Tehran, if he'd allow Zahira to continue her studies at the university. In a future dispute, would the boy take his wife's point of view rather than his mother's? Mohammed wanted to find out. But their intelligent, gregarious, headstrong daughter would ultimately decide whom she wanted as a husband. It would never be the laissez-faire random meeting so common in the United States. It would never be like her friend Lisa's misbegotten affair in Italy.

Aliyah stared out her window at the quiet dusty street. A man stood in front of her gate. She couldn't see his face, as the man, in a black tunic sticking out from under a blue-black raincoat, faced the street and stood erect like a soldier. She closed the curtains and stepped away, panicked. Why would someone stand in front of her house in the middle of the day? Should she call Mohammed at the university and ask him to come home? Persecutions from religious councils enforcing one edict after another on moral dress or behavior, or investigating accusations of heresy, were not common now. Certainly Mohammed's position at the university would make him a natural target if professors and students became suspects in a government crackdown against agitators. But that was not the situation now. Moreover, Mohammed and their family were supporters of the Islamic Revolution in Iran. Why was this man in front of her house?

Aliyah found another, smaller window from which to study him. His hair was grayish black. He seemed a bit hunched over, perhaps elderly. Was his hand shaking ever so slightly inside his left sleeve?

"Good morning, most dear sir," Aliyah said as she stepped across the threshold of her front door. The old man turned his head, startled, and she recognized him as her neighbor, Mr. Jalabi. He spent many evenings on his steps smoking cigarettes with his friends and reminded her of don Pedro.

"Oh, good morning, Hanum Kazemi. I did not know you were already here. I saw your keys on the door. I was worried."

Aliyah turned around and saw her house keys dangling on the front door. She must have left them in the keyhole when she returned from Ibraheem's school. "Oh, thank you, Mr. Jalabi. Thank you very much." As was her custom, Aliyah did not look him in the eye or offer to shake his hand.

"I have been waiting here for over an hour," Mr. Jalabi said, a bit irritated. "I thought you were still out. Somehow, I assumed you left them on your way out. I've done that sometimes when I'm in a hurry and my mind's a muddle."

"I am so sorry you had to wait, Mr. Jalabi. Thank you for looking after my house; I greatly appreciate it. May I bring you a bowl of fesenjun later for your dinner? I am making it today for my family, with chicken, walnuts, pomegranate sauce, and a touch of tamarind. I learned that from my mother in Mexico."

"Oh, thank you, Hanum Kazemi, that would be kind of you. Perhaps, if it is not too much trouble, mine should be without any tamarind. As a young man, I loved it, but now it gives my stomach too much of a rumble."

"That will be no problem at all," Aliyah said, finally taking her keys from the doorway. "I'll bring it over, or I'll have Majdy bring it over when she returns from school. Thank you, again."

After Aliyah had finished preparing the pot of fesenjun—it would have to cook for hours to get it just right—she wrote a letter to her mother.

May God Be Merciful on All Of Us, and Guide Us
Querida Mamá:

Today I was thinking of you as I was cooking a dish for my family. Remember that chicken dish we cooked with tamarind when we couldn't find any pomegranate sauce at Big 8's in Ysleta? That's what we are having for dinner tonight, but I only use a bit of tamarind here because it's too spicy for Mohammed and the children.

I know I haven't written to you in a long time, but I thought it was important to do it today. I was thinking how important you have been for me, and how perhaps you have been disappointed with me for many years. I know that you wanted me to be Catholic. I know that you have never forgiven me for becoming a Musulmana. But I hope you know that what you taught me, about behaving well, respecting myself and my family, following the Word of God, all of these things are central to my life. Your teachings live on and do matter. Perhaps it doesn't really matter which official "God" we follow as long as we do it.

I remember what you once told me about Elena, my friend from Ysleta High. I didn't agree with you, and I was angry with you for criticizing my best friend. Years later, when Lisa and I went to Europe one summer during college, I saw what Lisa was doing and I didn't want to do what she was doing. That's when I started to see what you had been saying all along. Lisa had been like me in so many ways and I was seeing where she was going. I wanted to stop. You were right about where I was going. You were right about so many things. And you should know that.

Mamá, I am trying to teach Zahira what you taught me. In her, I see Abuelita. Zahira has her will, her determination, her willingness to fight for what she wants. Did you know that Zahira, to prepare for a series of final exams, stayed up two nights in a row studying? Then she went to a spiritual retreat with her friends and another family. Afterwards the mother called me and said Zahira was more energetic than her own daughter, who could never seem to get up in the morning to help Zahira cook breakfast for everyone! Zahira reminds me so much of doña Pepita. I know Zahira is her own person and will perhaps do something I never even imagined. But in strange ways who we were in Ysleta and El Paso lives on in another world thousands of miles away.

Mamá, I love you. Thank you for being such a good mother to me, even when I didn't deserve it.

Your daughter,
Aliyah

The War in Ysleta
MARCH 2003

The song from a detergent commercial startled Pilar awake. She immediately felt the hardness of the black rosary beads she clutched in her hands, the dull, throbbing pain of her sixty-eight-year-old knees, the spasmodic flutter of her heart. Glancing around their living room, dark except for the bright flashes of the giant TV screen, she saw Cuauhtémoc was gone. He must have walked back to their bedroom by himself. How long had she fallen asleep on her knees?

Pilar pushed herself up. A sharp pain rippled up one leg and then just as suddenly disappeared. She walked, half-hunched, through the kitchen and to their bedroom, fearing Cuauhtémoc had fallen down again. Slowly she pushed open Julieta's old bedroom door. They had moved their bedroom there years ago, for it was the biggest and quietest room in the house, and also next to the furnace. She saw Cuauhtémoc's walker reclining against the wood paneling. Her husband was lying peacefully asleep in their bed. Pilar closed the door as softly as she could and walked back to the kitchen.

The television was on CNN again; it was three in the morning. The United States had given Iraq's Saddam Hussein an ultimatum earlier this month: step down, disarm, or face immediate, catastrophic consequences. The United States, Great Britain, and other allies had landed troops in Kuwait, near the border of southern Iraq, after Turkey had denied the United States use of its airspace for what appeared to be the invasion of Iraq by the U.S. Army. The United Nations, agreeing with President Bush, had declared that Saddam Hussein possessed weapons of mass destruction. These myriad television abstractions

203

puzzled Pilar for only a few moments. Weapons of mass destruction? Nuclear bombs? Who were they targeting? Israel? Saudi Arabia? The United States? Why were they working themselves into such a frenzy on Iraq and Afghanistan? Sometimes Pilar turned to Juárez TV stations for clarification. Ominous national news rarely touched Ysleta. The news from Washington was about as relevant as the news from Europe. Today, however, the news ripped her heart to pieces.

Pilar sat in the kitchen, ignoring the blow-by-blow of the ground assault through southern Iraq. The air strikes were like red and green fireworks. *Marcos is not there yet,* she repeated to herself. *He is in Arkansas, training. He is not there, dear God. Maybe this war will end quickly. Dios mio, please let it be quick. Please protect him, mi Virgen, protect him like your own son.*

Pilar wiped the rivulets of tears from her face. Light-headed, she almost slipped off the high kitchen stool she sat on. She needed to get some sleep. Pilar walked to the living room, clicked off the TV set, and turned off the lights. Lori and the kids were coming for dinner. Pilar had promised to cook them flautas. After she woke up she needed to go to Walmart for the brisket and help Cuauhtémoc get dressed. She hadn't cleaned the dog's doings in the backyard in three days. She needed to pick up the rents from the Olive and Magoffin departamentos and see whether don Manuel had swept the hallways as he had promised he would. There was so much to do! What would happen to this family if she fell apart, if she didn't get enough sleep, if she smashed the pickup on Socorro Road because she fell asleep at the wheel? It was time to rest her body for tomorrow's battles.

~

At a few minutes past 5:00 p.m., Lori's red Subaru stopped on San Lorenzo Avenue. Noah and Sarah jumped out of the car, both with blue backpacks in hand. Lori carried a stack of dark brown accordion folders, for both her course at UTEP and her teaching job at John Drugan Elementary. Pilar lifted the brisket slab with tongs and a fork and checked if it had simmered enough in its onion broth and was ready for shredding. She could smell the cloves of garlic she had embedded in the meat and the salt mixed with pepper, a sharp, tangy scent. She stuffed strands of meat inside corn tortillas, lanced them with a toothpick to keep the roll from popping open, and quickly fried them in vegetable oil. Drops of hot oil, which popped out of the pan, burned tiny round welts on her fingers and hands.

"Ay, mis niños, come give this viejita a hug and a kiss," Pilar said, her arms in the air, the tong still in her hands.

"Hi, Abuelita!" nine-year-old Sarah yelled, running up to Pilar and hugging her so tightly the five-foot-five Pilar almost fell over. Sarah looked exactly like her mother, with gorgeous blue eyes, tall and athletic, and the smoothest, shiniest shoulder-length blond hair Pilar had ever seen. "We having flautas? I love flautas! Can I help you, Abuelita?"

"Not until you finish your homework, young lady," Lori said, smiling at both of them.

"And this young man? Can this be my grandson? You're as tall as I am, mi precioso! Come over here. You will never be too old for a hug from your abuelita." Pilar marched over to thirteen-year-old Noah, kissed his forehead, and squeezed him tightly. It took every bit of strength Pilar possessed not to burst into tears. Noah was a carbon copy of his father.

"Hello, Abuelita. We miss you," Noah said quietly.

"Ay, Lori, it is so good to see you. I'm glad you're staying for dinner," Pilar said, also embracing her daughter-in-law. "You take the kids to the cuartito in the back. I cleared everything from Cuauhtémoc's old drafting table and put two chairs back there, so the kids will have enough room to do their work. You can use Pancho's old room. I cleaned his desk and made sure the bulb in the lamp works. Nobody will bother you."

"What would we do without our abuelita?" Lori said, staring appreciatively at her kids. "But I'm setting the table. I just have to grade some papers for tomorrow, and I'll be right out. Where's Cuauhtémoc?"

"He slept all day. His back is really hurting him. He has another doctor's appointment tomorrow, but I think Dr. Salas doesn't want to operate on him. Cuauhtémoc's too fragile. But the doctor told us about un aparato that might reduce Cuauhtémoc's pain."

"Go on, you know where the room in the back is," Lori said as Noah and Sarah walked into the hallway, toward the back of the house. "When you finish your homework, I want you to show it to me, okay? Don't play with the dog, and I'll come and get you when dinner's ready." As soon as Lori heard the wrought-iron back screen door bang shut, she put her accordion folders on the kitchen table. "Is he still losing weight?"

"Ay, m'ija, yes. Twenty-five pounds," Pilar whispered, glancing at their closed bedroom door in the hallway. "He doesn't want to eat. But maybe this machine will help him. He is depressed and in pain."

"If there is anything I can do . . ." Lori said, her voice trailing off as she picked up her accordion files again. "Marcos called me yesterday and their training is almost over. Only a few weeks to go."

"Jesús, María, y José. And they are definitely going to Iraq?"

"Yes, that's what he tells me. He's not worried. He tells me they're only a supply unit. They won't be on the front lines. But who knows once they get over there. Have you seen the news?"

"It's about the only thing I can do sometimes. It's like a curse. The more you watch, the less you want to hear, the more you have to know."

"Pilar, Pilar, I don't know what to do . . ."

"Oh, m'ija, please don't cry. He'll be all right." Pilar placed the tongs down and gently wrapped her arms around the taller Lori, whose blue eyes seemed to be swimming in thick puddles.

"I don't want anything to happen to him."

"We need to have faith in God at moments like these," Pilar said softly, holding Lori by the waist. Her poor daughter-in-law had no one but her friends at work to talk to. Lori's father had abandoned her mother when Lori was a teenager. Barbara, Lori's mother, had died of breast cancer five years ago. Long ago, when Marcos had first brought

Lori to Ysleta, Pilar had been intimidated by the appearance of this statuesque blond and her perfect, twangy English. What would this Americana think of Ysleta and these poor Mexicanos in this ramshackle adobe house next to a canal? But Lori had converted to Catholicism for Marcos. She kept as immaculate a house as Pilar did and was a dedicated mother. Pilar could not have asked for a better daughter-in-law. Lori had indeed become her hija. "I went to church to pray for Marcos every day this week," Pilar continued. "I talked to Father Hernandez—this is his last year before he retires—and he's going to give a special mass for all the men and women in the military. It's next Sunday. Let's go together."

"I would like that very much. I think it would help the kids too. Especially Noah. He doesn't say much, but he has nightmares and sometimes he gets up at five in the morning and turns on the news quietly, to see if anything has happened. I would tell him not to do it, but I think that might be worse for him."

"Maybe you should come over more often, two or three times a week. I'll cook dinner for everybody. It takes the stress out of your work, I get to see my niños, and we are together as a family. I talked to Pancho today, and he told me he and Isela are more than happy to pick up the kids whenever you have to stay late at school. The pobrecitos have never been able to have children, and you know how much they love Noé and Sarita."

"Thank you very much, Pilar. That means so much to me."

"You go do your work, and I'll call you when dinner's almost ready."

In less than an hour, Pilar had a pile of lightly brown flautas on a plate, a pressure cooker filled with yellow Mexican rice, bits of tomato and onion speckling the mix, a salad with slices of fresh tomato and cucumber, shredded carrot, and garbanzo beans, and a wide, flat pan with frijoles. She had prepared the frijoles from scratch yesterday, soaking the pinto beans in cold water for hours before she cooked them in the pressure cooker with bits of onion and bacon and added salt and just a pinch of pepper and mashed them. Pilar woke Cuauhtémoc and helped him sit down at the head of the table. Then she called Lori and told her dinner was ready.

"Wow! This is delicious, Abuelita. Can I have another one?" Sarah begged. Lori filled their glasses with low-fat milk.

"Of course, m'ija. But first eat your salad. Salad's good for you."

"Did you listen to your abuelita?"

"Mom, I'm done with my problem set. Can I go play with Elmo when I'm finished?"

"Yes, but I need to look at it and see if there's anything you need to check again."

"Pilar," Cuauhtémoc said, "could you get me un poquito chile jalapeño? And I don't have any frijoles yet."

"I'll get it for you," said Lori. "Pilar, you sit down, you've been working all day in the kitchen, and you're the only one not eating yet."

"No, Lori. It's okay. Por favor, siéntese. Let me just bring the frijoles and that's it."

"Thank you, Lori. But I'm used to my señora serving me," Cuauhtémoc said, forcing a smile. What once had been a stocky, muscular physique was now spindly, rickety legs and thinning arms that occasionally quivered for no apparent reason. "Pilar, how many years have you brought me dinner?"

"Here's the jalapeños and the frijoles. Ándale, try the jalapeños, Noah, see what happens," Pilar said, grinning, as the boy inched away from the small bowl with the green chile, sliced carrots, and onions as if it were a ticking time bomb.

"Pilar, please sit down next to me. I'm doing the dishes, okay?"

"Forty-six years," Cuauhtémoc said dreamily, reaching to stroke Pilar's cheek as she finally placed her plate in front of the empty chair next to Cuauhtémoc. She bent down to make it easier for him. Before the children had walked into the kitchen, Pilar had removed Cuauhtémoc's walker and returned it to their bedroom. "Forty-six years we have been novios."

"M'ijo, why are you so quiet? You're not getting sick, are you?" Pilar asked Noah.

"I love the rice, Abuelita. It's better than anything they give us in school."

"I'm afraid your abuelita is a much better cook than I will ever be," said Lori. "Did you know two of her recipes were included in a cookbook published by the church?"

"Two? Which ones? Can we buy the book?" Noah said, his face suddenly animated for a few seconds. He wolfed down a final spoonful of rice and grabbed another flauta from the stack in front of him.

"I have a copy already. I'll show it to you when we get back home. That's probably enough for you right there. Let it sit for ten minutes—remember our rule?—before you get seconds."

"M'ijo, it was a soup recipe, and I think a cookie recipe."

"Cookies?"

"We met at a plaza in Juárez. You were wearing a white dress, remember? She was the most beautiful woman I had ever seen."

"Ay, Cuauhtémoc, I'm just una vieja fea now. Let's just eat our dinner. Look at how your nietos eat! These children were hungry."

"Abuelita, may I bring you a glass of orange juice? You have nothing to drink."

"You are such a sweet child! Of course, you can. Gracias, mi preciosa. Can you reach the glasses? Here, I'll bring a glass down for you, and you can fill it up and bring it to me, okay?"

"Pilar, my fork, it looks like it has something on it. Me traes otro por favor?" Cuauhtémoc asked curtly, waving a fork in the air next to his ear. Pilar walked back to the kitchen and grabbed a new fork from the utensil drawer. Sarah followed carefully behind her with a glass filled about a millimeter from the top with orange juice.

"Thank you so much," Pilar said, after Sarah had carefully placed the glass of orange juice in front of Pilar's plate. Not a drop was spilled. She ran her fingers through her granddaughter's hair and kissed her cheek. "I love your hair. You have the most beautiful hair I have ever seen."

"Thank you, Abuelita. I like your hair too."

"Oh, these greñas? I didn't even have time to comb them today."

"Just leave the plate right in the sink, Noah. And you can go outside, but not outside the fence, okay? I'll call you in if I find anything wrong. Don't let the dog jump on you too much," said Lori.

"Ese perro cochino. Nobody plays with him anymore."

"Abuelita, what's 'cochino'?"

"It means 'dirrtee,' Sarita. But he's still a good guard dog, and he's affectionate."

"Maybe I'll go play with Elmo too. Can I, Mom?"

"Of course you can. You finish reading your story?"

"Yes, I'm finished."

"Un cafecito, Pilar, por favor. Here's my plate. And a toothpick, if it's not too much trouble, mi amor."

As Lori washed the dishes, Cuauhtémoc sat contentedly, yet alone, at the head of the table. His green eyes stared into space. Pilar knew he would be happier watching the news in the living room, so she helped him move to the velvety red couch and brought his coffee to him, as well as a cup for herself.

"Véngase, Lori, leave those dishes alone. Come and watch the news with us, and we can finish the dishes later."

"I'll be there in a few minutes; let me just finish these pots and pans."

Pilar turned on CNN.

"No, cámbiale. I don't want to see that viejo right now. *El Noticiero* is on," said Cuauhtémoc.

"Ahorita, un momento," Pilar said, motioning with her eyes toward the kitchen as she heard the running water suddenly stop. "Lori's here," she whispered.

The TV commentator spoke: "Illegal aliens are crossing our unprotected borders in record numbers, and what is our government doing about it? Nothing but putting their collective heads in the sand. The security of this country is at stake, after 9/11, and we'll report on the latest Washington political machinations that succeed in leaving us vulnerable. Reports from the nation's capitol, the Arizona border, and more. Please stay with us."

"Lori, sit here. It's more comfortable. You want me to bring you a cafecito?"

"I'm okay, Pilar. The kids are having so much fun here. I would like to come back for dinner again, if it's not too much trouble. Perhaps in a couple of days."

"Of course, we would love that. You don't even have to tell me ahead of time."

"Anything on Iraq?"

"In a minute, after this report, I think."

"Pilar, will you bring me a pillow? Un poquito mas café también, por favor, while you're in the kitchen."

"I really don't like this man," Lori said, twisting on the velvety red couch as if she had seen a cockroach crawl across her shoes.

"Well, he doesn't like ilegales. He's a racist, I think."

"I don't know about that. But it's the same thing night after night. Can't he focus on anything else? There are certainly bigger problems in the world."

"Change the channel, Pilar. I'm going to bed if you don't."

"Look, you see, it's over. El Canoso is next."

"Oh my God. We're bombing Baghdad."

Pilar placed her arm around her daughter-in-law's waist. Lori smiled bravely for a moment, then a few tears plunked softly onto her jeans.

Ese Mayello:

Well, I'm here in fucking Arkansas. It's like Ysleta, rural, but puros gringos. Not a Mexican around, at least not one who's not in the military. We ship off to Kuwait, and then Iraq in about a week, they tell us.

How are you? I told everybody back home to write to me. Sundays we get to write home, and read letters, and it's about the best part of the week. Are you still writing your stories? Send me a few. I could use the distraction. They're probably better than the shit magazines we get here. Have you heard from Mom and Pop? I talked to Lori, and she says Papá apparently still has back problems, and Mom is doing all the work. Ese, you don't think Pop's going to die soon, do you? I worry about that. He's not losing his mind, but his body's falling apart. It's the diabetes, all the work he did for so many goddamn years, his diet. Shit, when it's time to pay for your sins, it's time to pay.

Mayello, I never told you this, but I'm proud of you. I'm proud that you went to Harvard, that you teach at Columbia. I know, sometimes I made fun of you, that you take care of the kids at home, that you were different even when you were a kid. Maybe it was just that I didn't know how to relate to you. Sometimes when we don't understand something, or someone, we make fun of them. I've always understood Pancho, and I get my parents, although I don't agree with them about a lot of things. Julieta? I've never really known what the fuck she's doing!

Ese, you should see the pendejos running this unit. We have trucks that break down every other day. We have to wait for parts that nobody has. The squad leaders don't know shit about desert warfare, or about being near the front lines, or about tactics. I mean, I'm no expert either. But we're the ones being sent to goddamn Iraq, and yeah we're only a supply unit, but God, they should get us ready the right way. Yesterday we had an exercise to navigate ourselves to a checkpoint in the mountains, using our instruments and basic knowledge of the terrain, and the idiot who was leading our squad got lost and had to call from his cell phone to have somebody pick us up from the middle of nowhere. Imagine if we get lost in fucking Iraq! The whole squad was pissed off, and some threatened to go to a commanding officer, but then nobody wants to cause trouble.

We're getting a new squad leader tomorrow. The old one's probably sitting at a desk sharpening pencils. It's idiotic.

I'm gonna end it here. We have another, final exercise about our mission in Iraq on Monday and Tuesday. I think we'll be fine, with a little luck. Send saludos to Lilah, David, and Benjamin. I know my kids would love to see you guys, so I hope you're gonna visit El Paso over the summer. Cuidate.

Your brother (who's proud of you),
Marcos

Dear Lori:

I love you very much. I miss you and the kids. I know I just spoke to you yesterday, but when we're on the phone, I feel we talk about the kids and what's happening at home, about things we should talk about. But when I write to you, I feel I can say things that I don't, or can't, say on the phone. Does that make any sense at all? Anyway, tomorrow we're finally off to Kuwait. They've told us the Army will have phones to call back home even in the middle of the desert, but I'm guessing those calls will be fewer and further apart than at the base in Arkansas, so I will be writing more often. I promise.

Lori, I'm ready, but I'm also worried. I know I'll be fine. Hundreds of thousands of soldiers are already in Iraq, and from the reports we're getting we're kicking Saddam's ass. By the time we get there we may just have a mopping up operation on our hands. But you never know. I'm not really worried that anything will happen to me. But I'm worried about how our supply unit will do, how others will react when we get close to the action, how I'll react. I don't want to disappoint my buddies, but most of all, myself.

I'm in the best shape of my life. They've trained us hard, and they've given us the best equipment. So things could not be better on that score.

Before you know it my one-year enlistment will be over, and I'll be done. I've never been to the Middle East, and I'm kind of excited to see what it looks like. That, and the extra time added to my pension, makes it worthwhile, don't you think?

I'm glad I'm writing this at night, when only one other guy is still awake, but at least he's at the other end of our barracks. I'm crying my ass off, and I just want to say I love you, Lori. Thank you for forgiving me. I'm glad it all came out years ago. That woman should never have called you. As I told you then, I had broken it off and I guess she didn't want to accept it. I am still sorry for all the pain I put you through. Those days, when I thought I would lose you, when I imagined I had ruined my family, and my children's lives, and your life, were the worst. When you gave me another chance, I felt free. You saved me by forgiving me, even though I am not sure I will ever forgive myself for what I did to you. I love you, Lori, and every day I am here I will think of that to help me survive.

> I love you with all my heart,
> Your husband,
> Marcos

Dear Pancho:

I hope you are okay, carnal. We've been here a little over two weeks, moving up Iraq, towards Baghdad. We're somewhere south of Nasiriyah, although I don't know exactly where that is. I assume the fucking military censors won't blacken that out, but they might. They tell us they read every piece of mail we send home. We've been warned not to divulge anything of "military value," whatever the hell that means. The Iraqis wouldn't know what to do with it anyway, they are a bunch of idiots. Much worse, thank God, than our bunch of idiots. One thing to say about the Iraqis—they're losing, but they're not quitting yet.

Man, you should see this place. We're in the middle of nowhere, and we're just a small supply team, moving gas up the road to the frontline troops. It's boring most of the time. I mean, El Paso's a desert, but not like this. There's nothing here, for miles around. Not a tree, not a road, nada. Completely flat, except maybe when you get near the Tigris or Euphrates Rivers. Flat like White Sands, but not white, not beautiful. On a few marches, we saw people who live in barracas on these little islands. Some little towns remind me of the worst parts of Juárez, with dirt roads, no running water, and lots of huts with straw roofs. Remember Barraca contra Calavera in Ysleta? Over here it's Los Gringos, Los Negros, and some stupid Spics, against Los Pinchi Musulmanes maniáticos. But here they don't line up one side against the other on opposite sides of a canal before they take the chains and knives to each other. You kill the bastards from half a mile away, if you can, and then drive up to look at what's left of the bodies. They use their mujeres and niños to lure you out, before they race out to try to pump rocket-propelled grenades into your fuel truck. Puras pendejadas.

Ese, Pancho, thank you for helping Lori out with the kids. She won't admit it, but she needs the help. She's probably just getting used to her job again, and I know money's tight. I mean, I made more as an assistant principal than she makes as a teacher, and she has less time to help the kids. So I know she appreciates it when you and Isela take the kids and help her do her work. Sometimes I wonder whether I should have stayed in the reserves for this long. But I don't have a choice anymore; I have to do what I have to do. When I come back, at least I'll be a lot closer to my pension benefits. I just have to get through Iraq, and this year. I miss my kids most of all. Give them a big hug from their dad. Hasta pronto.

Your bro,
Marcos

Queridos Mamá y Papá:

Yo estoy bien aquí en Iraq. Estamos solamente llevando gasolina a las tropas cercas de las diferentes batallas y realmente no hay mucho peligro. Siempre que llevamos las trocas con gasolina tenemos soldados que nos protejen, y también tenemos armas para protejernos.

Yo los estraño, y a los niños, y a Lori. Pronto, yo espero, estaré otra vez en El Paso con ustedes. Y hago lo mejor para pensar en cosas buenas, y no me pongo muy deprimido. Gracias por mandarme la oración de la Virgen. Siempre la tengo conmigo, y estoy seguro que me va a protejer durante los tiempos más difíciles.

Aquí te mando una foto con mis amigos en Iraq. El güero es de Cincinnati y el negrito es de Nueva York. A los dos les encanta la comida mexicana y me dijieron que quieren probar tus flautas cuando me visiten en Ysleta, después de todo esto.

Con cariño,
Tu hijo Marcos

Dear Lori:

Thanks for your letters, and the letters and drawings from the kids. I love getting them, please keep sending them. They remind me of why I am here, why I should be here. There's a friend of mine who broke up with his girlfriend a month before he was deployed, and he gets a few letters from home, but not many. I let him read my letters, and it cheers him up. I hope you don't mind.

It is incredibly boring most of the time, except when we have to do our job. Suddenly it's a few nerve-racking hours, or a couple of days if we're on an extended run, and then it's quiet again. Please don't show this letter to the kids. We've seen many Iraqis slaughtered on roads, sometimes by us, sometimes, probably, by their own soldiers. They enforce a no-retreat *policy on soldiers who are often no more than teenagers, or old men. I've seen a few guys from other units come back wounded. There have been reports of a few deaths in American units we work with, but nothing firsthand, not in our unit, and I'm grateful for that. People have shot at us, as our gas trucks roll by their little towns and settlements. But we just keep moving to complete our mission. The worst incident was actually a friendly-fire one, when some idiot in a Warthog mistook our infantry for an advancing Iraqi unit! I heard about it, but luckily it was no one I knew.*

You know, Americas High School sent me this packet of letters and drawings from kids I've known there. It was really a nice thing to do, and I passed it out to my friends so they could see El Paso and Ysleta and Mexican-American culture. Most have never been even close to the border, and so they don't know anything about it. They imagine it's like Mexico, or that half the people are illegal aliens, or that everybody's living in shacks. They have sort of a New York Times version of the border.

I know the district hasn't been especially great to you about my deployment and my pay, but I'm glad that they did speed up your paperwork so you could have a job again. I'm sorry you've had some run-ins with Central Office, but I think we'll be fine.

I love you, Lori. I can't wait to see you again. Please give a hug and kiss to the kids, and let my parents know how I'm doing.

With all my love,
Marcos

Dear Mayello:

Thanks for the calendar. My New York buddies got a kick out of it. I liked how you marked the date when my one-year deployment is up. I can't wait. But I've heard they've started extending the deployment for some other Reserve units. There's an incredible amount of bitching about it, and I know it's screwed up. But the military owns us, and we just have to do our job. I haven't heard anything about my deployment being extended, but to tell you the truth I'm not looking for any good news. Lori more or less knows, but don't say anything to Mom and Dad about it, when you call them on the weekends. How's the weather in New York City?

You know, this fucking war is a mess. We've killed thousands of Iraqis, we've taken over the country more or less, but it's starting to "simmer," as some of the older guys say here. That means it's still going even when it's officially not going. It means some of the idiots planning this war didn't have jackshit for plans once we wiped out the Republican Guard. It means we haven't found Saddam, and it means we just killed some assholes who are not Iraqis, but from Syria and I think Saudi Arabia, mercenaries or whatever. Our forward unit, the ones we were supplying with gas, showed us the bodies. I'm okay though, and I guess I should thank God and la Virgen, and our fucking Stealth bombers.

Ese, I wanted to say that I've been thinking about your writing. Thanks for sending me your new stories. I liked the one where you combined our lives, Pancho's, yours, and mine, and made that story about that kid from Ysleta who finds a snake. I showed it to my friends, and they loved it. You're talented, man. Keep it up. You know, I don't think I've ever written so much as I have over the past few months. I don't remember ever writing a letter before I got deployed and now I've written dozens. Maybe not dozens, but certainly a lot, to Lori, you, Mom and Dad, Pancho. You never know when you're going to get the chance, and when you do it's not too hard to write about what's going on, your thoughts. And I hate being in line for these fucking phones and computers that work, and don't work. There's no privacy.

I mean, when I write I get to sit down quietly, usually in the library, which is just a tent with books and magazines. I get to push away all the fucking bodies I've seen without their heads, or without an arm, or hanging out of trucks. Do you feel this way? That you can push the world *away a bit whenever you write? It's quiet and I'm alone, and I like being lost by myself for a while, and then sending a message to somebody, to you right now, knowing that somebody will read it later. Hello, from the middle of nowhere. I know I'm gonna be fine, and I'll probably be home soon, maybe just past the original end of my deployment. But when I drop off a letter to you in New York, it's like I've sent a piece of myself away from this godforsaken nightmare, from the boredom and the blood, from our being so far away from home. I was wondering if you feel this way when you write a story.*

Man, will I have some stories to tell you when I get back home. Take care of yourself, bro. Send me more stories!

Marcos

Dear Noah:

Hey, buddy, how are you doing? I'm fine here in Iraq, and I miss you and your sister and mom a lot. I know you guys miss me a lot too, and I can't wait to get back home.

I wanted to tell you how proud I am of you. You are a wonderful son, and I know you are trying your best in school and at home. I know it's hard—Mom told me about your nightmares. But I'll be fine, and you need to help mom as much as you can. Please don't get angry with her for telling me. I'm glad she told me. She loves you as much as I love you, and we need to stick together as a family during this tough time. You have your sister, and your abuelitos, and your uncles and aunts. We are all together trying to make sure everybody is okay.

I am doing the best I can, I have thousands of friends here helping me, and I'll be okay. So please try not to worry too much. Most of the time we are just sitting around waiting for another mission to deliver gasoline to the units that need it. I'm not even on the front lines, where the worst fighting happens. Sometimes when you watch the news too much, you get a distorted picture of what's happening over here. It's really boring most of the time and I am not in danger. I would probably follow Mom's suggestion not to watch the news too much, because it's just going to give you a sense of the worst, the disasters, which is what people want to see anyway. If I told you the most exciting thing that happened yesterday was that I farted (!) while we were driving our gasoline truck and everybody had to open the windows, do you think they'd play that story on CNN? It was very funny, but it wasn't their kind of news. So please don't worry about me. I'll be home before you know it.

Noah, please remember that I love you and that I am very proud to be your father. I have shown all my buddies your picture, and I tell them I used to look like you when I was a kid. Give a great big kiss and hug to Mom and your sister from me. Tell them I miss all of you.

Love,
Dad

Lost in the Desert
DECEMBER 2005

They were in the clouds. Ismael looked at his sons, David and
Benjamin, nine and four years old, one with curly black hair, the other
with sandy straight hair. Asleep, they reclined against each other. The
plane's swaying caused their heads to bump softly together like melons
in a basket. The honey boys, as Ismael called them, did not wake up
after they transferred planes in Houston. They had so exhausted each
other, with their jokes, teasing, petty arguments, and laughter, most
of all their laughter. Across the aisle, Lilah read her *New York Times* to
distract herself. Again on the verge of tears, she momentarily stared at
Ismael. He reached across the aisle and patted her thigh through her
blue jeans, indicating he was okay.

Two weeks ago, Pilar had called him at two in the morning. "M'ijo!
Mataron a Marcos! Mi pobrecitos Marcos!" His father got on the line
and explained: "Two soldiers came to Lori's house today, and a priest.
Marcos's truck ran over a bomb and his patrol came under attack. Three
soldiers died. One of them was Marcos. It was Marcos, m'ijo. One of
them was Marcos."

Tears involuntarily rolled down Ismael's cheeks. He had last seen
Marcos over Christmas three years ago, before he had been called to
active duty. Marcos had returned to El Paso in between deployments
in Iraq—but not when Ismael and his family had been visiting for the
holidays, not that June in 2004 when Ismael had flown to El Paso for
a reading in Clint, not the year when Ismael and Lilah had decided to
spend Thanksgiving in Ysleta. Except for Julia, who hadn't been back to

Ysleta in at least five years, Ismael had been the family member who had not seen Marcos in the longest time.

That night Ismael had told his parents he would call them in the morning, hung up the phone, and sat in the dark, remembering. He had found it hard to breathe, as if wads of cotton had been shoved down his throat. After a few minutes, their bedroom door had opened, and a yellowish light had poured into the living room darkness. Lilah, in her billowy white nightgown, had walked gingerly toward him and asked, "Hey, bear, what's wrong?"

Today, outside the plane's window was nothing but the aftermath, that unforgiving earth, what had been left behind. Ismael imagined the prehistoric sea that had once covered this desert. He imagined the mountaintops as little islands above the treacherous waves. He imagined breathing for a moment and drowning, breathing and drowning.

~

"Why can't they open the casket, Cuauhtémoc? Why? I want to see my son before he is buried! I have that right!" Pilar sobbed, collapsed in a corner of the priest's antechamber at the Old Ysleta Mission. Decades ago, when the Martínez family had first arrived in dusty Ysleta, the silver cupola had easily been the tallest building for miles, a glittery signpost to the cotton fields and adobe shacks and irrigation canals of Ysleta. Today, the ancient church and its cinder block annex of the Mount Carmel school and chapel were surrounded and dwarfed by the perfectly plastered chocolate brown walls of the Tigua Indian casino, its Running Bear gas station, and a two-story Carl's Jr. restaurant across the street on Alameda.

"Pilar, por favor."

"I want to see my son!"

"Mamá, the military sealed the casket," Ismael said quietly. He and Lilah stared at each other, frozen. Ismael's mother sobbed uncontrollably a few feet away from them, crumpled on the floor, next to a dark, wooden wardrobe. Ismael's father, who couldn't bend over without his back collapsing, sat meekly on a beige metal folding chair next to Pilar, not touching her.

"They killed him! They killed him!"

"Pilar, I want to see Marcos one last time, too. Even Father Ortega talked to the military chaplain at Fort Bliss for us. It's better this way."

"Why? Because they left him in pieces! Oh, dear God, what have we done? I don't want to live anymore! My baby!" Pilar's deep, guttural sobs erupted from her chest, and their bleak force stunned everyone in the room. Lori, half-sedated, and the kids waited with Pancho and Isela at the casket in the church. Pilar had refused any medication.

"The priest is here. Lilah, help her get up, por favor, m'ija."

"Señora Martínez, Dios Nuestro Señor will help you through this most difficult time. You need to be strong for Lori, for those children. They will need the entire Martínez family now more than ever."

"Father, they slaughtered him!" Pilar half collapsed into the priest's arms.

"Pilar, we don't know the reasons for God's will. But we do know Marcos is with Him now. We know we will see our beloved son one day again, on Judgment Day. We will see him, and that will be a day to rejoice in His glory." The priest clasped Pilar's hands in his own. Cuauhtémoc stood up gingerly, one hand on the back of his chair, the other on Pilar's shoulder.

"Father," Pilar blurted out, staring at the priest intensely. "How do we know pobrecito Marcos is in that casket? Maybe Marcos was captured, and it's somebody else."

"Pilar."

"Listen to me, Father! How do we know? I want to see my son! I am his mother and I have that right! I gave birth to him!"

"Marcos's body is in that casket. I talked to the military chaplain. There is no doubt. No doubt at all. Please Pilar, let's go join the others in the chapel."

"They left my Marcos in pieces! How can that be God's will? We were a good family! We worked all our lives! We came to make a better life. Father, how can this be? We are cursed!"

"The answers to your questions only Jesus Christ our Lord knows. God wanted Marcos with Him and that's where your son is now. Take comfort in that. Marcos is looking at Lori, at Noah and Sarah. He wants this family to stay together. Pilar, please look at me. You are not cursed. We are going out there, and we are going to pray for Marcos's soul. We will help each other get through this, to remember all of us are a part of him."

Pilar shook her head, but stayed silent. Father Ortega was on one side of her, his hand firmly under her elbow, and Ismael was on the other side, clasping her trembling hand. Old Cuauhtémoc, who could hardly walk ten feet without tottering unsteadily, walked with Lilah at his side. All marched slowly out of the priest's antechamber and into the shadowy chapel, and sat around Lori and her children. Lori and Pilar huddled next to each other on the front wooden pew, the casket a few feet away. The casket had been draped with a new American flag, and a detail of Fort Bliss soldiers in dress uniform surrounded it. Their brass buttons shined under the dim, grayish light of the adobe church. Their white gloves were almost phosphorescent. Eleven-year-old Sarah gripped her Uncle Pancho's beefy hand, and fifteen-year-old Noah sat next to them. Zahira, who was with her new husband, Ali, sat next to Noah, her hand lightly on his shoulder. Her mother, Aliyah, was recovering from a bout of pneumonia and had not been able to make the trip. Tears poured from Noah's green eyes, exactly like his father's, yet Noah's face was like granite. In her black chador, Zahira uncannily resembled her great-grandmother, doña Josefina Del Rio, with piercingly dark brown eyes, sharply cut cheeks, and a jaw that jutted out, as if ready for any challenge. After a few minutes, the heavy wooden doors creaked open. Dozens of people streamed into the ancient adobe chapel, to pay their respects to this son of Ysleta.

~

The funeral took place the next day on Mount Carmel's cold cemetery grounds. The brittle yellow grass was like bits of tangled wire embedded in the earth. The wind whipped up small twisters among the tombstones and the irrigation canals beyond the chain-link fence. On the horizon, the Border Highway and the newly expanded Zaragoza International Bridge teemed with cars and eighteen-wheelers. They released a low, pulsating screech as they zoomed over the black asphalt. The thirty-foot-high border fence, the color of rust, loomed like a gigantic old screen against the horizon. The sky was overcast and claustrophobic, threatening to unleash a few raindrops. Dozens upon dozens of Pilar and Cuauhtémoc's neighbors were present, as well as soldiers who had known Marcos at the Army Reserve, Mrs. Vega from South Loop School, teachers and administrators from Americas High School where Marcos had been an assistant principal, schoolmates from Ysleta High School, now in their forties, and many others. After the shiny tungsten-colored casket had been mechanically lowered into the rectangular pit, strangers shuffled past Pilar, nodding and shaking hands with Pancho, Ismael, and Zahira and Ali. Others simply hugged Lori, or kissed Sarah and Noah.

It wasn't long before many returned to their cars, perhaps to finish their Christmas shopping, or to get back to their tamales and their families. Soon only the Martínez family and a few close friends remained amid the gusts of wind and the flat, sandy landscape. Father Ortega huddled next to Lori and the children who sat at one end of the pit.

"We should never have come here, Cuauhtémoc. We should never have come," Pilar said, staring across the burial pit to her grandchildren.

"What are you saying? Our son did his duty for his country." Cuauhtémoc's hand trembled even as he gripped the chair.

"We didn't belong in Mexico and we don't belong here. We've been abandoned in this evil desert. We had nowhere else to go. But why did we come here, Cuauhtémoc? Why?"

"We came for a better life. We came for our children."

"To bury them in this sand?"

"It's not anybody's fault."

"Cuauhtémoc, it is our fault. It is the fault of the people who slaughtered Marcos. It is the fault of this government who sends its citizens to the ends of this earth to die for no reason. It is the fault of God for not protecting him. We should never have believed in these stupid dreams. Nobody belongs anywhere anymore. The only place we belong is buried in this earth." Convulsions seized her body. Pilar gasped for air as if underwater, her face uplifted to the sky. Tears poured down her cheeks.

~

Ismael waited until dark, until all the guests had gone, until the pots full of tamales, or menudo, or the trays with chiles rellenos stopped arriving at the door, mostly from older people whom he did not immediately recognize. They hugged him and called him "Mayello." His mother had fallen asleep after Pancho had finally convinced her to swallow a sleeping pill. Ismael waited until Lori had left with Sarah and Noah, and after Lilah had hugged and kissed Lori like a true sister, promising to spend the day with her tomorrow. Pancho and Isela drove Lori the two miles home, and would stay with her tonight. Ismael waited until Lilah had turned off the lights for David and Benjamin to sleep in Pancho's old room, until his father Cuauhtémoc had gone to sleep. Zahira and Ali had long ago said good night and retired to don Pedro's old room in the back. Alone, Ismael boiled whole milk to calm his nerves, just as his mother had done for many years.

"M'ijo, you're up. What are you doing?"

"Just drinking leche caliente like you taught me, and waiting for you."

"Mayello, you remember when we first came to Ysleta?"

"Of course, Mamá. It seems like yesterday. How could I forget? It was as dark as it is tonight, but darker. That first night, without lights, without anything. I was scared. I felt like we were at the bottom of the sea."

"Mayello, what are we going to do without Marcos? What can I do anymore?" Pilar sat slumped in front of the round Formica table. The quiet in the kitchen that had once resonated peace was now only a void.

"Mamá, I don't know. I wish I had said good-bye. I wish I had never left Ysleta. I wish Marcos and I were still kids playing in the canal."

"I love you, do you know that? You have always been a good son. I love you and Marcos and Pancho, and even Julia, even after everything she has done to this family. Her children are at least good children."

"Mamá, here's a cup for you. I do the same thing almost every night, too."

"Gracias. Ay, I feel so betrayed. By my God, by this country, by myself. Why did we come here? Why did I let you go to college so far away from home? Why did Marcos go so far away from home? Why did Julia abandon us? I swear, I don't want to live. I'm just so tired. If I didn't have to take care of your father, I just wouldn't want to see another day."

"Mamá, please stop crying. I don't know when, but it will get better. Marcos left us Noah and Sarah, and Lori. He left us his life, Mamá. That's what we still have. We have it here, in our hearts. We have it when we remember him. Mamá, you and Papá gave us a wonderful life. You taught us to make our own decisions. You taught us to be proud of who we are."

"Nothing matters anymore. Father Ortega is coming tomorrow, but I don't want to see him. I don't want to hear his lies. I don't ever want to believe anymore."

"Mamá, I have something for you."

Pilar held her head, her eyes closed.

"Mamá, I wrote a story. It's about our family, Mamá. A family from Ysleta."

"A story? Mayello, I have always been proud of you, you know that. But I don't know if I can read anything right now. I don't even understand many of the English words you use. And now my mind seems as if it's been chopped to pieces. Marcos was so proud of you too, Mayello. He was always proud of his little brother. He would always brag to his students about his brother the writer."

"Mamá, it's not about me, it's about our family. It's about Ysleta. It's about how we lived, how we tried. It's about how we were together for a time. I, I didn't know what else to do. How else to remember him. How else to remember us."

"M'ijo, you have always been very thoughtful, perhaps the smartest of my children. My heart, dear God, my heart feels like it's been buried with Marcos in that dust at Mount Carmel. But it's the only thing we have left, these memories. And maybe with time, something else, something besides this awful pain."

"It's just a story, just words. But it's what I can do. It's how I can make sure no one ever forgets."

"Then it's not nothing, m'ijo. Then maybe someone will read it, and think about his family, and how much love they had a long time ago, and how to recreate it, how to fight for it, even if they begin in la nada like we did, even if they suffer so many stones and arrows flung at their hearts."

About the Author

Sergio Troncoso was born in El Paso, Texas, and now lives in New York City. After graduating from Harvard College, he was a Fulbright Scholar to Mexico and studied international relations and philosophy at Yale University.

Troncoso's stories have been featured in many anthologies, including *Camino del Sol: Fifteen Years of Latina and Latino Writing* (University of Arizona Press), *Latino Boom: An Anthology of U.S. Latino Literature* (Pearson Longman Publishing), *Once Upon a Cuento* (Curbstone Press), *Hecho en Tejas: An Anthology of Texas-Mexican Literature* (University of New Mexico Press), *City Wilds: Essays and Stories about Urban Nature* (University of Georgia Press), and *New World: Young Latino Writers* (Dell Publishing). His work has also appeared in *Encyclopedia Latina*, *Newsday*, the *El Paso Times*, *Pembroke Magazine*, *Hadassah Magazine*, *Other Voices*, and many other newspapers and magazines.

His book of short stories *The Last Tortilla and Other Stories* (University of Arizona Press, 1999) won the Premio Aztlán for the best book by a new Mexican-American writer and the Southwest Book Award from the Border Regional Library Association. His novel *The Nature of Truth* (Northwestern University Press, 2003) is about a Yale research student who discovers that his boss, a renowned professor, hides a Nazi past.

His award-winning website is at www.SergioTroncoso.com. He writes the blog www.ChicoLingo.com about writing, politics, and finance.